STRANGERS ARE JUST FRIENDS YOU HAVEN'T KILLED YET

A NOVEL

by

RYAN BRACHA

For Rebecca

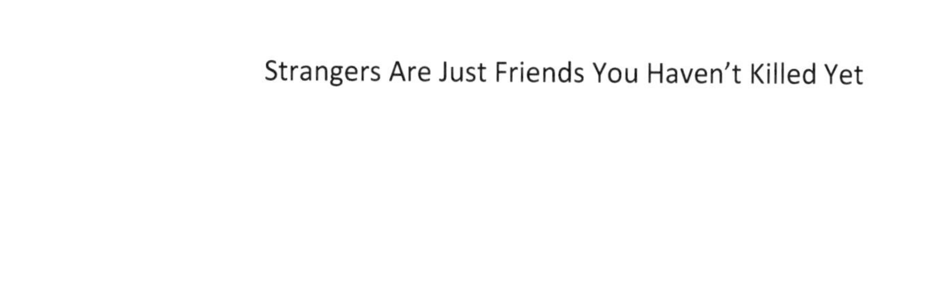

PART 1 - STRANGERS AND FRIENDS

Alan

Thursday 15th October 2009

The waiting room felt kind of cold. Not cold in that tense jaw, backache sort of way. More the sort of cold that crept up on you, and you weren't even aware of it until you realised your toes were numb. The kind of cold that a jumper could fight off, but a vest would surrender to with barely a sniff of an argument. With this in his mind, Alan felt glad to have worn an extra layer, his favourite V-neck sweater sitting neatly over his white shirt with the embroidered collar, it felt good to be proven right, even if there was nobody to prove wrong.

The queue - a term he'd be hesitant to use in any other circumstance, it appeared to be more like the queue system used in a barbers' salon, based on an unofficial trust that you knew who was ahead of you, and those who had arrived after you weren't sure who arrived when, so were forced to ride it out until they were sure it was their turn - hadn't budged since he'd arrived, and a young woman who'd arrived shortly after Alan was beginning to ask a question he'd been wondering himself for the past five minutes. She was pacing, the impatience etched across her scowling face seemed, to Alan at least, to come as natural to her as a smile to a child. It was an impatience he imagined brought very little success, she was destined to wait here like the rest of them. *Good things come to those who wait*, Alan mused to himself, allowing a thin smile for the briefest of moments.

His eyes darted the room every few seconds,

taking in the rest of the "applicants", all of whom probably had as good an idea of what they were waiting for as he did, in that they all didn't have a clue. He was never as impulsive as he had been this last week. Alan had always been a quiet one, he'd readily admit it, he'd much rather keep his head down, and get on with his own life. At the same time though, he was very aware of himself as so, and would often make failed attempts to force himself to make eye contact with the people who served him in everyday life. He'd climb onto the bus staring up, down, anywhere that wasn't directly at the driver, or conductor, and would cut his own hair to avoid trips to the barber, where he'd invariably be hammered into making, and keeping, conversation. As a result, his unkempt crop was in danger of resembling a slightly askew wig, shorter on one side than it was the other. Made all the more noticeable by the even lines of the arms of his glasses. The unpleasant aroma of his wax jacket followed him around, even on warm days when he wasn't wearing it, or now, as his coat was taken from him on entry to this place, whatever it was. He was aware of it, but he had no other coats, and what else was he supposed to wear when it was cold? Besides, new coats meant spending money, and money was exactly what he didn't have. He'd been laid off last year when his employers decided they'd be much better off having their stock knocked together in Vietnam, or some other godforsaken country that way out. He'd been from job to job before that, Alan wasn't exactly the kind of person who made friends easily, so was often made to bear the brunt of his workmates merciless jibes, which in turn would send him packing to his next menial occupation. After he'd been laid off he decided that signing onto Jobseeker's Allowance would perhaps be the best thing, and he'd only have to be in contact with the woman in the Job Centre, and whoever was in the post office every two weeks. This didn't afford him much in the way of extra spends, and he would often find himself falling behind on the council tax (he was well aware that he was eligible for benefits in that department but God forbid he go into the office to claim it!), or sitting in darkness for two days because the electricity had run out and he couldn't afford to get it out of the emergency credit. He was sure his parents, God rest their souls, wouldn't have wanted him moping about it though, so he made the best of what he had. He'd go for walks on nights when he had no electricity, so he didn't have to sit in darkness, and it wasn't so bad in the summer because it would still be light when he was ready for bed. Sheffield was a wonderfully green city, he could quite happily stroll down Eccleshall Road and spend whole days in the botanical gardens, and at seven when it closed he'd amble back down to Millhouses park and sit by the river. He knew it wasn't an ideal way to live, and this was exactly the reason he was here. He needed money.

What led him to this point, aside from a rather unpleasant and uncompromising bailiff who went by the entirely inappropriate name of Mr Small, chasing six hundred pounds for a council tax debt that started out at three hundred, was an advertisement he'd seen in the free newspaper you get on the bus, *"Live in Sheffield? £10,000 could be yours"* and then a number. It was only a few words, and he came close to throwing the whole idea away but he'd kept the paper to do the

Sudoku quizzes when he got home and he saw the advertisement again. Just before the electricity ran out. Out on his walk he stopped by a telephone box and called the number, and an automated message instructed him to leave his contact details and was told he would be informed by mail whether he was a successful applicant. This was three months ago. He'd got the letter yesterday, "Mr Foster, thank you for your application for the chance to win, you have been selected as one of the eight final applicants all with the chance of winning the cash prize. Be at the statue of King Edward VII by Fitzalan Square at 2pm on Thursday 15th October and you will be met by a representative. Bring this letter with you. Thank you." It was a pretty vague instruction and seemed shady to say the least. He'd been tempted to simply throw the letter away and get on with life, and had even got as far as leaving it on top of the recycling box. He didn't want to have to meet a representative. Something inside him kept pulling away though, like a small child tugging on the sleeve of its parent, requesting a sniff of attention, it didn't stop all day, and eventually the small child would have been squeaking "Dad, Dad, Dad, Dad" continuously as its parent ignored the incessant tugging. The next morning he watched the clock turn nine, ten, eleven o'clock. The letter had found its
way back into his hands as he stared at the hands tick round. It had got to half-twelve by the time his mind was made, and he found himself waiting for the 53 bus. The next ninety minutes passed in a haze, as if he'd somehow been detached from his body and somebody else had climbed aboard the good ship Alan and decided to drive for a while, he resented this somebody

for thrusting him into this unknown world of potential adult interaction, but try as he might, he couldn't get back behind the wheel.

He arrived at the statue on time, and found himself surrounded by scores of students from the university down the road. He caught himself watching a girl, she was only wearing a t-shirt and jeans yet the only evidence that she was cold on this autumn's day were the erect nipples she was displaying, her perfect breasts dancing in the tight Ramones top she was sporting. *They are two of the greatest things that I have ever seen. I want to hold them, to kiss them, take her in my arms and-* Totally in the moment, he wasn't even aware of somebody standing beside him until a man's voice broke the spell.

"Beautiful aren't they? The woman's form is a thing to be worshipped Mr Foster"

Alan turned with a start to see a tall, muscular man encased in what could only be described as the world's most expensive suit, at least in Alan's opinion. His ice-blue eyes looked like they could puncture your soul, and an immaculately cropped blond haircut covered his head.

"How do you-?" Was all Alan could squeeze out before the German bodybuilder interrupted him.

"All in good time Mr Foster" His accent told of nothing, except that he was perhaps European with a magnificent grasp of English, or English but having had spent time at length abroad. Either way, he'd come from, or been, further afield than Alan could ever have dreamed of being. He'd been to the Isle of Wight as a child.

"My name is Mr Berg, follow me from a distance, don't

ask questions"

And so here he was, waiting in a room, queuing for heavens-knew what, having followed the mysterious Mr Berg for only a short time. He'd watched the blonde monster enter an iron door halfway up a back street, leaving the door open for Alan. There were two doors inside, sandwiching a large metal drawer and a sign "Please remove your coat and place it in the drawer before entering". The door on the left closed, the right hand portal open, leading to a narrow corridor down which Alan apprehensively stepped until he reached another door, pushing it to reveal a white room with about seven or eight people all watching the door expectantly, hoping for some sort of answer to the question on every one their lips "*why are we here?*". Feeling somewhat guilty at having let down the occupants of the room with his lack of new information he made his way to a free chair, seating himself three seats to the right of a gentleman of around his own age, but of what would appear, by the look of his proudly buffed shoes, to be a vastly different background, economically speaking. His balding head was mostly covered by grey hair twisted back into itself in tight curls as if it had a fear of venturing any further from the warmth of its keeper's skull, as if braver strands once grew from the follicles now left barren around his crown, and the rest of them had become reclusive and withdrawn. He looked to be semi-responsive to a conversation opposite them, smiling when something was deemed humorous, but not actually contributing. Alan fancied that the fellow would eventually shift himself over to the other side of the room to take part. Two seats away to his own

right, a long haired man, about thirty years of age, was listening to music on his headphones and rhythmically tapping his fingers against his ripped denim clad knees. The tinny "*tiss tiss tiss*" of drums and a mild fuzz of guitars told Alan nothing of what he could be listening to, and he was glad that his new "friend" was otherwise busy, or the newly acquired intruder into Alan's mind would force him to indulge in conversation. Further round the room there was a young coloured fellow leaning forward and staring into his hands, his right leg nigged away through either impatience or nerves. He seemed to have the right idea, absorbed in his own world, refusing to raise his eyes to acknowledge anybody else, Alan made a vague effort to replicate his actions. A balding man opposite, his chubby sweating head popping out of a thick black sweater like the thumb of a hand wearing fingerless gloves, was forcing his gaze upon Alan, intently chewing gum. Aware that he was being watched, Alan would flick his eyes at the man, only to look away the second eye contact was made. *He looks dangerous.* This continued for what seemed like hours until he looked up. The balding man smiled.
"Y'alright mate?" His voice was soft, like he was younger than his appearance would have you believe. Alan imagined that he would be very much at home fighting drunkards in one of the city's multitude of pubs, or teaching karate to young lads in the local church hall. He certainly wasn't somebody Alan would very much like to know and engage with. He afforded the balding man a smile then felt himself blush as his eyes shot to the floor once again. The man laughed quietly, muttering that Alan could suit himself. A young

man and woman, the recipients of the fellow to his left's quiet attentions, were conversing together in the corner, it didn't seem like they knew each other, more likely getting to know one another to keep the time passing. She was a very attractive girl, her blonde hair in dreadlocks intertwined with pink streaks. He was slouching in his chair, his face forward yet talking out the side of his mouth and his eyes strained as far left as they could go. Alan wondered why he didn't just turn his head to speak to her, but *hey-ho* he thought, *nowt as queer as folk.*

The door swung open a few minutes later, revealing the impatient girl, her hair tied tight back, and what appeared to be a stuck-on scowl.
"The fuck is this? The fuck's 'appnin?" Were the words which formed the room's introduction to her eloquent ways, thus concreting her status as one to avoid in Alan's book. Mind, this whole bunch were ones to avoid in his book. She threw herself into an empty chair enthusiastically, exhaling in a huff. As the door swung shut, Alan wasn't sure if anybody else heard it, but a faint click of the door locking seemed to seal all of their fates as being together in this -whatever it was -until the end.

The mumbled hush of the room continued, Little Miss Impatient was pacing, her nicotine addiction grabbing her by her throat and not letting go, until a crackle then a hiss broke the suspense.
"James Crosby, enter" There was the familiar voice of Mr Berg, and a click as the door through which they'd all entered locked, then another as the one at the other end of the room unlocked. The slouching lad next to the dreadlocked girl jumped up with a start, he must

have been James Crosby, first of the eight.
Every other pair of eyes in the room was on him, the music fan to Alan's right felt moved to take out his earphones, opening up the tiny speakers to unleash a slightly louder version of the *'tiss tiss tiss'* but still proved fruitless in its quest to be anything more than obscure to his own admittedly rather blander tastes. James Crosby stood up and looked around the room, and in an effort to appear defiantly nonchalant he shrugged to them all and smirked. "Someone's got to be first eh?". It cracked open the tension in the room as the dreadlocked girl gave a small nervous giggle and the young coloured fellow smiled with huge brilliant white teeth. Little Miss Impatient scowled. Alan didn't look at James for long, but despite the effort, he could see there was a definite fear in his eyes as he slowly edged toward the door and slipped through it. The click denoted that it had locked, sucking James from the room. It certainly looked like this was the beginning. The beginning of whatever it was.

James' removal from the group had done something to it, like it had shaken all (most) of their shackles of unfamiliarity loose. Alan and the coloured fellow remained still and quiet, as the girl with the dreadlocks asked what everybody's names were, the previously self-entertaining long haired chap shifted himself around and lent forward in order to engage with her "Tom, you?" and she responded with the revelation that her name was Ruby, and looked toward the man to Alan's left, who attempted to get something out only to be stifled by phlegm in the throat, which he cleared "Um, Geoffrey, ahem, Geoff"
"Nice to meet you Geoff, how about you?" and a

moment of silence ensued as Alan looked up to see six faces looking expectantly at his own, which was starting to take a shift toward a deep shade of red as the silence seemed to go on between them all forever.
What in Heaven's name am I doing here? I didn't think I was signing up for this, whatever this is. Just tell her your name you fool, it was a simple enough blasted question. I don't want to tell her my blasted-
"Sorry, my name is Alan. Alan Foster. Good to meet you Ruby"
She returned his reply with a warm smile. *How difficult was that? Hmm?* Little Miss Impatient begrudgingly gave up her name as Lisa. She looked very familiar now that Alan had taken the time to study her face. He was sure she lived somewhere close to him, or-
"You fuckin' lookin' at you pervy bastard?" her face came into focus as he realised he'd been staring.
"Sorry?"
"Yeah, you fuckin' will be you old cunt, you fuckin' stink" she started out of her chair toward him until the tannoy crackled into life.
"Sit down Miss Wallett"
She stopped in her tracks and studied the walls around her for some sort of surveillance equipment raising her middle finger to the tiny black box above the door through which they had all entered the room, a red spot blinking away to denote it's live and recording status. Somewhat bizarrely she removed a scuffed formerly white training shoe and attempted to throw it at the camera.
"Fuckin' let me out you wankers!"
"All in good time Miss Wallett, you may wish to put your shoe back on and calm down, you are going to

need to preserve your energy"
The mysterious and threateningly calm nature of this sentence silenced the room, and sent a nervous shudder through Alan's body, suddenly nobody felt the need to continue introductions, let alone chat or throw footwear around the place. His throat burned from the bile rising up from his stomach, and for ten minutes nobody uttered a word. The already familiar crackle, hiss and unlocking of the door.
"Alan Foster, enter" *No turning back now at all old fellow*. He rose unsteadily and shuffled tentatively toward the door, feeling like when he was younger and in trouble with his father, who would sit threateningly in his favourite armchair and growl for Alan to come to him, and he'd take maybe one or two steps toward him pleading that he was already there, and his father would point to the spot directly in front of his slipper clad feet and say "here" and they would both perform the ritual on a continuous loop until he was close enough for his father to lash out like lizards tongue and pull a young Alan toward him and give him the thrashing of his life. He felt that same kind of fear just now, but this was more a fear of the unknown, rather than the fear of a relentless punishment at the hands of his father. As he passed the door's threshold he turned to face the others in the room, then was snatched from it as quickly as that lizard's tongue of his father's grasp.

David Harston BA(Hons)

Saturday 17th October 2009

The naked body of twenty four year old Graham Capper was discovered at six o'clock this morning in Meersbrook Park with his throat cut. This is the first time I've ever had to write about a murder. How do I do it? What is my angle? This might make page nine in The Sun, but it's going to make the front page in the rag I work for. He was found by an old woman walking her dog, inevitably. They usually are. Or a jogger. The old dear, she must have shit herself.

I got into journalism by mistake really. At university I wanted to do music, composition if anything, but my parents wanted me to take a more academic route, so I applied for Media Studies at Sheffield, which was essentially fucking about with cameras, computers and editing software, but as long as they thought I was doing a degree with "studies" in the title, then they were off my back. My mum proudly informing everybody she knew that I was "the first Harston to go to uni" and so it was, my parents hopes of a work-free future resting solely on my shoulders, my sister Kelly having succumbed to the draw of the instant cash afforded by getting herself a minimum wage job straight from school. My time at uni wasn't a particularly bad, nor good one. Nights generally spent getting, or trying to get weed, sex or alcohol sandwiched between days generally spent getting, or trying to get a degree. I played bass in a band called "The Ancient Art Of Seeing Into The Future" which enabled me to keep up my passion for music, get a steady flow of notches on my bedpost, also to earn extra money to keep me from rolling terminally into my overdraft. We had a regular spot at the student union bar so were never short of gigs, and we even got a slot at the Leadmill supporting The Stands, but most local bands get a support slot there at some point, it's just a case of who makes it past that next hurdle. We didn't.

The band was Craig MacNichol, lead guitar and vocals, we fleshed out whatever he thought might work, it was his band y'know? He was the pure talent, seriously, he must have come out of his mum holding a fucking guitar playing Layla or Whiskey In A Jar, one of those kinds of blokes you just wish you were born with the talent of, then spend the rest of your life trying to emulate. Back at the start, I'd got a job at a nightclub, as a barman. Craig was pootling about collecting bottles and plastic pint-pots. It didn't matter whether we were into the hardhouse, off-your-tits on pills variety of music, a job is a job, we were two indie-kids each trying to stretch out our student loans. It was our own mutual disdain toward the people we were serving that brought us together. As heathens in the "Church of Ecstasy" we were both bound together as hippie-scum there purely for the financial gains. So we found ourselves retreating back to his after the club to smoke hash and listen to bands like Flaming Lips, and Modest Mouse. Bands I'd never heard of but would definitely have to learn the ways of if I were ever to infiltrate his group of pals. A lot of the time we were smoking hash and strumming our guitars, making up songs about the people we'd encountered that night, recording into his old Compaq PC microphone and editing as we went. It was before CD writers came as standard so we'd find ourselves hitting record and play on a decrepit ghetto blaster hooked up with jack leads to get the stuff onto tape. I still have the cassettes somewhere.

He'd got a band together already, Alex on drums, Matt was their bassist and a kid called Mike on keyboards. And they weren't bad at all. I'd like to say I brought the band an altogether complete sound but I didn't, I simply replaced Matt, who'd dropped out of uni and flitted back to Portsmouth without saying anything to anybody. I later found out that Matt had got a fifteen year old girl pregnant and wasn't prepared to stick around for the fallout, especially as she didn't even know his name, she'd collared him in a pub a few weeks later to tell him she was keeping the baby and wanted him to be involved. It was testament to her immaturity that she didn't know he was looking at a statutory rape charge if he stuck around. So off he went. Craig approached me about replacing Matt the night of the new millenium. It was the usual all-nighter and it was twenty quid an hour, partly on the basis that it was such an illustrious occasion, but primarily because most of the staff had rallied together to voice their disdain about working on such an occasion. I personally didn't care, a night is a night is a night, what is the special wonder of seeing in a year that, as far as I know, means nothing but the anniversary of two thousand years ago? But the other staff thought it would be a once in a lifetime opportunity to do what they always did, and didn't want to miss out unless they were being paid handsomely to do so, so Craig and myself got ourselves a hefty bonus for pretty much nothing. The best part of it was that the place was dead, everybody else across the country had also decided it was such an important night, that they'd like to spend it at house parties with their friends and family. So we sat chatting on our break, about Matt, and what his possible reasons for leaving town were, TAAOSITF were due to play a gig about a week later, and nobody could get hold of Matt. Craig asked if, on the event of Matt not showing up, would I fill in? We'd played a lot of their songs at his already on stoned nights in, and they did a lot of covers I'd previously learned, so it seemed rude to turn him down. Actually, it wasn't that it would have been rude to turn him down, it would have been rude to kiss and hug him and thank him for the opportunity, because that's what I wanted to do.

A week of intense practice, and about an ounce of skunk later, and I was there on stage at the student union bar, standing to the left of Craig. We had a little smoke machine providing suitable dramatics for the by-now-standard drawn out intro, Alex manically tapping on the hi-hat, Mike building up the atmospherics on his Moog, and myself thumbing a steady bassline whilst Craig plugged in his beautiful metallic red Les Paul with his back to the audience. The dumdumdumdumdumdumdumdum of my bass increasing with Alex's hi-hat being joined by a crack on the snare every eight beats, and the atmospherics building to almost earbursting decibels. Then it would quickly dissipate and silence would ensue. Then Craig would look at us all, and we'd go mental. The usual first track of the night would be "Fingers For Guns", a catchy number about being skint and having to hold up the local Spar to buy drugs. It was inspired by a smack head that Alex had read about who had held up a shop using his fingers as a gun, but had later seen the woman he'd threatened to "shoot" in town, and collared her to apologise for the stress he must have caused. Fucking idiot. It translated to a pretty fucking good track. We worked through a few of the band's other more popular tunes like "BoyGirlBoyGirl" and "Two Black Eyes" throwing in a handful of covers of The White Stripes, 22-20s, The Hives, that kind of thing, working down to the band's interpretations of obscure stuff by Leadbelly and The Palace Brothers. The feeling of being onstage, even if it was only fifty students we were playing to, was immense. Admittedly most of the crowd were friends, and a handful of people who'd seen them before Christmas at The Harley, when it was the last Saturday night that a lot of the students were having before they went home for the break so it was packed and the chance of acquiring fans was a high one. Despite the knowledge that we were preaching to the converted, I felt like I was changing lives, that I was knocking down walls and building bridges. This would quickly fizzle out as I downed a selection of ales paid on at the bar, but the need for that buzz came again when I woke up the next day, a girl called Natalie on the other side of my bed. It seemed like musicians got whatever they wanted, quickly, and this was what I wanted to do.

So I joined the band for the time being, we were still chasing Matt, and we'd got at least a gig a week booked for the next three months. Craig was also the band's manager, he was on a different world that lad. My academic work started to deteriorate inevitably, but it didn't seem to matter in the moment though, we had our music, drugs, and steady conveyor belt of disposable women. Thinking about it now I'm unbelievably embarrassed at my behaviour, but back then it was all for the day. Before I went to uni I'd had one girlfriend, and had smoked a little bit of a spliff, and had, in the first week of our course, admitted that I'd 'smoked cannabis but never marijuana'. Afterwards I couldn't even begin to tell you who I'd slept with, or what drugs I'd consumed, let's just call it a lot, on both counts. It worked itself into my routine and I found myself off my tits at lectures. Rather than stay off, calling in sick every now and then, I'd go all night, vacuuming coke and dropping pills with the other guys then rock up at my media theory lecture stinking of beer with bright red eyes. The worst thing was that the other lads were doing things right. With them, they knew when they could party, and they knew when they had to stay in. This was their lives. I remember one occasion, I asked Alex if he was coming to student night at Kingdom one Monday night as a continuation of one of our sessions and he refused, citing an early morning lecture as his reason, and he asked me if I ever stayed in. I simply ignored the question and went into some tirade about how boring he was, and that he'd end up missing out on something. I think that was my own problem, I was scared of missing out on something, whether it was a line of charlie, or a stolen kiss or fuck from some girl who had a boyfriend back home. I don't think I ever considered what might happen if I dropped behind with my studies. Until the time in the second year that I was called in to have a discussion with the head of faculty and my main lecturer.

I felt empty from the moment I knew I had to see them, to the moment I saw them. But it didn't stop me doing a line and having a spliff before I went in, and it didn't stop me doing this:

"No, what you're doing is trying to persecute me. I have a life outside this institution. I don't need to hear you talking to me like that, you're power crazy. No, Jim, you can't tell me what I'm doing, unless it's within the confines of my education, and within what I need to do to attain my degree, you don't own me, and you don't have the right to dictate what I do out of this place. Yes, I have strayed onto the very beaten path of socialising so much that I can't control myself when I go out, but I'm doing what I can to keep hold of my education, because I care about my future. I just can't stop caring about my future. You may see me as just another number, or name that you see every day when you figure out which of us sheep you're supposed to be teaching, but I have a life, I have a mind. I have a fucking choice of whether I'm going to learn or not. My tuition fees are paid, I have attained the minimum of attendance you require from a student in order to qualify for a degree, should my work be of the necessary standard, and as of yet, I think it's imperative that I inform you that I haven't had anything less than a 2:1 quality piece of work, so get off my fucking back" This, on paper, looks like I had a point, but you have to take into account the fact that this memory is clouded by the drugs I'd taken, and that the meeting went on for about half an hour, whereby I was essentially stripped naked and flogged until I agreed to do what I had to in order to finish the course. Literally speaking, I wasn't actually stripped naked and flogged, but I may as well have been.

Talking to Craig about it later, to my utter dismay he agreed with Jim and Ian. I couldn't believe it. He was a future rock star and I was in his band. It was

like a child being told Santa didn't exist. This guy was somebody whose absolute approval was something I was constantly striving to get hold of. It wasn't a gay thing, far from it, it was just that I would have given up everything to have his talent yet I was simply an adequate bass player. I had sat earlier that day acting like I had that talent, like no matter what happened at uni, I would always have that skill to fall back on. Yet I didn't. My skills took me as far as they needed to for the time being. I was told at school by a biology teacher, I forget his name, that I would forever get through life on my natural ability, but that as long as there were distractions, I would get distracted.
"Dude, we're a student band, not the Stones, you don't need to be Cliff Richards, but you don't need to be Keith Richards, just calm it down a bit, you'll be dead with a needle in your fuckin' arm before we even get a single out". It was a bit of an exaggeration but he had a point and I didn't want to hear it. I decided to lay low for a few days, so I bought a bag of weed and chilled out in my room, thinking about what had been said to me. The decision that culminated from my two day hermit show was that I needed to cool it, stick with the band and sort my life out. It was probably the best thing I could have done to cut myself off from the world. It was the fact that I couldn't sleep without blitzing myself with cannabis that got to me first. I couldn't remember a time anymore that I'd had a night of natural sleep, even though I'd only started on the drugs about nine months earlier. It was crazy, the first night I stayed up until four in the morning, watching Ceefax on BBC2 rolling a constant supply of joints. I'd set my alarm for nine so that the next night I'd be so knackered that I wouldn't be

able to resist sleep. The best laid plans and all that. Of course I got no sleep, and finished off my weed. I clearly had a problem, and needed to fix it.

By the time I'd finally emerged from my room I looked like shit. I felt like shit. And I no doubt smelled like shit. You must think I'm pathetic, classic idiot thinks he's a megastar, running before he could walk, yeah classic fucking cliché man, but in retrospect I know I didn't even nearly hit bottom, I had people there who cared enough to slap my face and tell me to grow up, which I don't think I have done entirely, even at 27 I still wait for the day where I make the transition from man-child to adult in my sleep. But at least I had a plan. I arranged to speak to a counsellor about my problems, and started to get myself sorted. I bought some sleeping tablets to aid me at night, and unless we were gigging I stayed pretty much teetotal, I allowed myself alcohol but the coke and cannabis were a big no-no. To this day I remain drug free. My attitude to my assignments in my third and final year was a vast improvement, and I would manage my time a lot better. I drew the line at going to addiction meetings for the simple fact that I didn't want to associate with yellow fingered, black toothed wife beaters who'd spent the most part of their lives frittering away their jobseekers allowance in the pub, then temporarily pawning in their wives' jewellery at Cash Converters.

I realise now, in my infinite wisdom, that this was erring on the side of blatant ignorance, but that was what alcoholics and drug addicts were to me, and I wanted no part of that thank you very much. The band ended up going their seperate ways, I'm sure you've heard of Craig MacNichol's band "Kissing The Kerb",

I've seen them play a few times at his invitation, the last time was at the Leeds Festival. Alex plays session stuff with a few big bands, and Mike settled down with his girlfriend and the last I heard they'd got three kids. Not my thing kids, not yet anyway.

So I slowly but surely turned myself around, and came away with a 2:1 degree in Media Studies, graduating in 2004. I had no delusions about making it big in Hollywood, so I opted for a slightly easier to break into, yet no less brutal industry of journalism. I don't know anybody big, but I don't anymore intend to, so I stuck around in Sheffield after my degree had finished and got a job at the evening paper working voluntarily to start with while I worked two jobs, then managed to convince them I had enough nous to do at least an adequate job. I've been working in my current capacity as a field journalist for three weeks, and with this Graham Capper murder they've really thrown me in at the deep end, in that I would be around the city getting various updates and throwing together witness statements in time for press this afternoon. The biggest piece I've had to do prior today was covering vandalism at Millhouses Park boating pond, half a page, on page five. This'll be big news in Sheffield for a few weeks yet, I'm sure, murders are happening all the time I know, but how many lads my age are stripped naked and murdered in public? And he wasn't a skinny lad, a photographer I know tells me he was pretty well built, he looked more like a bouncer than a gay cruiser, but appearances can be deceptive, who knew what double life he might have led? Beating up homophobic pissheads at some nightclub, then cottaging around toilets after hours. This could be an angle nobody's looking at it from. It's coming up to nine in the morning and press deadline is two thirty. I better get some answers pretty quickly, I need to impress, I could get an exclusive on something quite immense. If the editors of a tabloid paper want to buy it from me then who's to stop me selling it on for a much higher cost by holding a quiet auction? Who knows where I could go? The world could then be quite literally, my oyster.

Graham

Compiled from Audio and Written Statements
Taken by DI Felix Matouba and DC Suzanne Milton

Sunday 18th October 2009

Maureen Capper (Mother): Our Graham was a gentle giant. He loved his rugby, he really did. He played for the Royal Oak team. He could have been the best scrum half around. I didn't even know what a scrum half was until he came home from school when he was sixteen, a big grin on his face, telling me he'd been picked for the school team and they were going to Belgium for a tour of the schools over there. That's his shirt over in the washing, I was going to wash and iron it today ready for the weekend. He plays.. played.. every week, if he hadn't been run over he could have been a star.
Karl Ollerenshaw (Employer): Capper collected glasses here on weekends. I know, a glass collector, but he was fucking good at it. You could watch him and his eyes would dart all over the place, he'd be all over the dancefloor, under tables and bars, the place was spotless. Usually we'd just send him round the place, and the others would wash and distribute to the bars as needed. He was never a loud one but he didn't have to be, have you seen the size of him? The thing he liked about his job was that he'd find money all over the shop. The amount he could come out with after finding cash on the floor was like twice of what the barstaff were getting with tips, now, I don't have a problem with letting the staff keep money they've found, it's not like my customers come back to me the next day telling me

they remember the serial numbers of the notes they dropped when they were pissed. Purses though, he'd bring straight to me, wallets, handbags, mobile phones, all of them full of original contents or in working order. He wasn't a thief, just a natural magpie.
Maureen Capper: He won a trophy too you know? His team won the under-18s cup. Oh his face was a picture. We were so proud of him.
John Capper (Father): He weren't sharpest tool in box, you know what I mean? He were thick as shit. But he didn't have a bad word to say about anybody. That was the thing with our Graham. He were a big bastard but he were soft as shit. That was his thing, rugby. It were like he had blinkers on to everything else around him, if there were summat he wanted to do, he had to do it. Like a big kid really. But that's the thing, he couldn't do owt else except rugby, so we pushed him to do well in that. He was signed for Leeds you know? Fucked that up though didn't he?
Maureen Capper: That day he won that trophy, there were some of those rugby people there. You know? Those people who come and see if you're any good? Well, they were there, and a man spoke to us after the game, told us they wanted our Graham to see if he was good enough for trials with them, no, sorry, to have trials to see if he were good enough to play for them. Sorry, my head is all over the place
Karl Ollerenshaw: I'll tell you a story about him, brilliant story. This one time, right, I'd been in the office with, well, a friend. Okay, a girl I used to see in the club, Lorraine I think she was called, regular in the club. We used to meet for, y'know? Well, anyway, I'd finished with her and went downstairs to bar one. The

big bar. We had four bars, one, two, three and the bottle bar. I went into the washroom and Capper was there, head deep in the glass washing machine. It must have been broken. Anyway, he was tugging away at whatever it was that was in there, and he catches a glimpse of me there, watching him. He makes this face, like he'd been struggling and made a big, cheeks puffed out kind of face, and he says "Jesus whip". Jesus whip. So I ask him what he'd said and he looked at me like I was mad, he says "Jesus whip", then says "It's a saying" so I gets him to explain to me what it meant, and he says, no word of a lie "You know? That whip that Jesus got whipped with?" As if it was insane that I shouldn't understand what he was saying, honestly, I just burst out laughing. Jesus whip. Obviously he meant *Jesus Wept.*

Alexandra Coles (Colleague): The Jesus whip incident actually happened to me. I wouldn't listen much to what Karl says, he lies. No, what happened was that a couple of the other glass collectors had phoned in sick, so it was just Graham on his own that night. The washing machine had broken, and he was having to wash all the glasses by hand until somebody arrived to sort it out. We were absolutely packed, and Karl had been on at me, asking why the bar was a mess, and why didn't we have enough glasses? The wanker. So because Karl was on my back, I went into the glass room in a huff and had a go at Graham, asking him to hurry up with the pots, customers were queuing with their old pots, but because of health and safety we couldn't rinse them or anything. So Graham turns to me and shouts "God Alex, I'm going as fast as I can, get off my back. Jesus whip!" and I just burst out laughing. I asked him later what he meant and he said it was the whip that Jesus got whipped with. As much shit as I'd taken that day, it only took him saying that to cheer me up. He could make you smile without even meaning to. He just played the bandits too much for my liking.

John Capper: The accident? Oh, that accident. Yeah. After he'd won that trophy, he was called up to Leeds by the scouts for trials with them. He were proper excited, he really were. So off we were up there, we dropped him off in Headingley and then me and the wife went round the city to do a bit of shopping. He got the call the next day to tell him they were gonna put him on their books, and they wanted to sign him up for the youth squad to start with, and then they could see where it went from there. The lads in his team took him on the piss to celebrate, his teacher even went out with them, they were all nineteen so he weren't buying them owt when they were underage, so don't you be going looking for him, he had nowt to do with the accident. Our Graham, he had it all to come, he really did, he woulda been an absolute star, me and Maureen wouldn't have wanted for owt. But the daft sod, he went and fell in front of a car when he were hammered. The stupid little bastard.

Maureen Capper: The cowards that hit him, they just drove off, left him there to die in the street. If I could see them now, I'd kill them, I'd ask them if they were happy, happy to know what they've done to my poor lad. I'd tell them what they've caused, a young career ruined. And they probably don't care. Nobody cares about anybody any more. They broke his arms and legs. I visited him every day for six weeks at hospital, took him magazines and puzzle books. Those wordsearches

were his favourites. He spent all of his time looking for words that weren't on the list of ones to find. Mostly swear words. He'd read them out loud to the other two people on his ward. The nurses didn't like that.
John Capper: When he got home he spent all his time in his room. The doctors told him he wouldn't play rugby again, the accident had done something to his arms. He couldn't lift them over his shoulders, they said he'd never do it again. It killed him it did. One day he was gonna be a sports star, the world at his feet, the next he was nothing but a giant cripple, and he knew it. Me and Maureen argued loads, mostly over money. We were trying to pay for him and ourselves but we needed to be around for Graham all the time too. We were trying to be supportive and civil to each other infront of him, but we'd spend all night arguing, and he could hear us. We were days from separation, then it happened.
Alexandra Coles: From the second we all got our coats on after our shifts, to the second we left the building, Graham would be standing putting his money into the fruit machines. When you asked him if he'd won, he'd say something that kinda freaked me out, I think he'd picked it up from the door lads from when they played, but when they said it, they seemed to be able to pull it off, I don't know if it was just a line that needed to be said by an ignorant sad chauvinistic bastard to sound like it was meant to do, like a joke. But when Graham said "No, it's just been fucking me up my arse with its big electronic cock", it just sounded creepy.
Karl Ollerenshaw: I used to have to shout him out of the place at the end of the night. Tell him I was turning the electricity off, and he'd shout that he'd just got up onto the board and to give him a minute, then he'd stroll

past me saying that the bandit had fucked him up his arse with its big metal cock, then start laughing, like he'd forgotten that he'd spent his wages in the last twenty minutes, and the joke was all it took for him to get over it.

John Capper: It was Maureen that found him on the floor in the bathroom, he'd taken a rusty knife from the shed and chopped into his wrist. There were blood everywhere. I wish to the heavens that it were me that found him, it's gonna haunt her forever that is. You'll just have to give her a minute, she still can't talk about it. So he were there on the floor with his arm half hanging off, the doctors said he was minutes from bleeding to death.

Dr Karen Fox (Surgeon): Of course I remember Graham Capper. We worked for hours to stabilise him, the biggest problem, if I strip it down to layman's terms, was that he'd torn through most of his muscle and tendons, as well as various major arteries, added to that were the flakes of rusted metal embedded into his flesh, he'd made a real mess of himself. I remember when they brought him in, he was in and out of consciousness, and he was simply murmuring about how his arms were useless, he didn't want them any more. As far as we could tell, he wasn't trying to kill himself, he was trying to hack off his own arm. He apparently confirmed this to the hospital counsellor later on, we're obliged to offer support to those who attempt suicide, although she's no longer in our company to concur, she left for America, she met a man on the internet.

John Capper: He spoke to the counsellor woman for months while his arm was healing. I think she helped him turn a corner. What was her name? Gloria something, nice woman. She got it out of him that he was trying to get rid of his arms, "If I can't do rugby I don't need them" were his words, she helped him get over that. Honestly, before he met her, he were never gonna make it to twenty two, after he met her he were a changed lad, he started working with a physio to get better. Again, it were like he were blinkered, all he knew were that he had to get his arms better if he were ever gonna play his beloved again, he went swimming all the time, they said that'd do it good. He got his job a couple of years ago. It were good to see him out of the house and meeting people. He used to come home and tell us stories the next morning about things he'd done, what funny things other people had done, it were really good for him.

Karl Ollerenshaw: I don't do proper interviews, I'll just get the applicants in and we have a little chat. You can tell a lot more about a person when they're at ease and just talking to you. If you sit and hammer them with questions they just clam up and you don't know anything about them. I definitely remember Capper's interview, he was sent here by the job centre. I won’t lie to you, usually the job centre applicants are smack heads or scrotes who last a night before they've nicked somebody's purse or they decide they can't be arsed. I prefer the ones who have been recommended by staff, they tend to be a bit more reliable. But Capper, he sat and talked crap about his family, his gambling, and rugby. He told me all about what had happened to him with the accident and the other thing. For some reason, that kind of honesty goes a long way with me, so I gave him a chance. I mean, I knew he weren't all there

upstairs but not many of my glass collectors are. That's why they're glass collectors.
Andy Freeman (Colleague): Graham got the staff taxi with me after work. It were weird, he'd sit in silence until there were just me and him left, then he'd just start talking and not stop. God, I heard about him betting on horses, and this chance he had to win ten grand, he spoke about that one quite a bit. Every night we got the taxi, he'd say "I'm still waiting to hear about that money, I can't wait. I'm gonna be rich" like it was a guarantee he was going to be in the money at some point. I think it was just some scam he was gonna get burned by, but that's him all over. He always got led down the wrong path by people smarter than him. I mean, if you're gonna try and cut your own arm off, you're not wired up right are you? I reckon he got killed by bookies or summat, he owed a lot of money out. I only know because he told me, it weren't a big secret. Honestly, he couldn't hold his own water that cunt.
Maureen Capper: I don't know anything about him gambling. He started to play for the Royal Oak every now and then. His dad used to go in there on Sundays, and they'd all got together and signed him up, he'd maybe get five or ten minutes on the pitch but that's all he needed. He felt like he was normal again, that he finally beat the darkness that he had inside himself since the accident. He was a different person.
John Capper: He had a job, money in his pocket, and he was playing rugby again. His life was getting to where he wanted it. Why did they kill him? You have to find this bastard that did it. I know he were never gonna move out of our house, but that was fine with me. The last time I saw him he said he were going to the city

centre. Said he was meeting somebody, a friend from work he said.

Andy Freeman: No, he weren't meeting anybody from work. Nobody ever saw him out of work. I don't know why he'd lie. Sometimes everybody'd go back to Ben's for a few beers and tunes, but Graham never did. He just didn't socialise with us. If I had to have a guess at who he was meeting, I'd stick with my first one of a bookie. Seriously, unless he was talking about what he'd done with his mum and dad the day before, or who his team were playing on Sunday, he was telling me about bets he'd put on. I couldn't tell you why it was only ever me he spoke to, I think a lot of the other staff thought he was a freak, Alex used to chat with him. I just humoured him. Maybe he saw that as me being his friend.

Maureen Capper: He always had money, how could he be in debt if he always had money?

John Capper: Our Graham weren't a gambler. I promise you. Please just find the murdering scumbag that killed him. Please.

Karl Ollerenshaw: By last week, Capper had taken out a sub on his next two weeks wages. I don't know what kind of trouble he was in, but this isn't as clear cut as you think it is. I don't know for definite, but whatever trouble he was in, he was in deep. If his parents don't know he was in debt, he was obviously hiding it from them. He idolised his dad, so I reckon he wouldn't want to let him down. He did mention that he might be coming into a lot of money soon, thanks to something he'd applied for, then he didn't say anything about it again. That's all I know about that, I just thought it might be worth mentioning.

Alexandra Coles: No, he didn't tell me who he was meeting. He said he was going to take me on holiday when he won some money. I had a soft spot for him but that was out of pity. No, I wasn't seeing him. Are you sick? He was a lovely guy, but despite that he was still a creepy guy.

Andrew Freeman: Has anybody told you the "Jesus whip" story? I was in the glass room with him one night...

Daisy Beckford

Taken from Internet Blog: Killer In Your Midst

Sunday 25th October 2009

Four bodies. All naked. All with their throats cut. Apparently there was no link between the victims. No pattern at all except the way they were killed. First was Graham Capper, a twenty four year old nightclub worker, his body found by a pensioner in Meersbrook Park 8 days ago. On the following Monday that of Lisa Wallett, heroin addict and at twenty one, already a mother of four, was discovered 2 miles away in Heeley by drunken teenagers. The next day, across the city a student finds the naked body of Ruby Spenner, local café proprietor, thirty one, with her neck sliced open. Again, no link. Several days pass without incident, but now I turn on the news to see the latest killing. As yet unnamed, believed to be a man in his early twenties, was found by a hysterical tram of commuters, as the body was left in plain view at the site of the demolished Tinsley cooling towers by Meadowhall. Four bodies, eight days, I suppose now is the time to worry.

Every paper you read is telling you it's the Sheffield Ripper. The Sheffield Ripper. What if he, or she, were to head out to Rotherham to make a killing? South Yorkshire Ripper? The New Yorkshire Ripper? Jack the Ripper killed prostitutes. Peter Sutcliffe supposedly predominantly killed prostitutes. This person has randomly slaughtered four people, none as yet proven as sex workers (and I truly believe there is a journalist out there who has tried to prove it so), perhaps the term itself is misleading to everybody except the every-day readers of The Sun? (To paraphrase a musician named Gonzales, A tabloid paper's readership, don't believe in shit, they need leadership). It's ridiculous that the killer becomes bigger than the crime just by the media's own falling over themselves to give them a suitably dramatic title. The basic facts that four lives have been snuffed out for what appears to be no reason seem irrelevant. What is relevant to them, is that there's a new monster in town, and we all have front row seats at the *theatre du tabloid's* telling of the story. You can ignore it, but the harsh facts are that 80% of this country are idiots. You only have to look at the popularity of X Factor and Big Brother to see this. Yes, there are good things to be taken from mindless dross on television, good things such as the opportunity to witness the emergence of yet another throwaway celebrity you can feel happy to despise. Good things such as the live breakdown of simpletons who, in their transparently bloodthirsty chase for fame, will emulate simpletons past and follow them down the long desperate road to Z-list fame and drunken nights falling down in front of a half interested paparazzi, nights afforded to them by exclusive interviews in, you've guessed it, The Sun.

Now it would be hypocritical of me to go into a tirade about the state of the media and of the nation, how the victims are generally ignored unless there's a montage of sad photographs, chosen by loved ones who must decide which haunting image they must subject themselves to on every front page on every newspaper on every new day. No, I cannot climb aboard my high horse without first making tribute to, and showing my

respect for the victims.
Graham Capper, The Gentle Giant. A loner by all accounts, nobody you would want to befriend, but by the state of his parents on Richard and Judy he was well loved at home. So what is more important? A hectic yet ultimately shallow social life whereby you may have a hundred friends, but not one of them can tell you your favourite film, or song? Or a life where friends are the luxury you can afford yourself whilst absorbing the unabated love in the family home? Most of us may retort with arguments about balancing the pair, but if you can't, what can you choose? Graham Capper was said to be on the slow side, but he was loved, and protected for the most part by his parents. You can read into mental health issues if you must, but this doesn't mean that he had earned his own murder simply by slitting his own wrists years ago does it?

Lisa Wallett, young working class mother with an unfortunate addiction to heroin. Even (and I say even begrudgingly) Lisa had things to live for. Heroin addiction is a disease, yet it is a curable disease. A disease of the mind and of the heart that drags it's wretched host down a detestable path, through shame, hatred and lies. Lisa had four children, none of whom were over the age of 7, and none of whom could understand what had happened to their mother. Please put yourself in their shoes from maybe, ten years down the line. How hard is that going to be, for both the children, and their grandmother? The grandmother that has to live with seeing her own daughter pulled into heroin addiction for a start, then has to identify the naked, blue lifeless lump of flesh she once gave birth to. The victims are only the first victims here, the victims are purely the butterfly flapping it's wings somewhere else a week ago, the real effect starts now.

Ruby Spenner, who ran a small café near Sheffield University, well loved by her customers, and reasonably successful at what she did. She'd found a prime spot and at the right time, and word has it that she was looking to expand into two or three extra locations. Interviews with her partner Gina, to whom she was married in a civil partnership last year, tell us that she was a likeable person, never had a bad word against people, and vice versa. Gina explained that Ruby was waiting on a windfall she was going to be in for, so they could expand the business together, yet she never got the chance. I try to be as subjective as I can in my blogs, but as I write this I cry. I don't know anything about any of the victims apart from what I have read, or witnessed on the news, but how can I not, even when I only scrape the surface of the loss and pain these people must be going through?

And so we wait to hear news of the fourth body. Another young life snatched from existence to leave behind family, friends, a boy or girlfriend, and possibly children. A young life that could have blossomed into anything. When I was a young girl, I wanted to be a hairdresser, then when I was a teenager I wanted to be a solicitor, before going to university I changed my mind several times and went on to study Leisure and Tourism. This isn't my biography. I simply wanted to express that people have dreams, be they changeable dreams of careers and ambitions, or static from-birth dreams of having a white wedding, somewhere exotic perhaps, with a handsome husband to dote upon. This person, and I so so wish that I knew his name, if only to show him the respect that he deserves, had dreams. He may not have been a deep thinker like you or I dear reader, there is every chance that he didn't have a proper thought at all in his short life, but even in that case, is it not arguable that he may have wanted a good job? Or something more material like he couldn't decide between a nice Audi or a more down to earth Vauxhall? Regardless of whatever he wanted out of life, the choice is no longer his to make.

Four bodies, eight days. I don't doubt that we will be seeing more. The people of Sheffield are terrified. At the supermarket I overheard the girl at the checkout talking to the man in front of me, My dad won't let me work here after 7 o'clock, he wants me home by dark. I wanted to ask her why, when two of the victims were murdered in daylight? Of course I have more tact than that, but it's true, forensic reports have shown that both Lisa Wallett and Ruby Spenner had been murdered around noon on their respective days of death. So should it not be more sensible of a father clearly looking out for his daughter's best interests, to impose a 24 hour curfew on her, and the rest of his flock? What rules might he force his family to live by had it been the middle of summer? Don't go out after 10:17pm? Of course not. I guess this is just the psychology of winter. My neighbours call in their cats and dogs mid-afternoon then lock up their doors and windows until morning. Again, there is no real logic to this. I hate to jest at such a time, but cats and dogs? I have not yet seen a report into the murder of a Labrador that had had its throat cut and it's fur taken. Neither has the killer broken into houses to take down his prey. Everybody in this city now believes themselves to be the next victim, and I continue to place the blame for this frenzy directly at the feet of the media. We cannot ignore that every editor of every newspaper, every news reporter, for all the humanity they claim to have, currently has the biggest secret smile inside. This fourth body guarantees that every word will be anticipated with baited breath, every sentence will be devoured and the reader will sit, hankering after more information that they believe will save their lives. Information which will more often than not, be useless. Information that these people want you to have. There's so much news out there, about the victims, evidence, potential suspects. Do you seriously think they're going to give it all out at once? Not a chance. No, we're going to be fed the news in miniature rations, enough to satiate our desire for knowledge, but enough for us to sit like intent children in front of the television. Eagerly anticipating that next slice of news. They can't do it for long at this rate though, the news will be pouring out of every channel, paper, radio station, following this story. Because the killer will make another sacrifice soon enough, and any news will quickly become old news.

Of course, there are other factors. The killer, for one. He, or she, has panicked an entire city. If the papers, or the police, had a clue as to motives, then they could get right down to cracking the case. But the killer has worked in such a way that the people they kill mean nothing to them, they mean nothing to each other. Probably the only people they meant anything to were the people they meant everything to. This is not to say the killer has found drips and drabs of society and stalked them, researched them if you will, found out everything about them, quite probably far from it. It is likely that this person has merely has killed out of compulsion to kill, and found themselves with a hunger to kill again. The first kill was perhaps only an opportunist crime, no more. And like Lisa Wallett after her first taste of opiates, this person now has to continue to chase the dragon if they are to ever feel as good as they did that first time. I'm no psychologist but could it not be argued that the killer then takes their victims' clothes as a trophy? Perhaps something to keep as a memento of the kill, to have at hand to ebb the growing desire to go out and kill again. Or to make it burn stronger than ever. On the other hand, they may not be as twisted as that. More calculated and thoughtful perhaps, simply taking the clothes to dispose of, destroying vital clues in the process. Either is worrying. The former would make them an unstable psychopath with an insatiable craving to spill the blood of others, the latter a cold, heartless monster killing for fun, and with enough control over their own mind to know to remove evidence. We can go round and round the houses dissecting their psyche. We can assume that they wet the bed as a child. We can assume that they weren't hugged enough as a child. We can make all the assumptions in the world but the truth is the only person who knows the reasoning behind this spate of unnecessary deaths is the killer.

Disturbingly, it could be anybody. I don't want to preach about the media sensationalising matters to cause panic and then go on to make it worse, but it's true. If we have a person roaming the streets of Sheffield randomly slaughtering people, then it could be any one of us that is next. And on the other side of the same coin, it could be anybody that is doing the killing. This is the only given right now. I don't mean for us all to look at our postman, our butcher, or our brother or sister through suspicious eyes. The police are doing enough of that. You can be guaranteed that every violent criminal that has passed through the doors of Her Majesty's hotels is under the microscope, being followed from whatever hostel they call home, to wherever they deem it necessary to go. And in my opinion the police are wasting their time. I promise you, this situation will roll on and on and on. And on. I can think of nothing more certain right now. I also promise you, that we are currently living within a pivotal time for Sheffield, this time we are in right now will stay with the city forever. We cannot ignore that this current climate will define an era for the city. The common cliché of Where were you when...? will apply to millions of peoples' lives when, or indeed if, the culprit is finally caught. In 2012, our favourite tabloids will feature the story when they scour the history books for a subject for On this day five years ago... and people will tell each other that they knew that person that was finally caught. They'll undoubtedly claim that they once slept with/ lived next door to/ are related to The Sheffield Ripper, claiming their exclusive place within stories that never happened. If it isn't a beautiful yet immensely dim fame hungry harlot sprawled half-naked across the centre pages of The News Of The World claiming that she once slept with the killer, but always knew there was something wrong with them (and you'll note with glee the juxtaposition of pictures featuring semi-naked model with story predominantly based on the murders themselves intermittently interrupted by sordid details of the night itself), it's the sombre real-life story of the one that got away in Closer, or Take-A-Break, pictures of somebody staring solemnly at the camera whilst standing back straight, hands holding each other to the front of their body, like they are offering their respects at a funeral. Either that or a close-up of them, chin resting on both hands as they lean on a table. Still solemn. There's no need to imagine it, you'll witness it soon enough. There's no better way of claiming notoriety than having once experienced a living encounter with a killer. Or a dead man who cannot refute your claims. Well, that and appearing on Big Brother.

As I write this a news report has identified the fourth victim as James Crosby, twenty two, an art graduate in the first year of his PGCE. A future teacher. Such a waste.

Daniel

Monday 19th October 2009

He hadn't slept in two days. Not after Saturday. Every time he closed his eyes he saw the struggle with the fat one. The blood. Punching him to the ground. Winding him. Standing over his hunched body and drawing his knife across his throat. It couldn't have gone on more than a few minutes. His twitching body. His desperate gasps for air that would never come, between coughing up thick dark blood over his own face and into his eyes. The fat kid's lungs eventually giving up the fight. His mouth ceasing to reach for oxygen. Daniel could picture this lifeless mound that until that moment, was a living breathing thing. Every time he closed his eyes he saw himself removing his victim's shirt to reveal a roadmap of stretch marks of varying shades of purple. He saw the left arm, marked with a wicked looking jagged scar, like he'd been on the wrong end of a chainsaw. Imprinted on his mind was the sickening sound of his victim's skin tearing as he caught the wound pulling the shirt from around his bulbous head and his own struggling to keep the contents of his stomach in their current location. If he closed his eyes he would picture pulling down the cheap denim jeans and pale blue underpants, and falling over as he strained to pull off the trainers. The white socks turned brown and crusted like they had been on his blotchy sweaty feet for days. Placing everything he had taken into his backpack with the knife and his latex gloves. Then running.

That was two days ago. Now, exhausted yet with

a renewed sense of exhilaration, Daniel was watching the smack head. She wasn't hard to find, that kind of person never was. He'd seen her out and about in the city on several occasions, usually begging for cigarettes or change to get the bus home to places he knew she didn't live because they changed every time he encountered her. One time stuck in his head more than the others. She had confronted him outside the bus station, demanding cigarettes. When he informed her that he only had one left, her accomplice- a skinny prick with a cap sitting high atop his skull, blackened teeth and a light layer of fur parading as a moustache above his top lip -yelled "S'alright mate, we only want one" and as he laughed and walked past the pair, ignoring the comment, they hurled a barrage of abuse at him for being "a tight cunt", he had considered that time that he should turn round and confront them, but it clearly wasn't worth it, they were probably rattling from smack withdrawals anyway, so they had enough to worry about without black eyes and busted noses adding to the mix. No, he'd decided that the thing that would hurt them the most, would be to turn round, take out his last fag, and light it, laughing. It went down like a lead balloon, they simply offered more abuse, this time racial, as he walked away, but it was a moral victory for Daniel. If somebody could only call you a black cunt then they weren't really worth kicking the fuck out of, they had no imagination, they were simple people with simple minds. He had friends that would stab people that only looked at them the wrong way. They were paranoid old West Indians that had grown up with the stigma that the colour of their skin was all people saw, so they stuck together and didn't give a fuck about the consequences. Daniel knew why they were doing it but he considered himself above it. He had a brain and wasn't afraid to use it. What pissed him off more were the ignorant folks who would engage him in conversation, telling him they weren't racist, that they had a lot of black friends, that their brother-in-law was black and he was a sound bloke. He had friends, black, white, Asian, and they were just his friends. Race was rarely mentioned, because it wasn't important, friends are friends are friends. That's why he walked away from the addicts' abuse, they didn't know any better. The skinny lad offering most of the abuse, in nasal whining yelps. Daniel knew that the second he turned round the kid would run away, he just couldn't be arsed with the effort. The girl simply screamed about him being a wanker.

The thing was, she wasn't actually that unattractive to look at. Big blue tired eyes, a petite button nose, tiny ears framed by lank greasy dirty blonde hair. Her downturned mouth that seemed to be a standard feature of that breed of human, would no doubt be hiding a beautiful smile, but she didn't look to be one that smiled unless she was heading home with heroin in her pocket. She was tall and slim, but not overly skinny like most of her opiate-loving peers, probably due to having had several kids and retaining some weight. He'd also seen her being arrested outside Boots by the cathedral, plain clothes police rooting through her carrier bag lined with security-tag nullifying tinfoil, she was screeching about having done fuck all wrong, but the fact that she was then dragged kicking and screaming toward an approaching police car told him she had been proved wrong on the "doing fuck all" front. Daniel hated smack heads. The city was full of them. That's why one less wouldn't hurt. No, one wouldn't make a difference. The fat kid had a certain sorrow to him, he'd spoken to him for five minutes but had forgotten his name. He was slow in the head, easy pickings really, he actually felt bad that he was his first choice once he'd had the time to think about what he'd done. The smack head on the other hand, she was ripe for it. She clearly had to die, if somebody hadn't got to her first.

He was already in the area she was residing in, it being only a mile from Meersbrook Park, the place of his first killing. The worst thing she could have done was go home. She was wide open. He figured that she'd panicked when the message came through, and thought safety would be there, so he hung around, laying low. Her flat was an upstairs one-bedroom flat. The front windows boarded up, having been smashed by angry dealers, people she had more than likely fucked over for cash, bored kids. The back window was still intact but he hadn't seen any lights on in the thirty-odd hours he'd been here. There was, however, a glow from the open door he could see through the window, so she was in the front room, and had been for about a day-and-a-half. He'd followed her home so he knew she was in there, and she would have to come out soon. None of her multitude of kids had been around, although an older woman had been there with a pushchair. The child looked too young to have been hers, so he assumed that she was the smack head's mother, bringing round her grandchild to check on her. She didn't answer the door, and the older woman scuttled back up the street, moaning that she would be waiting half an hour for a bus now. Daniel had been nestled in undergrowth between two corrugated iron garages for what seemed like forever, and was beginning to question his own sanity that he'd seen the girl come here in the first place. Like he'd been imagining that he followed her here. The images imprinted on his mind wouldn't let him sleep anyway, but he was getting pretty fucking uncomfortable. He wanted to get up, stroll around and stretch his legs, but something inside him told him to stay put. He was a part of this now, he'd made his bed and he would have to lie in it.

It was about noon when he heard her door go. He saw her looking around, full of paranoia. Then he watched her hurriedly meander into an alleyway across the street. Now or never thought Daniel, and he lifted himself out of his haven of greenery. He felt his legs numb up, then pins and needles take over. Stamping his feet for a few moments, he remembered his prey, then hobbled across to the entrance of the alley. Approaching it at an angle so as not to be detected, he stuck his head round the corner, she was quickly dancing down the path. It was about half a mile long, and she was about a hundred metres in. A small glance around showed nobody. So in he went. The pins and needles wore off as he followed from a distance, rapidly gaining on her. He was as quiet as he could be, so there was no way she could have been turning round to respond to his noise, more her own paranoia he reckoned. She had turned her head round, and spotted him. He froze. She turned round and froze herself. They looked into each other's eyes for seconds. Each registering what was happening. She knew. She had to know. She had to recognise him. She ran. He ran. He

felt himself gaining ground on her easily. His feet pounded the ground, the two days lack of sleep gone and forgotten now he was pursuing his prey like a cheetah does a zebra. Suddenly she stopped about halfway down the alley and turned to him. He stuttered to a halt about thirty feet from her. Around them, six or seven feet of greenery, beyond that a playing field on one side, a residential car park on the other. Perfect thought Daniel. The smack rat didn't take her eyes off of him as her hands were vigorously patting around her body, searching for something. Her face full of panic. Crying. He stood watching her nervously, she revealed a knife and waved it toward him.
"Come on then ya fuckin' cunt! Bring it on! I'll cut ya bastard 'ead off!" she yelped through her tears, "Why'd you come for me? Eh? Why did you fuckin' come for me?"
Daniel stood in silence. Facing her off. Shaking, never taking his eyes off hers, getting his breath back. The only thing he could hear was his heartbeat. She lunged for him, screaming as she hurtled toward him. As she reached him flailing the blade around he punched her square in the face knocking her off her feet and into unconsciousness. Her head hit the ground with force and bounced up as her body settled on the floor. She was still but breathing. Glancing around quickly he dragged her into a hedgerow with his hands in her armpits, dropped her limp body once they were under cover, and pulled the blade and gloves from his bag. Grabbing a handful of her greasy, almost wet hair he lifted up her head and inhaled and closed his eyes as he felt her blood pour down his hand as the knife sliced into her neck. He heard the flickering of her blood

spray against the leaves in the hedgerow. Exhaling he reopened his eyes and looked down at his work. Her glistening oesophagus exposed, blood leaking down her neck and soaking into her t-shirt and forcing it to cling to her chest at which he afforded himself a peek before remembering himself and continuing to remove her clothes, the soaked red t-shirt first to reveal her bare, small and perky breasts, her tiny nipples smeared with a crimson which continued down her body, and the insides of her arms dotted with dark red specks running up the veins. The stained and oily tracksuit bottoms proved to be far easier to remove than the jeans he tore from the fat one's blue legs. As much as he'd hate to admit it, he felt a stirring in his crotch as he peeled off her panties to expose the shaven and flowered flesh of her vagina. She would definitely have been fuck material if she hadn't messed up her life. Or wasn't dead. Something inside him was tempted but he remembered the warning and continued the stripping, filled his bag with her clothes, and calmly strolled out of the hedgerow, into the alley and onto the street. If anybody had heard any of the commotion, the was no evidence of such.

This time there was no sickness, nothing to denote that Daniel was a newcomer to bloodshed. What he did feel however, was the adrenaline pumping through his veins. Excitement running through his skin, his muscle, his blood, right the way through his bones, joints, and marrow. He was almost turned on by the power he had held over this girl's life. Nothing this time felt surreal. It was more like nothing had ever been more real. He had actually enjoyed killing her. When he had held her head up by the hair, drawing the knife across her throat, he felt alive. I'd kill to feel like this again thought Daniel, then smirked to himself. Of course, he'd have to, whether he liked it or not.

He watched the bus pass him into the station, as he huddled into himself, alone on a bench. A young woman caught his eye as he scanned its occupants, a faint glimmer of recognition sparked between them. *Keisha.* An old girlfriend from school. Regret ambled through him as he looked away from her. He'd treated her badly, when she'd failed to back him up when he was trying to punt his mix-tapes and get spots at the grime nights he regularly attended, she had cast doubt over his potential, so he'd kicked that bitch to the kerb, called her all the names he could think of, spread rumours, cast doubt on her integrity. He'd been harsh, but the bitch should have had faith in a man. He watched an old woman pulling a tartan trolley was talking to herself, she was wearing a fleece coat covered with scenery depicting wolves howling at the moon. He'd never understood the popularity of those things. He could walk through the city and be guaranteed to witness at least twenty of the fuckers, ranging from horses galloping in a forest, through Scotch Terriers playing with wool (wool? Dogs play with wool?), and bears prancing around. He'd die from hypothermia before he ever wrapped himself in one. He rose from the bench, hauling his backpack up and swinging it over his shoulder. There were two ways to the Wicker Arches from here, through the bus station, or round Pond's Forge, the former being the quickest. Chancing his arm he found himself striding through the automatic doors to an announcement that "Sheffield Interchange, is a smoke free zone" in an obvious nod to the trio of lads all sharing a shady cigarette in a huddle. As he coasted by them the tannoy sparked into life again, this time "Put yer bloody fags out yer bloody idiots!" as some guard had been watching them on the video screens, raging into a walkie talkie at some poor sap who had to go face down three teenagers over mans breaking the law. He bristled with a sudden paranoia. Cameras. Man had been a fucking idiot. His paranoia leapt a further few notches when he felt his mobile vibrate against his leg. The only phone he had was the one they gave him. A message had come through. He did an about turn on the spot and passed the teenagers, not smoking anymore but harassing a middle aged guy in the bright yellow jacket, sent there to police them. As he walked away he took the mobile out and checked the message. *Get out of there ASAP*. Fuck's sake.

Christophe

Saturday 7th September 2009

His telephone rang. Removing it from its perch on the front of the dashboard of his immaculate black Vauxhall Astra 1.9L CDTI he glanced at the blue flashing window and flipped open the mobile.
"Mr Hoxton" he greeted.
"Christophe, what's the news?" his immediate superior getting straight to the point, he wasn't one for offering pleasantries and small talk at the best of times.
"Well sir, the applicant is perfect. No close family and seemingly no friends. Today he was at home all evening, then left the house at nightfall to wander the streets, before returning at around ten-thirty and going to bed. He spends two or three days a week in darkness sir, his electricity is on a meter, and he doesn't appear to have the funds to keep it running constantly"
"So he's in dire need of money?"
"Exactly sir, it's my belief that it would be easy to get him involved"
"Good work Christophe, keep me updated"
"Yes sir"
Replacing the telephone into its perch, Christophe returned to his reconnaissance. The audio from the applicant's house was now at a minimum, the guy having been in bed for the last hour. It wasn't hard for Deitmann to get the bug in there, but for what it was worth all this guy did was talk to himself. At first Christophe thought he'd got somebody else in there that never left the house, an elderly parent or some such, or a pet that he liked to have around as company. It

became evident after a couple of days that he was just speaking to himself. He'd discussed the local politics, what he could possibly have for his dinner, and the merits of a sweater over a vest. Christophe had never encountered a person as dull as the one he was staking out.

Until five years ago he had never spent time out of Paris unless it was a holiday with his parents to Morzine, God knew why they were so smitten with the place. All of his friends would be taken to Italy or Greece on holiday in the summer but they would go year after year on skiing holidays to the French Alps. Over the years he became a familiar face amongst the locals, and foreigners who appeared every year as instructors, bar staff, or cleaners. He would leave his parents to scenery chasing and go party with his seasonal friends. He knew other Parisians who would use trips to Morzine as an excuse to steal, take advantage of the foreign tourists and staff. A friend of his named Hubert, from the St Germain district would come out here on a single train ticket, a few francs, and the clothes he was wearing. Four days later he would leave with over ten thousand francs and a suitcase full of snowboard accessories having stolen the gear and several downhill mountain bicycles. Being there with his family he would tend to sway toward the party lifestyle over the criminal, and often went three or four days without sleep as he fucked his way through half the tourists. His own predilection toward emptying his balls at every opportunity meant he would regularly wake up beside girls or guys, occasionally both. If he awoke alone he would furiously masturbate to ease the tension in his pants. Christophe felt it to be a harmless hobby. He'd rather be a fuck monkey over a kleptomaniac like Hubert any day. As long as he was careful, and both parties were happy with the arrangement, where was the harm? Most of his conquests had partners back home themselves, and they all knew that what was happening was for one night only. A female friend, Claudie, an instructor with a beautiful ass, who was impervious to his advances would ask him how he could do it, how he could take such an impersonal approach to something so intimate. He couldn't answer her, had he even been listening, as a stunning blonde had approached the bar behind Claudie and he was already working through his game plan to get his dick inside her.

Usually he'd advance upon them, a glint in his eye, a cheeky grin on his face, his ears already pricked up, like a radar for whichever language they were speaking. He spoke, to varying fluency, seven languages. It was better if they were English, *Les Femmes Anglaise* were easier to bed. They tended to be more receptive to his way of thinking, they knew he wouldn't be sticking around in the morning, and they knew what it was. French girls, especially the locals, were a lot more dubious about his intentions, if they had met one guy like Christophe, they had met a hundred, and they were so much sharper of tongue than the English. He had overheard one French girl ask an English guy to light her cigarette for her. The poor man patted his pockets and shrugged, explaining that he didn't have a match, but asked her if she would like a drink anyway. The girl looked the man directly in the eye and said dryly "A man without a match, is like a man without a dick" then turned on her heels and went elsewhere for a flame. The poor guy, he watched her walk away, and looked around, hoping nobody had witnessed this brutal rejection. Christophe smiled at him, offering a sympathetic look, then shrugged as he took his own lighter to the girl, and added fire to the end of her cigarette. He didn't even smoke but he knew the score. Later on they would be fucking until the early hours. Not all French girls were unapproachable.

There was the odd occasion that he would find himself with another man. The Germans were probably the worst offenders for homosexual behaviour in his experience. He didn't take it in the ass, no way, he wasn't that way inclined, but he would happily stick his dick the ass of a guy who was that way inclined. He'd only done it four or five times but it was the rush of the orgasm he lived for, not the person he was coming into. Those times were opportunist fucks, simply a case of being in the right place at the right time, he'd never actually go out looking for men, it was them that had to approach him. He'd fucked an American girl once, the smell she gave off was stomach churning. With every slap of him pounding his dick into her chubby ass a sweaty, pungent aroma filled his nostrils, so much so that he could taste her pussy without even having eaten her out. The Americans were a disgusting race, they really were. Sure, the Germans were a race of fags, but they knew how to keep clean. The English were sluts with no morals, but they knew how to fuck. The Americans, no, they were for grudge fucks. Every American he fucked, he would do it with as much ferocity as his body could give. He remembered choking one girl when she was sucking his dick, as she hungrily gobbled his meat into her mouth he took a hold of her head and forced it further down onto it, a choking moan and a gagging sound before she pulled away and threw up onto his stomach. He had tossed from the bed and spat on her, branding her a filthy cunt, ejecting her from his chalet half naked, covered in vomit and sobbing. After that he had returned to his bed and masturbated; satisfied at his treatment of the Yank.

This was how he spent his annual fortnight away. Back in Paris he would trawl the streets of the arrondissement of Montmartre with Hubert, moving from bar to bar until they found themselves at a club, or more often than not, a brothel. Hubert would pick the pockets of sex tourists, there from all over the world, looking for an easy lay from the area's mass of hookers and transsexuals. Another favourite trick of Hubert's was to sell small deals of shitty drugs at extortionate prices, whispering Hashish, Coca, Ecstasy to groups of foreigners as they passed him. The best customers would be groups of men, having what the English called a Stag Party. They could see them all from a distance, shouting to each other when they were only a metre apart, laughing and jeering at one another whenever they passed one of the area's XXX cinemas and strip clubs and the girls would come out touting for business. Christophe could see them discussing whether or not they had the balls to go and see what was inside. He'd also seen the same kind of people drunkenly laughing and acting like children when they were standing looking at pornography in the sex shops, shouting the titles of DVDs and magazines to each other. It was sad to see that the women were just as bad, like they had never seen a porno before. It was a strange thing. Down in Morzine, the women were sophisticated fuck machines who, behind closed doors, could swallow his come over and over again, and be very good at it. But put them with their friends in a sex shop and they turned into *les enfants,* giggling with each other whilst they pretended to suck a dildo. He knew never to approach groups of English girls when he was in Paris, as they acted the exact same way as they did in the sex shops. Sure, one of them might give him a smile but they would never leave each other, they would turn coy, and one of them would throw abuse at him until the rest took this as their cue, and all of them would drunkenly shout at him until he made a hasty retreat and they would turn and giggle at their own behaviour. *Les enfants.*

Between the bars and the club, Christophe and Hubert's brothel of choice was usually *Kiss Me.* Sabine, a Tunisian hooker, would come over, kiss his ear and whisper to follow her to a back room. Sabine was his favourite, she was only short, but she had an ass to die for, a pussy that was pristine, and titties that stared at heaven as she rode him. He knew she had to moan to make the customer think she was enjoying it, to make them want to come back. He felt that with him, it was different, she would scream down the house, dig her fingernails deep into his chest, tearing out chunks of his flesh, the pain spurring him on further, thrusting upward from the bed until he could feel his dick almost in her stomach, hitting the roof of her pussy. Then he'd flip her over onto her knees and slide his tongue deep into her ass, the bitter rubbery taste of condoms from clients past, but that wasn't his concern, he loved the taste of her ass and it turned him on to see himself so close to a girl's most intimate parts. He'd met her in a bar when she was on a break, and they'd spent the whole of the hour talking at length about their lives, the subject of her occupation never coming up until she passed him her card as she left, whispering that she wanted him badly, giving him a long lingering smile before turning and heading round the corner to *Kiss Me*. He'd never even considered taking the time to finish his drink as he hopped from his stool and chased after her, already removing the Euros from his wallet. They still accepted Francs in the brothel, but the Euro had by then taken over as the currency of choice and he had encountered some hookers who would only fuck for Euros anymore, so when in Montmartre, he would only ever carry Euros. It was a pain, as he'd always been a fan of the Franc, his parents had refused to convert, and his father's *Boulangerie* still dealt exclusively in the Franc, so it was a belief bred into him since its inception that the Euro was a bad idea. Not so much of a bad idea that he wouldn't use it to buy himself a blow job, but still, on principal he was against the Euro.

May Twentieth, 2004. The day that changed his life and the way it was going. Up until that day his life plan consisted entirely of seeing himself as a sexual vagrant, who, rather than worrying about where that next meal might come from, his anxiety was over when and where his next sexual instance may occur. With the benefit of hindsight, he should have seen it coming. The times that he would sit aboard the Metropolitan train, his eyes fixed intently on lone women, waiting to catch their gaze, so he could offer them a confident smile and silently mouth Bonjour to test the water. Every now and then he would get a return on his investment of effort, but usually he'd receive a scowl, and his prey would return their attentions to Le Figaro or Cosmo, occasionally glancing back up to make sure this lecherous pig was not still staring. Christophe would be sure to never alight the Metro at the same destination as the recipient of his attention if they hadn't reciprocated a smile, as it was a sure way of being arrested. Or worse. He knew from experience that girls have boyfriends, husbands, brothers, all willing to lay a fist upon the face of a man who couldn't take no for an answer and the only women who responded to a man with a bruised cheek and lip engorged with blood in Paris were scum, no, he'd get no sympathy for his wounds, just the attraction of some Moroccan selling train tickets at *Barbés Rochechouart* for a 1 Euro mark up. Yet on the day that changed his life, Christophe didn't listen to the voice in his head he recognised as common sense as he'd undertaken his silent wooing of a beautiful girl across from himself who'd already made it clear that he was going to get nowhere. She was slender, had smooth blonde hair, thick secretarial spectacles, and very expertly wore a fitted grey suit which complemented and accentuated her round breasts beautifully, white blouse appearing from underneath the buttoned jacket, on his random meanderings across the city he'd seen her climbing aboard at *Trinité d'Estienne d'Orves* and had always attempted some form of contact yet she had never replicated his enthusiasm for a liaison. Something in him wasn't going to be deterred that day, she was like nobody he'd ever fucked, sure, he'd had sex with some stunning women, but she was almost celestial. An angel. He'd got off at *Jules Joffrin* and followed her from a distance onto *rue Ramey* past a selection of shops and into a narrow alley at the end of which there were a hundred or so steep steps that led to the back of *La Basilique Du Sacre-Coeur.* It wasn't until they were in the alley that he'd finally attempted vocal contact, the passageway surrounded by residential buildings clawing high to the sky line around them, shading the miniature street from anything that remained from the day's light, almost leaning in to watch the humiliating spectacle that was about to play out before them, hanging baskets and balconies full of flowers providing the residents with suitable flora in lieu of real gardens. The girl's foot had paused at the bottom step as he'd yelled out for her to stop, confusion became recognition became disgust and disapproval, she'd then turned back to the steps and hurriedly worked her way up them. In a heartbeat Christophe had begun to sprint to catch up to her, constantly calling out for her attention "Arrete! Arrete!", reaching the steps he'd bounded up two and three at a time to draw closer to her. At the halfway platform that was sandwiched by two sections of the stairwell he paused to watch her clambering up as quickly as her petite legs could take her, and before he could restart ascending she'd mistimed her step and hurtled face first into the steps. He watched with horror as her body crumpled and then rolled down the stairs toward him, tumbling erratically, her head striking the iron railings one after the other leaving splatters of crimson on the concrete. Her body flailed helplessly until it twisted round and her skull became stuck between two railings but the momentum of her falling took the rest of her down, breaking her neck instantly, and she came to an abrupt halt. Christophe stood, mouth open, unable to comprehend what he had caused. A thin stream of blood snaked down the steps in his direction, breaking into sticky tributaries around tiny pebbles that dared to stand in its way, he stared at it, silence all around him but for a gentle breeze in the baby trees that surrounded him. The girl's lifeless lump twisted and unrecognisable from the radiant angel he'd seen on the train. His mind was empty, his eyes and ears barely registering what they were being told was reality, only his heart and his lungs working to show that he was a functioning human.

Then he ran.

God only knew why, or how, but two days later he received a telephone call.

Ruby

Tuesday October 20th 2009

She tried to blink, the ruby liquid flowed into her eyes. She tried to call out but an empty gargle brought an agonising pain to her pounding skull. This was it. No prayers, no final song. Just a cold void getting gradually more and more vacant. Her ears were ringing. A heavy boot pressed onto her stomach as her attacker tried to remove her jeans. How could she have been so stu-
BACK-
she went, to 2002, to Gina, and herself, first meeting. Back during happier times. The feeling she'd had when their eyes first met in Somerfield's, there was no faking the shortness of breath, the open-mouthed awe at her beauty, there was no denying her genuine shock at the effect this woman was having on her. She needed to know and talk to her, to feel, and taste her, to absorb her. She was generally wary of instant infatuation but this was different, she could feel it, and had to approach her.

It turned out she was called Gina, she was single too, the same age as Ruby, and they had both lived within a couple of miles of each other at most points during their lives, so couldn't believe they had never bumped into each other. It mattered not to Ruby, they had bumped into each other now, and that was all that mattered, and she wasn't considering letting this particular beauty slip away too easily. They chatted for a few hours over a coffee, discussing books they had read (Gina loved Chuck Palahniuk and Irvine Welsh, Ruby was more affectionate toward Elmore Leonard

and Chris Brookmyre as far as American and Scottish authors were concerned, authors whose books that were a lot more action packed, rather than full of internal monologue, in her humble opinion), ex-partners (a conversation instigated by Ruby, intended, of course, to decipher a final idea of whether she was barking up the wrong non-lesbian tree. She wasn't able to contain her delight when she'd heard that Gina's ex was called Amanda, and just wasn't ready for the full time commitment that Gina felt she needed), music they were into (Gina: Neil Young, Pink Floyd, Fleetwood Mac. Ruby: The Coral, The Charlatans, Stone Roses), politics (happily they both agreed that immigration was a good thing, human rights were one of life's important issues, although if the prick at Number Ten had been set alight, neither would be in a hurry to drop their pants to provide the necessary urine to dampen the flames) and family (Gina was from a large family in Doncaster, her granddad having come across from Poland during the war, setting up camp and keeping her grandma perennially pregnant while he brewed up firewater in a still he'd kept in the outhouse. Ruby was an only child to a well-to-do couple from Derby who had died when she was young, forcing her younger self to live with her Auntie and Uncle, and her inheritance came through five years ago, which she used t-
FORWARD-
she went, no longer fighting the inevitable. A strange calmness filtered into her, seeping in through the red stained-glass effect that her blood soaked eyes were encountering. No more a panicked, shock induced shivering wreck, now more an aged elephant, wandering off to die with the understanding and

knowledge of its own mortality. Her legs, and lower torso were dragged into the air with her attacker's final struggle to pull the ankles of her jeans from the unwitting grasp of her feet. A blinding light overcame her when her body thumped back to earth and sent her nerves into overdrive, slowly being replaced by the serenity she was feeli-

BACK-

to 2002. Happy times. She didn't want to lose them. So Ruby plucked up the courage to request Gina's company that night for a few drinks, which, to her delight, was exactly what Gina was going to ask herself. They exchanged numbers and went their separate ways, both unaware of precisely how attracted the other one was to them. Ruby got home and slumped into a happy pile on her sofa, looking at the number on her mobile. Gina. Scrolling through her menus to Create Message several times, typing in the beginning of a message, deleting most of it, then typing some more, then deleting it, just hoping that the right thing to say would bubble through her mind, down through her neck, shoulder, elbow, wrist and into her fingers, which held the final say on what message she would eventually finish with. As she showered *Hi Gina, hope you don't mind me texting so soon, it was really nice to meet you, I can't wait for tonight. Ruby x* sat unsent in her Drafts folder. It sat unsent in her phone as she dried and straightened her hair, and again as she selected outfit after outfit after outfit for her big date. It sat unsent as she climbed into her taxi to the city centre, and she decided she had done the right thing, not wanting to appear needy or over-anxious, so her fingers did the work and deleted the message from the phone.

As she slipped the phone back into her bag she felt a flutter in her chest upon that delightful vibrating alert, seeing Message received from Gina on the display she flipped open the phone with more enthusiasm than she would care to acknowledge, desperately hoping for it not to be a *Hi sorry I can't make it, take care and have a nice life.* It wasn't. She was relieved to read *I'm there. What do you want to drink? G xxx* and resolutely decided to take it easy on the alcohol tonight, there couldn't have been a worse time to get pissed and make a tit of oneself than a first date. Especially this first date. She chose Archers and lemonade, and sat back for the rest of the journey to the pub, an air of calm-
FORWARD-
calmness still washing over her as he removed her cardigan. Her attacker muttering, sobbing, apologising. James. Her newest friend. Who had sat by her side, speculating in the waiting room, discussing what possibilities lay beyond the white door. Whose hand she had squeezed when he was called in first, gave him a reassuring smile and told him she would see him on the other side. Yeah, she saw him alright. Saw him-
BACK-
in the pub they discussed the books again at length ("he's been quoted as being a nihilist, but a lot of his stories have the old We're all going to die anyway so what's the point? vein running through them so surely that makes him a fatalist?") and found that they had a mutual appreciation of modern literature and a mutual disdain of rave music. They both liked an occasional joint, but wouldn't overdo it since their respective flirtations with the world of the whitey (Gina had embarrassed herself by passing out in her own sick in a

friend's garden, shivering and barely noticing somebody else's taxi pulling up, then pulling away as it decided that that sicky looking bitch wasn't getting in. They had to wait two more hours as a result. Ruby had fallen asleep on her kitchen floor after a ridiculously silly night of flirtatious showing off with Debbie Booth at uni. Half a bottle of vodka and a quarter of soap bar was enough to put her on her arse and determine that her future with cannabis was a purely a ships in the night kind of deal) and had both sampled their own portion of cock and decided that while it was a nice enough experience, the whole male gender would never get past the mental age of eighteen, thus would never be grown up enough to understand a woman, and her needs, both mentally and physically. Gina did, however, admit to having tried it again recently, but out of sheer lust and frustration at her split with Amanda, the bloke was well hung and he knew what he was doing, but it just didn't feel particularly right.

The thing with Gina, Ruby contemplated, was that she held no airs or graces, she was a stunning woman, yet was either unaware of it, or refused to act upon the benefits that such aesthetics brought. She seemed as happy in The Frog and Parrot as she could be in a grimy sweaty fetish club in Leeds as she could be at the opera, silently appreciating Carmen. She could probably hold court with a gang of yobbish shouting Blades fans, effortlessly batting away their affections as if they were gnats, before getting dolled up and talking the mayor into letting her off of a parking fine. She was petite and blonde with massive blue eyes that fit just right into her small round face, atop a very kissable neck that gradually cascaded down past full round breasts that stretched the fabric on her Deathcab for Cutie T-shirt, with an impossibly slender waist, and she carried herself with an unassuming confidence that threatened to disarm even the most confrontational of people. It was quite spectacularly illustrated when a young local requested that she *Get them fuckin tits out love* and turned to take in his friends' amusement, and as he turned back he barely had time to register the shock of her taking a generous handful of his balls and squeezing, and quite curtly saying *There's a four tit limit on this street, and I can see four standing in front of me, so I won't be getting these fuckin tits out. Love.* And kissed the lad on his bright red cheeks. Normal play was resumed when they got within a reasonable distance and the young bloke started shouting again. Ruby felt an overwhelming urge to kiss Gina, but felt it subside when the sensation of Gina hooking her arm through hers-

FORWARD-

he left the waiting room, the look on his face said shit scared but who wouldn't be? Nobody knew what the hell they were doing there. She sniffed up an unusual smell that appeared to be emanating from the bloke across from her, she knew it from her youth but couldn't place it. Almost like crayons. His hair was uneven, and his glasses reeked of NHS. And he reeked of something else, but she couldn't for the life of her figure it out. The young black lad in the corner kept his head down, his braids a mite neater than her own heavy dreads, a yellow and purple sports top over a white T-shirt, if she had to guess she would probably have gone with a basketball top but couldn't be sure. The big dopey kid was muttering to himself, and the bloke with the headphones on would no doubt be prodded and asked if he was who they were asking for when his name was called. Another man directly across was grinning inanely any time something amused him, a creepy glint in his eye, oh, and the God-awful heroin addict who occasionally hung around near the front of the shop she knew as Lisa was also here, which should have set alarm bells ringing bu-

BACK-

their first night together. That night. The day they had met. Was perfect. They had walked arm in arm from pub to pub. Each bar brought them closer. In The Frog and Parrot they had stood around chatting, by The Grapes they were sitting closer, each yelling into the other's ear to speak over the live bands. By the time they hit the club they were holding hands and kissing at every opportunity. Ruby felt herself get uncomfortably wet every time Gina's hand slid over her thigh, each time her middle finger stretched slightly further up the leg, until her hand was high enough up the leg to be sandwiched between both thighs. Before, if Ruby was ever caught staring at the object of her affections, she would find an alarming distance in their eyes, and would quickly avert her gaze. However, with Gina, if she was caught, Ruby would be rewarded with a smile that was illuminated by those giant eyes, and then Gina would lean in, and slide her tongue down her throat, as if to silently reciprocate in her own beautiful way.

They found themselves in a taxi to Gina's flat in Broomhill, Gina gently stroking Ruby's thigh, biting her lip and mouthing fuck me to her new beloved, who would get slightly embarrassed, but still, no less horny.

Back at the flat, Gina stripped and gently played with herself while Ruby removed her top an-
FORWARD-
peeling her T-shirt over her head and arms seemed to be a struggle for him. Then she heard him vomit beside her. No, he had half vomited beside her. Most of it had splashed onto her naked torso. He was still crying. *Poor awkward James. If I knew then what I know now* thought Ruby *you would be fucking dead you fucking cunt. I'm here dying. You fucking-*
BACK-
they slowly moved against each other, working into a rhythm, Ruby's hands crawling eagerly over Gina's naked body, her hands sliding down between her legs, feeling the wetne-
FORWARD-
the wetness of the blood on her face and chest was becoming stickiness, as it dried in the autumn wind. She could no longer see anything, the whiteness becoming ever present. When James removed her T-shirt her head cracked against the concrete beneath it, him not aware that she was still alive. Barely. Only the white light and the noise were apparent to her. The noise of his crying, his apologies to her. Using her name. *I'm sorry Ruby, I'm sorry-*
BACK-
she was on her back now, her hands desperately reaching for Gina's head between her legs, her tongue working at the clit, ferocious yet at the same time perfectly tender, two of her fingers working into her pussy, and pushed themselves deeper into her. Coming up to meet her face, Gina smiled and asked her if she was okay. No time given for a reply, Ruby pulled her

new lover closer, and licked her face to taste herself, and then kissed her deeply, teasing the nipples standing firm and dark between her fingers, attached to possibly the best tits she had ever seen. Sometimes it was hard to believe in love at first sight, sometimes not so har-
FORWARD-
she knew he was close to her because he was talking into her ear. She couldn't feel anything anymore. But she could hear. She heard him kiss her ear, sending that pathetic whine first class direct to her ear drums, she heard him apologise for the eighth or ninth time, and sniff up a giant mucous filled snot followed by the slimy horrid sound of him swallowing it, taking a breath, and apologising one more time-
BACK-
the next morning she turned over to see Gina smiling at her, then gripped her hand and said *hi you* before leaning in for a morning kiss. Something she rarely dared do through fear of unleashing some vicious morning breath, not this morning-
FORWARD-
his footsteps subsided and birdsong filled the air. Nothing else. The serenity returned. A slight smile slowly trickled across her face-
BACK-
Gina smiling at her. *Hi you.* Kissing. Nothing else mattered.

Terry Collins

Tuesday 21st October 2009

Summat weird's goin' on here. Am tellin ya. You know they've only gone an' found two more bodies. Two birds, different places like. Throats cut, no clothes on. I mean, what the fuck is goin' on? I tell you who I reckon's behind it. Pakis. Muslims. Terrorists. They're killing us off one by one. Now, you might think I'm bein' racist, but am I fuck. They've been doing it for years. It's not enough that they come over here to take our money, send it back to their own country so they can spend it all there. They're killing us, it dunt hafta be that they're blowing us up, they're doin' it on the sly. Back int' seventies right? I wa' workin' for t' council after me accident. Some Pakistani bloke waltzes in right? I'm there, behind my counter, an' he comes in an' sez "Where's free bank? I looking for free bank". Free bank right? So I sez to 'im, I sez "There's Barclays round the corner, other banks up there" pointing further up the street. He sez "No, I come England yesterday, I looking for free bank". I had to explain to 'im that there's no such thing as free money, you hafta work for it. You know what he was looking for? Social Security. Fuckin' DSS. See what am saying? They don't hafta be blowin' us up, they can just bleed us dry from the inside.

There's talk that it's a serial killer. The paper sez it's the new Yorkshire Ripper, I mean, it's gotta be summat. Our Tina reckons it's the government. I mean, if it is the government, why are they doing it? What's the point? That's what I wanna know. She's pretty thick our lass. When she reads, she reads out loud. Mary next door, shiz telling people they shunt go out at night. You think that's summat people are gonna do? Get fucked, course they fuckin' aren't. Little dickheads out by the bus stop, pissed an' shoutin' at folk, they aren't gonna stay in. Our Kev, he's out while after midnight, then he comes in off his face, wakin' our Tina up when shiz gotta be awake for work at five. No, kids are gonna go fuckin' nowhere. I tell ya what, if there is a serial killer, he dunt want to be hangin' round our end, our Kev an' his mates'll tear the cunt to shreds. You know why that is? Coz they've all become fearless little cunts. Our Kev's mate Daz right? Stuck nut on 'is teacher dint he? You know what they did to 'im? Fuck all. Sure, they sent 'im 'ome from school for a few week, but he were back, claimin' he were hardest int school 'cause he'd fuckin' nutted 'is teacher. He were only there a few week before he stopped goin'. That's the way this country's goin' nowadays, we're not allowed to crack our kids anymore, so they know they can get away with whatever they fuckin' want. Growin' up right? I used to get the belt at school for askin' for seconds just 'cause there were folk still not finished eatin'. These days the fuckin' dinnerlady'd get a fuckin' buncha knuckles in 'er fuckin' trap just for tryin' to stop 'em havin' seconds. How'd the fuck that happen? That's what the fuck I wanna know. Seriously, how is it have kids become suddenly our superiors just cos we can't smack the little fuckers? Wanna know? Esther fuckin' Rantzen. I mean, yeah, if am honest ad admit there's more paedos nowadays an' I'm all for castrating the dirty cunts, but not every cunt is a paedo, ya know? We're not livin' in Victorian times for fuck's sake, we've all got fuckin' common sense enough not to send us kids out to work int' mines or cotton factories soon as they can fuckin' talk, an' we've enough sense not to send 'em out to a park fulla rabid twitchin' kiddy fiddlers, but when a parent dunt have a right to give his kid a fuckin' whack for givin' him lip or nickin' cars and bikes, that's just fucked. You know what else is fucked? Where's all the youth clubs gone? When I were younger, we had stuff to do, places to go. Even our Shane, he's a bit older than our Kev, he's not mine, our Tina had him to some bloke when she were younger, I've pretty much brought 'im up like, but aye, our Shane, he had youthies about ten years ago, where'd the fuck they go? Now they can either hang around getting' wankered ont rec, or they can cause a fuckin' nuisance out front of our yard, not for long like, I fuckin' tell 'em, go on, fuck off, hang outside one of your mates' fuckin' yards. Watch 'em try and gi' me lip, I'll fatten the fucker.

Anyway, you've got me talkin' about summat else, where was I? Oh right, yeah, this fuckin' serial killer. Fuckin' paki bastards. Hey, I 'ope Allah's not listening, hahaha, he'll have me fuckin' guts for garters. No, fuck 'em, they've come to our country, taken over little blotches, they're like fuckin skin cancer for our once great nation. You could sit a fuckin' satellite over the country, with little red dots, hahaha, fuckin' red dots, ya geddit? Anyway, little red fuckin' dots for each one, then watch it over each day and watch the rash grow, you wunt believe it if you saw it. I dunt hafta see it, because I fuckin' know mate. Fuckin' Jack Rackies. You might think I'm a right cunt, like, a racist cunt, but it's not all races, ya know? I ant got a problem wi' all these Polish comin' into our country, these cunts that moan that they're takin' all our jobs could've had them jobs ages ago if they actually wanted to do 'em, but they'd rather sit on their arses claimin' shit, than sew shit, or clean shit. No, they've spotted a chance to work for a better life and they've taken it, fair play to 'em. It's what I'd fuckin' do if I lived in some Polish shithole int backa beyond. You see what am sayin'? If you're prepared to actually do some work then I ant got no problems with ya. All my life I've worked me fingers to the fuckin' bone. And it's not all them from over that way either, Mr Binder, little funny Sikh fucker, runs the shop down the road, is fuckin' mint. Seriously, you could have a proper laugh an' a joke wi' that cunt all day, he dunt gi' a fuck about nowt, just guz about 'is business an' chills wi' every cunt. He sorts us out wi' blue movies an'all like, ya can't go wrong wi' a cunt that sorts blueys out for ya. I do fancy our Tina, dunt get me wrong, an' shiz fuckin' mint at suckin' me cock, but there's not much better than a pissed up wank on a Friday night while she's out at bingo and the lads are out wi' their mates, an' watchin' some young bird teck it all ways an endin' up covered in spunk, I wunt normally admit it but av had a few beers, so I dunt mind, I actually dunt mind watchin' a fat cock slide into some young bird's arse, the fatter the better, them sort that meck their faces screw up, that's what I wanna see, I don't mind watchin' em lezzin' up, but to be fair, where do I put me senn when am havin' a wank? If it's just birds lezzin' up then you relegate yourself to that bloke who stands at the side not gettin' any fanny, just watchin', wishin' you could prod one of 'em while they feel each other up. No fuckin' thank you very fuckin' much. No, you've got to see cock so you can meck that cock your cock, you know what am sayin'?

Yeah, so am not sayin' am racist, far from it, got nowt against a lot of Asians, nowt against most of these illegals comin' in, long as they play by the fuckin' rules, av just got a good nose when it comes to bad 'uns an' right now, me nose is pickin' up a distinct whiff of curry, y'know what am sayin'? You want another one pal?

So what the fuck is a supposed serial killer gunna get outta comin' round our way? Fuckin' two black eyes an' 'is cheeky little tail between 'is legs. That's why we dunt need to worry out our way. You don't come from the Manor, you get fuck all from the Manor. Simple as that. The cunt needs a death wish to come up our end. Did you hear about that young lass? Got off tram at wrong stop, young Polish girl, think she were about twenty, didn't have much English to her? Was on totally wrong tram, decided to get off an' wait for next one back to town? They're still lookin' for the kids that raped her. Four of 'em, none of 'em older than fifteen apparently, took turns to fuck her. Awful mate, fuckin' awful. No, fuck that, if I were after killin' folk I wunt come lookin' up this way, it dunt seem like there's enough crime to go round the criminals, so they make their own just for entertainment anyway. Fuck that. Seriously, fuck it right up its own arse with its own fuckin' cock. Fuck it. You know what I saw the other day? You know what I saw? Watched a young Paki kid get his head stoved in wi' a shovel. Did you read about it int' Star? Nowt to do wi' me, nowt to do wi' most of the village. Just one of them things. I saw it then I heard from Mickey Dutton, their Ashley wa' there like, the Paki kid had come bringin' his lip, tellin' young Ashley Dutton he were gunna teck his rings off him. Obviously Ashley telled him to fuck off, that young Jack Rackie sez to young Ashley that hiz gunna come back and cut 'em off 'is fingers his senn! Can you fuckin' believe it? He's sez he's gunna come back to cut the rings off his fingers! Needless to say, he got the fuck all that he deserved. Him an' his mates come back up to where young Ashley's got a few of his mates gathered by now. Tooled up to fuck. The four Pakis got shit kicked out on 'em. Proper shit kicked out on 'em. That's what I saw, comin' out of here, just up by Netto. A proper ruckus goin' on am tellin' ya. Tram's goin' fuckin' nowhere, cars goin' fuckin' nowhere. Little brown arms swingin' against white faces. Little white faces layin' the fuckin' nut on little brown faces. Then one of our lads got stabbed. Dirty fuckin' bastards. It were Colin Tommo's lad, you know him? Fuckin', go on, what the fuck's his name? Lee! That's it, Lee Thompson, he gets his self fuckin' stabbed! On his own turf! So one of 'em disappears, goes to his yard, brings back a spade and plants it straight ont side of the head of one of them fuckin' scummy little cunts. Game over. He fuckin' dint stop 'til old Mary O'Connell brings her fuckin' nebbin' head out dunt she? Chelpin' that he's gunna kill some cunt. Sirens galore. Ten minutes later the young Jack Rackie's bin stumblin' about the road, his mates drag him into the car an' peg it off, probly off to Attercliffe. Our boys scarper an' young Lee gets tecken to hospital. Fuck knows what happened to the brown kid, any luck he's fuckin' dead.

So they're obviously takin' the piss, comin' to

our country an' takin' liberties. Is it not your round mate?

Ada

Tuesday 27th October 2009

Hoxton had been standing over her for the last hour. She wished he would just disappear for a bit. Let her get on with her job. He had a habit of lingering whenever any of his subordinates were around. There was never any conversation, just a few bleeps from her computer system, punctuated by random sighs and tuts from Hoxton, clearly not seeing what he wanted to. There were four remaining, two having been dispatched today. Time and caution were definitely important factors from here on in. If the remaining seekers did their jobs efficiently she could be home by Thursday.

Home. Budapest. However, home at the minute was a room in a hotel on the edge of the city, not that she would get much time to spend in this room in Sheffield, the farmhouse being the home from home from home. Sheffield. She had never heard of it until recently, and wondered why the hell they didn't choose London, or Manchester. A little bit of research told her it was one of the bigger cities in England, famous for making forks, The Human League and ABC. Its surrounding towns were rife with heroin, poverty and teenage pregnancy. The Look Of Love indeed. It seemed a harmless enough place though, and could see this year's outing to be a run-of-the-mill operation. On the drive into the city she was pleasantly surprised by the greenery of the hills that surrounded the busy grey centre, then instantly brought down to Earth with the sheet of miserable red and grey high rise blocks of flats that overlooked the city and her hotel. Even from a distance she could make out, on its face, a tattoo of graffiti which served as a warning to outsiders, and as a territorial pissing by its inhabitants. She couldn't imagine the brains behind Smoke or Chops being the kinds of brains she would like to pick. Probably more the kinds of brains she would much like to smash in with her very able bare fists. But this wasn't that kind of a trip.

Checking in had been a chore. She had been surprised to encounter the bored inattention of a chubby squat woman at the check-in desk, quite obviously put out by the fact that she was being forced to do the job for which she was paid. These kinds of people irritated Ada. Yes, there were people who didn't enjoy their place along the employment spectrum, who were more than welcome to voice their disdain, and the more sensible specimen would accept their lot or simply get out of the situation they had found themselves in and take control of their own lives and destinies. The worst type however, were the ones who just didn't know or care enough to get out, the idiots that represented the shit and sawdust of the rat's cage known as the world. That is what this woman was, a person who had by some miracle attained herself a position of prominence within the public service industry. Not prominence in the way that she claimed any degree of authority, no, more in the way that she was inexplicably the public face of this establishment, yet had a total lack of presentation about her, or respect and enthusiasm toward the strangers she encountered on a daily basis. Strangers that ultimately paid her wages. The worst part was when Ada had opened her mouth and the woman picked up on her Eastern European accent and looked visibly disgusted by her presence in the hotel, regardless of her flawless grasp of the English language. The look was that of somebody who had opened their gifts on Christmas Day to find nothing but steaming fresh piles of shit in lieu of real presents. It had inwardly angered Ada, because she was here on very expensive business, and she herself earned an extremely handsome salary for what she did, and she had begun to question herself, was she going to allow herself to be looked down upon by this thing? She had killed better people that the rotund piece of shit that was standing opposite her. Politicians, doctors, people who had taken the time to attain themselves an education, all who found their demise to be caused by her hands. Eventually she had regained her composure and began to look upon the woman with pity, she was a native, and Ada couldn't afford to make trouble for herself, so instead decided to rile the beast by waving the highest denomination of British currency at a lingering porter, and politely requested that he take her bags up to her room, slipping the fifty pounds seductively into his breast pocket. He was actually quite cute, and could see herself fucking him before she left. She always liked to take just one of the locals to bed on any of her work outings, of which this was the fourth, just to see what it was like. This porter was barely into his twenties, and had an eagerness about him that endeared her to him. As he had walked in front of her he was incessantly asking her questions about her business, what brought her to Sheffield, how long she would be staying. She had always found it beneficial to be as vague as possible, especially in her line of work, the more you said, the more people remembered you. And it didn't pay to be remembered. Her part of the set-up was the riskiest time-wise. No, the porter wouldn't be the one she would fuck, too close to home. But she was definitely going to be fucked by the end of this trip.

She had to arrive only days before it begun, and then leave day after it had ended. Christophe and his team had been here for six months, and would stay on for a few weeks after to tie up loose ends, so they could stay relatively low key. They all had to stay low key, but she was the most at risk in terms of the timing of the whole operation. What she had in her favour though, was that nobody could ever suspect her, in the reality of it. She was only a tiny thing, and always liked to give an impression of helplessness, be it that she didn't know how to operate a coffee machine, or that she couldn't lift her own suitcase. It didn't matter that she had black belts in several disciplines, or that she had killed, or been a part of the deaths of more people than she weighed in pounds, although nobody but a handful of people knew that, and what everybody else didn't know, couldn't hurt. Actually it could, but only if she decided it could.

Her role in this year's operation was erring on the side of technical adviser and supervisory tracker of participants, which, perhaps surprisingly, was a very easy role in England. The seekers were erratic but efficient, their prey were holed up and hopeful. Her particular favourite, and favourite with the backers, was the young black man, Daniel, he'd accepted and undertaken the task at hand with an admirable ease. Having watched them all being given their specific roles, for her he was the one that stood out, he had acknowledged what was expected of him with a nonchalance that belied his youth and demeanour when she first laid eyes on him. In the waiting room prior to the introduction of the game he'd kept low key, in comparison to the girl Lisa, who had unwittingly thrown all her cards on the table before it had even begun. It was almost as if he'd known something was amiss, and was waiting to see how the situation played out. He was smart, and a definite good choice for a role as seeker. In stark contrast, however, was James, a man who had simply sat in his temporary responsibility as a hider, waiting for his own demise. He knew he could be found, and he knew what he had to do, yet still sat, hoping, if that was the right word, that he would not be found, and he would never ever have expected his life to be snuffed out by the hand that did it. The large boy known as Graham, the man-child, an easy target, too simple to understand what was happening to him, as if he were playing war with his friends using snapped branches, and leaves strapped to his head using laces taken from old training shoes. Ruby, the girl with the dreadlocks, lured in by the boy James, strangers yet friends. Christophe had done well with their acquisition. The game didn't need more than a handful of strong competitors, it needed easy pickings, token sitting ducks. Eight strong competitors and it became dangerous for all because it could go on for months, eight sitting ducks and it could become dangerous because of their weaknesses. Their eventual breakdown. The players wouldn't have any favourites. Every race needed a favourite. The dark horses seemingly intent on messing up for Daniel right now were Thomas, the long haired man that Christophe predicted an premature death for yet had managed to avoid exposure at all turns, Geoffrey, the middle aged man who, to everybody except Ada, had disappeared off the face of the Earth yet, again by Christophe's predictions, was apparently due for an early demise, and Alan, the loner, who by some miracle had come into some sort of element, having dispatched one of his seven competitors.

Admittedly, Daniel was still the favourite, though, from Hoxton's sighing, was not his particular favourite. Most of the money had been laid down on Daniel, and it was not unknown for foul play to occur even over and above the required amount. This was where Ada was key. In the past, backers had attempted to get messages to their competitors in order to sway the way the game was going. Hoxton's syndicate had gotten wise to it fairly quickly, and created the role of tracker. Anybody found to be forcing the way of the game were disqualified, and usually shoved from this mortal coil with the very able hand of a bullet from a silenced pistol. And more often than not, that pistol was held by the very able hand of one Ada Birczik.

As it stood, Thomas and Geoffrey were hiding. Alan and Daniel were seeking. Ada could see herself very much at home come Thursday morning.

PART 2 - A PAIR OF SPANNERS IN THE WORKS

Thursday 29th October 2009

9:37am
The tone sounds in my ear, another call. Fucking joy. For sure I adhere to the speech with catatonic enthusiasm equal to that of a small boy in a catholic church and roll my eyes at Janine across the partition and mouth "Foreign" to her. Her quizzical furrowed brow and a mouthed 'what?' cause me to repeat my action. She still doesn't get it, so I quickly scrawl down the word on my notepad. She mirrors my rolling of the eyes and shrugs. There's a call of her own coming through.
"Good afternoon and thank you for calling Electric Company, you're speaking with Janine, how may I help you today?"

It's a speech I've heard at least a hundred times a day being poured from my own mouth, and ten times that from all around me, from my fellow work rats. It's a speech that my ex-girlfriend Lynsey, caught me reeling off in my sleep. I sometimes catch myself about to say it when I'm answering my own fucking mobile. I need a new job.
"Good afternoon, thank you for calling Electric Company, you're speaking to Tom, how may I help you today?" How could I possibly help you? Your wife has left you and you need to vent on an ear that can't bite back? You need to act like the job I do is so far beneath your own personal station in life that you can forget that you're as utterly anonymous as I am? Is appreciation a concept that's as foreign to you as the cunt I'm currently dividing every word into LOUD. MON. O. SYLL. A. BIC. NOI. SES. FOR? DO. YOU. UN. DER. STAND?

Of course you fucking don't, because I'm here, far away from you, a safe distance, biting my tongue and experiencing visions of tracking you down. Fucking you up. I need a new job.

I wasn't always this bitter, of course I wasn't. I remember tackling each call like it was the first of the day, with an enthusiasm that my new colleagues remembered feeling themselves at some point, but could no longer understand. They always told me it would change before long, and for sure I believed them, but I reckoned I was the exception to the rule, that I could battle on and retain my individuality in an ritualistic environment, full of time withered work rats, filing through the turnstile, hooking themselves up to the shackles, chained from the ear to their own personal hell. All around me I'd hear "Shut the fuck up! Let me speak!" as another would have a shaking, nail-bitten finger pressed firmly over the mute button. Enjoying little bite sized chunks of rebellion but never quite pushing themselves far enough to take on a full meal. Sticking it to the man while he has his back turned. How very punk. The call centre equivalent of silent farting in a lift. All around were people idly going through the motions whilst looking at photographs of random friends on Facebook, playing internet games, scribbling down little pictures of cocks and balls or stick men onto their notebooks and barely registering what the person on the other end of the line had to say. People who had no desire to better themselves. I, on the other hand, savoured every call as a different story to tell my girlfriend when I got home, I saw each person as an individual chapter in a grand novel of my day, I'd try to put my own spin on their call, leave them feeling on top of the world, I was on the front line in the war on high priced energy!

Three years later I'm the same as the rest of them, no matter how much I try to kid myself, and it's my own fault. I stayed long enough to let it get me down, then once the disdain set in, it worked through me like a fucking infection, blackening my veins, filling them with hateful globs of pus. It looks like the only antibiotic would be a foray into pastures new, but then I'd only let the scorn harvest itself again after so long. As long as I'm serving the general fucking public, I'm going to be well and truly fucked off. For sure I can kid myself that I'm a people person, but I'm no more a people person than this serial killer that's doing the rounds. The Sheffield Ripper. Mr Ripper, if you please. I wonder to myself whether I've perhaps ever taken a payment from Mr Ripper, if you please. I contemplate whether he keeps his finances in order -or if maybe he's doing it because he's nothing left to live for- whilst the bellend on the line struggles with his own basic grasp on the English language to tell me his electricity isn't working. No shit, for sure he should have paid his fucking bills. "Sir, if you had found yourself with troubles making payments you should have called us earlier and we could have come to-" He cuts me off and goes into a vaguely intelligible tirade about how he had paid all his bills but a third party came onto the line and stole his card details, and Electric Company had taken him to court and he couldn't make it because he'd had bird flu but that was another story. His words, not mine, I think. Fucking idiot. I consider releasing his call, releasing him, back into the wilderness of darkness, coldness, hunger and whatever emotions that may come his way in a world without electricity, or the vocabulary to even express them. This brief consideration is shot to pieces as I catch the pensive glare of Chris, quite transparently listening to, and scrutinizing my performance. I can tell he fucking loves it, the prick. He started at around the same time as me, but he's kissed all the right arses, sucked all the right cock. I never considered him to be a bad lad, but the longer I worked with him the more I considered him to a be an utter fanny. With Chris in mind, I turn on the charm and patience with Johnny Foreigner, and with eyes directly on the pretentious bellend, headphones on, listening to my performance, I watch his smug face drop as I tell Mr Foreigner to go fuck himself, to get back to Eastern Europe if he's so unhappy with the way that England's utility providers are treating him. In slow clipped tones, partly so he understands exactly what I'm saying, but mainly so I can enjoy our glorious leader's mood take a dip in quality. Fucking quality. It's all about the quality, quality of the call, the quality of service. For sure, I'm good at my job, but the job's no good for me. I can't be allowed to do it my own way, I have to do the same as the other ninety people around me. Not any more, our glorious leader, you can stick your fucking employment opportunity right up your fucking arse, if there's enough space for it next to your own fucking head. Just for fun, I quickly wipe clear all debt that Mr Jonathon Foreigner has built up in his tenure as a legal immigrant in fair Blighty, and watch our glorious leader throw down his headset and start my way. His barely contained rage threatens to spill over as he nods toward the small room in the corner. "Aux 4 please Tom, can I have a quick word?" the tears in the eyes already condemn this fucker to lose his rag. I push the button to put myself offline, remove my headset, and smile at Janine, watching Chris head over to the room. She frowns and looks at me as if to ask what's up with me. I smile, and wave at her, intending to look somewhat mysterious but she spoils my little moment by sticking her customer on mute and asking me what's up. "Promotion, congratulate me" I respond dryly. Regardless of how good her tits are, she's slightly gormless our Janine, so as her face lights up like a council estate at Christmas, I feel obliged to dismiss the notion as quickly as it arose, and tell her I'll see her around, savouring that confused look again before I head off to see what our glorious leader has in store for me in his little realm of punishment. For sure, he's a proper dickhead.

The sweaty windowless room is the backdrop to our little showdown. Two low bucket seats and a nondescript coffee table. A smiling image of some goon with glasses staring into the distance under the slogan "A smile costs nothing" hangs above our glorious leader's head. He's a boyish looking lad, couple of years younger than my twenty-seven, you can tell he has to shave maybe once every fortnight, if indeed he shaves at all. He reminds me of a joke we used to tell when I was younger and we ribbed each other about bum fluff, something about 'How does Chris get a shave in the morning? He gets his mum to blow on his face like a dandelion clock, like phoo! one o'clock! phoo! two o'clock!' I have a little smile at that one and shift my focus back to the bell end in front of me. His already blotched red cheeks take it up to the next level of dedication to displaying their owner's discomfort as he clears his throat.

"Tom, what the fuck were you playing at?"
I shrug, and hope that my bored demeanour can wind him up.
"You're a good bloke Tom, good at your job, you could have been a team leader, what you done this for?"
That's right Christopher, the much practised art of sphincter cleaning, that's the way to open me up. Get right in there, my hoop needs a good wash. That's the stuff. You cunt. I'm saying fuck all. I harden my bored gaze into a firm stare, and I must have started to involuntarily clench my teeth because his beady little marbles flicker to my jaw, just under my ear. For sure, he's starting to falter. His eyes well up again. Fucking poof.
"Fine, if that's how you want to play it, get your fucking things. You're suspended without pay, pending an investigation. Bear in mind I witnessed everything, so I don't imagine there'll be much hope-"
"Spineless cunt"
Chris splutters to a halt, blinking away the tears that are rapidly amounting in his eyes, whether they're tears of fear, or of anger I can't tell so I ball up my fists just in case it's the latter and I have to snot him. His face reddens and twists as he struggles to find words, or even thoughts, then he inhales deeply and attempts to compose himself. As he opens his quivering gob to speak again I cut him off.
"Wanker"
Jackpot. He slams his hands on the coffee table barrier between us. Give it to me Mr Bossman.
"You're a smart twat you Tom, always givin' it the big fuckin' yap yap, answer for everything. You've always been like it, that's why I'm sat here sacking you and

you're here getting sacked by me" He points at his mincing man-sucking lips and finishes up with "You can't keep this shut!"
I smile at him.
"Wanker"
"See? You just have to have the last word, all the fuckin' time!"
"It seems to be so, prick"
He sits back, spent. The shitbag weasel cunt. I'd hoped he'd be more sport than this. What the fuck is wrong with people in this industry? Am I the only cunt with any balls? This country. For sure it's gotten to the point where there's so much competition for business that we have to pander to every bellend who threatens to go elsewhere with their hard earned, hard stolen, and hard begged money. What? You've never paid a bill on time in your life but you'll still go to NPower if we don't stop pestering you for that money that YOU owe US? In that case, we apologise, go forth and fritter away your readies on booze, fags, that half pound onion ring burger with cheesy chips from Mario's takeaway, perhaps even that shiny new bag you really REALLY need. I digress.
"Just get out, you clearly have no interest in keepin' your job, we may as well get somebody in who actually WANTS to work for a living" he flounces his hand around in as nonchalant and dismissive a manner as he can muster up right now. It simply comes across as more than just a little gay. I get out of my seat and lean over him, breathing right in his face. Usually I'd give a shit about my breath when in such close proximity to other people, but I let him take the warm stench of coffee, tobacco and the rotten back tooth that's recently

been giving me a shitload of jip while I lean in and let him know I'll see him around.

So I'm out of there, handing in my badge and my gun with the chubby wheezing pensioner that masquerades as security. It's only when I leave the building that I realise exactly what I've done and what I'd take to be regret hits me. For sure I'll miss a few of the people there, not all, just a few kindred spirits that made the place more bearable. I decide to make a conscious effort to call a couple of them tonight. Also to be missed is my pay packet, but I figure that I can walk into something else easily enough. Right now though, I want a beer, it wasn't a coincidence that I chose to fuck it all up on pay day.

10:56am

On the train into Sheffield I'm slightly deflated, there's none of the elation that I've anticipated, only a feeling of 'what now?', and I'm going through the events of the day in my head. I don't give a fuck about what I did or said to make our glorious former leader uncomfortable, he's a cunt, it's just that, well, I don't know what it is. Fuck it, I'm getting pissed. I call Justin to see if he's out for a few pops.

"Tommy boy! What you on wi' mate? You not at work like?"

"No mate, kinda walked out"

"Yeah? How come?"

"Got fucked off wi' it pal, thinkin' I might have fucked up a bit though, wanna come into town for a bit? I fancy a bit of company like"

"Where you thinkin'?"

"Frog and Parrot?"

"Half an hour mate, want some fetchin'?"
"Course I do brother, see y'in a bit"
"In a bit"
Justin, part time 'to-friends-only' coke dealer, and all round good cunt, known each other since school. We work in our own circles of mates and don't get so many chances to hook up but he's one of the best, I'd trust the bloke with my life.

So I'm shuffling along in my own world down West Street heading up to the Frog, the harassed West Indian security guard battles a pisshead fresh from the Wetherspoons outside the Spar. In my current mood I feel like dragging the camel-coated, trousers and trainers cunt from his grasp and kicking him to death to relieve him of his own foul stinking existance, and whatever it is he's hiding from within the confines of one of Sheffield's multitude of chain-pubs whose clientele inexplicably merge from all walks of life. For sure, stick a fucking Wetherspoons in the middle of Afghanistan we'd all be okay, all Jihad related disputes would be settled with drunken fisticuffs then forgotten about over a roll up in a heated smoking area, no planes full of suicide bombers any more, just a happy world of affordable binge drinking. I don't kick Camel Coat to death. Instead I walk on and part a trio of young students, a prematurely balding mincer and his two fag hags, stopping off briefly at the paper shop for some cigs and chuddy. I spark up a snout outside the Frog and Parrot while I wait for Justin, and watch some youths fucking around on the skate park at Devonshire Green. My eyes are drawn to a solitary figure standing at a window in The Cube, a high rise city apartment block of rooms that are essentially bedsits for people

with too much money. Five hundred quid a month for a room. Load of shit. Before I know it I've smoked my ciggie and am already picking at the lip of my box open to take out another. I look at it and half decide to put it back in the pack but half decide is by no means fully decide and I light it up. Justin should be here soon. I glance back up to the window in the high-rise, nothing there. I won't be affording one of those places any-
"Scuse me mate" A wax work of a teenager has appeared beside me, hands tucked up inside his stained and ripped Henleys hooded top, he's a good few inches shorter than me, and dancing around like he needs a piss or shit, though it's more than likely a hit of something or other, but who am I to judge? I'm as unemployed as this poor cunt right now. I look at him neutrally, encouraging him to go on.
"Ah cunt buy a fag off yer could ah?" he's holding a handful of coppers out to me as if to entice me into this lucrative transaction. How long he's been sitting up by the Tesco Express to save up for a ciggie I couldn't possibly guess, but I'm not about to fill my fucking pockets with his coppers, he can keep them. I take out a cig and pass it to him, waving away his offer of cash, hoping he'll fuck off sometime soon but no.
"Ah cunt nick a light off yer could ah mate?" I roll my eyes and grin "You want a fuckin' lung an'all?" as I hold a flame up for him and he's giving it the 'sorry mate, sorry mate' performance while he sways the tip of his freshly procured snout over it until it crackles into life. The bliss on his spotty little chops is immediately evident as he stands and lets the nicotine power into his bloodstream. Then he's away, thanking me whilst he's doing his best to keep the smoke in his lungs.

There's no sign of Justin when I'm stubbing out that second smoke so I head into the pub for the first of many anticipated pints and a fat line of chee-chee.
It rarely gets too busy on a weekday afternoon in the Frog so I'm served straight away by a tidy little piece with red hair that I've never seen in here before who gives me a cheeky smile, takes my order of two pear Kopparbergs and turns round to bend into the fridge for the bottles. I feel a little twitch in my cock when her jeans ride down a bit and reveal a lacy red thong. In my mind I'm already staying back with her tonight, lifting her over the bar and pulling down those tiny pants and ramming two fingers into her fanny while I poke around her arsehole with my tongue. Dragged back into reality she's standing asking me for a fiver. We share a split second moment as our skin brushes together when I hand her the note, then I take the bottles up the steps to the top window to keep an eye out for Justin. I'm watching the fox behind the bar like a hawk, trying to catch her eye, but a whispered voice throws me off track.
"Fucked her the other night, she was unbelievable" a big bastard in a suit, with blonde hair, is sitting on the next table with a coffee or tea or something, grinning at me and raising his eyebrows.
I turn to look at him incredulously. "What?"
He downs his coffee, closes the laptop in front of him and slides it into its case as he begins to ready himself for leaving. "Word of advice, if you take her home then drink a couple of Red Bulls, because she'll go all night, she fucking loves cock", it's like Jean Claude Van Damme talking out of Dolph Lundgren's mouth here so I'm not about to square up to him, but I feel obliged to

retort, and I instantly regret the "Yeah, alright" I sarcastically come up with as it sounds feeble and defeated, only compounded by the large flashing pearly whites as he laughs and winks at the barmaid as she looks over and waves at him. Jammy cunt, for sure. "And she isn't a real red head" he says as he heads down the steps. In that moment my day goes from bad to a hell of a lot worse, then back round upon itself to just great as I spot Jean Claude Van Lundgren holding the door open for Justin to make his welcome entrance. Bring it on!

11:45am
He wasn't one for being selfish. The redhead, Jessica, was pure filth and she really did love cock. Christophe felt the obligation to let what he saw as a fellow fuck monkey know the score, but mused that he really should have known that Englishmen were a lot more backward in going forward than they let on. Yeah, put them with their friends and they'll fill with bravado quicker than a balloon attached to a gas canister and they'll walk away with a disease ridden whore of a woman for the night. Alone however, they'd see a thing of real beauty, admire from afar, drink in every curve of their true object of desire, yet do nothing except go home and masturbate furiously, more than likely with tears in their eyes. It was all about confidence. The strength of character to feel, to know even, that you can get whatever you want if you are truly confident that it will be so, but also to stay on the good side of arrogance. And so it was, that the guy in the bar was reduced to childish sarcasm when faced with what Christophe saw as a genuine piece of advice, an

opportunity to stand tall and take what he wanted, which was almost certainly that neat little pussy wrapped around his weak English cock.

He did enjoy the bar, The Frog and Parrot. It was in an unusually metropolitan area of this grey city, full of life, it made him miss Paris somewhat. He'd been there this afternoon with his computer, keeping tabs on the participants, one of them, the black guy, Daniel, was fifty metres away from Geoffrey at one point, but missed the opportunity and they were now miles apart. In three hours the roles would change. He'd have stayed in the bar drinking espresso all afternoon if Ada had not called him, hissing down the line that he should stay out of plain view, that he was putting the operation at risk, too many people would see him. He tried to explain that if he hung around in the shadows, sneaking from place to place then he would surely be more of a suspicious figure than if he were to simply blend into the city. Was this not a city of commerce? Of businessmen socialising and taking meetings in less formal environs, such as coffee shops, and quaint little bars? Most certainly it was, the businessman of today is younger, more vibrant, energetic! The businessman of today wants you to know he's important, he thrives on you hearing what a great deal he's lining up. But no, Ada was as cold and insistent as ever, and she was his superior, in the professional capacity. So he did as he was instructed and left the bar, politely allowing a busy-faced guy through the door, and skipping over the road to the car park, and the Astra.

Ada, if ever there was a true walking talking definition of the word unattainable then she was it. Christophe knew she didn't trust him, at least as far as the job went, and that wasn't something that had ever bothered him. She had never wanted him on board and had been very vocal to him about her misgivings, but he didn't see why that should stop them ever fucking. She loved to fuck a variety of strangers on the job, so why not keep it close to home and let a meeting of sexual visionaries come to fruition? He could play the long game, no doubt about that.

11:59am

"Then I sat and called him a spineless cunt, fuckin' wanker, prick, an' he sat there close to tears. Close to fuckin' tears mate, am tellin' ya. He's not had a bird in all the time av worked there. Fuckin' mincer mate. I'd have a bit of respect for the cunt if he'd had a pop but he dint, just sat there and fannied it. Proper fannied it" Justin's fetching a couple of lagers back to the table and I'm babbling, this coke is fucking unreal. Little redhead is looking over now and then, whether she's suspicious over our alternating trips to the bogs, or whether she wants to ride my face I don't know, but right now I do not give one fuck. Justin's a top cunt. His chee-chee is a beautiful reflection of exactly what a top cunt he is. I love the boy.

"So what you gonna do about a job pal?"

"Fuck knows brother, I'll cross that little bridge on Monday for sure, for now though me and you are gonna get fuckin' LARRUPPED!" We grab our pints and chink them together in celebration and I go and inspect the jukebox that's currently knocking out whatever it chooses due to a lack of funds being pumped into it. It's popular with students in here so it's a pretty eclectic selection on the old box, quid for five goes an'all, not

bad. I slam a nugget into the slot and the first thing that goes on is Poison by The Prodigy. Right tune. Justin seems to think so too because he's currently nodding at me in appreciation and drumming away with his hands on the table. I eagerly select four more tracks and sit back down.
"You put on?"
"This, Clash, Kasabian, erm.."
"What Clash?"
"Guns Of Brixton"
"Nice"
"Yeah man, can't remember what else I put on now, fuck it, it'll be a surprise"
"Too right pal"
And we chink our glasses again and in what must be some sort of psychic connection we take it upon ourselves to nail our pints in one. My round.
"D'ya want?"
"Same I reckon, wanna get a coupla shots this time?"
"Why not"
So I'm at the bar. Little Redhead is behind the bar. I really would like to do bad things to her. Jammy Jean Claude Van Lundgren, I bet he didn't fuck her. I order two lagers and Jagermeisters and try to look deep into her eyes, those emerald beauties sparkling in the front of her head. She smiles at me every time she looks up from the pint she's pulling. I'm feeling good so I make a show of looking her up and down, lingering on her tits. If she's embarrassed by it she's not showing it and she gives me a coy look as I hand over the cash.
"And one for yourself.." I trail off, hoping she'll finish the sentence for me, which she does. "Jess"
"Jess, beautiful name, beautiful, it suits you, one for

yourself Jess" she's giggling now, fucking loves my patter, coke does wonders for the confidence for sure.
"Thanks"
I flash the nashers and wink as I spin away to the table. She's fucking well getting it tonight.

13:06
He'd spent most of the day flitting between Norfolk Park and the City Road Cemetery, risking it the Saturday night before to get some sleep in the cemetery itself, reasoning that he was less likely to encounter wandering public, or the seekers, in there. He was pretty much correct aside from a dangerous half an hour when a middle aged couple from the Manor roamed in for a drunken fumble after midnight, it looked like it was supposed to be a drunken fuck, but for the old boys lack of a hard on, and her mocking his supposed manhood. The inevitable outcome was him grabbing her roughly by the hair, throwing her to the ground and kicking the shit out of her, then dragging her out of the graveyard and on to wherever it was they lived. It seemed pretty harsh but there was no way at all Daniel was going to get involved, there were rules to this shit that he had no inclination whatsoever to break, even if nobody else seemed to have a grasp of that. For one, stay on the move. The fat kid, Graham, had spent all of his time wandering aimlessly round Meersbrook Park, he may as well have had a target painted onto his massive back. There was a definite degree of, something, naivety? Stupidity? Something, about the fat kid, that had made Daniel pity him. He was never going to last more than a day or two. Secondly, they needed to stay away from their own home. The smack head, Tina,

in her urgency to get back to whatever it was that was there, walked straight into his trap. It was always going to be the case that she did that, because they had to stay out of very public places, and in all fairness, every motherfucker in Sheffield knew her face, she had to get away to somewhere, she just did it very predictably. So the message came through that he was back to seeking, and with his renewed vigour that a couple of hours sleep had afforded him, he had to get on the move, track down whoever he could. They had mixed it up a bit this time round, there were only four of them, and he was the only seeker for the next twenty four hours, he had to make the most of it. Daniel was definitely in no mood to leave this Earth early.

13:30pm

We've been raping the jukebox for the last hour. In his coke fuelled enthusiasm Justin has stuck at least a tenner in there to ensure the sounds are ours until, and definitely long after, we depart. A few students have started to filter in for some early afternoon drinking and seem to appreciate the choices. Never had no problems with students really. My old man gets proper wound up about them, gives it the big-waste-of-taxpayers money diatribe every time they're protesting over immigration or the environment on Look North or Calendar, but in the bigger picture, there's 2 universities in this fucking city, they're not going anywhere and neither are the students. Having said that though, there's a few of them bickering about Mr Ripper (if you please), this one cunt in a battered porkpie hat sits fondling a wispy piss-poor effort at a goatee beard, and is taking three weeks to get his point across. Without reading his autobiography you

can already tell he's addicted to the scene, perennial first year failure, been at the uni for 10 years but never made it to the second year. The freshers call him a legend but he's just a cunt. For sure, well-read is not intelligence in my book, knowing what words mean is not knowing when to use them. He's going on;
"I mean, it's fundamentally incorrect of the media to force upon us the assumption that the perpetrator of these criminal activities is of the male gender, I mean, there have been many female multiple murderers heralding from these fair Isles in the decades prior to the current one. I mean, take Myra Hindley as a prime example of how the supposed fairer sex can-"
"That's SHITE! Fuckin' Johnny Long-Words cunt! What the fuck are you talkin' about?" I've slammed my hand onto the table and turned in my chair to face him. The others round the table have shat it. A big shit-eating grin spreads across his face, his blackened teeth stink of a million roll ups.
"Dude, chill, I mean, I'm simply purveying my personal opinion to my gathered associates" he sweeps his hands around the table to show me the others as if I haven't seen them already. I'm aware that I'm grinding my teeth, partly because of the coke, but generally because this fucking tosser is irritating me, and while I consider knocking the crusty bellend on his arse, some bird has stepped in. "Sorry, but this IS a private conversation we're having, it's not of your business". Another lad stands up beside her in what I take to be a potential show of solidarity, but it turns out he's actually fannying it and pulling at her shoulder giving it "Come on Daisy, forget it" and it does the trick in defusing the situation as I'm suddenly faced with the choice of

belting her or belting him, and in all honesty, I could lose face in front of-
"Daft cunt!" Justin's flown in and cracked the crusty wanker full in his scummy chops, fair play to him because he's proper knocked him out, I mean, his eyes roll right up into the back of his head and time stands still for a second as everybody takes in what's happened before all hell breaks loose and this Daisy bird is screeching at the obliging fit redhead to call the bobbies, and I've snotted her knight in shiting armour a good one. He falls onto the crusty cunt and it's looking like a pussy pile-on by now. We're looking to the rest of the table for one of them to step up and have a pop but it's not happening, one of them's holding his hands up, palms toward us in a gesture of peace and the whole thing's in danger of fizzling out 'cause there's no noise in the place except the Daisy bird stood there in defiance calling us a pair of animals, and her knight in shiting armour has slid to the floor and is holding his face and crying. Justin looks at me wild eyed, then back to the Daisy bird, and for a minute it looks like he's gonna belt her an'all but he starts laughing.
"You bird, only fucker here wi' any balls, shame you're a fuckin' gobshite" and he goes back to our table and downs his pint "Come on pal, these cunts've ruined me buzz". So we're out of there laughing our tits off, leaving the crusty porkpie cunt to his (in likely his own words) 'enforced reverie' and the rest of the fanny squad doubtlessly shell-shocked, and readying stories to tell in the Union Bar of how ten local drug-crazed thugs pounced them for no reason. Justin had it right though, for sure the only cunt in there with no actual balls was the only cunt in there with any balls. That's the thing

with gobshite birds though, they tend to know that the law of averages says you're not likely to give them a crack, so they'll push their luck as far as they can. I personally wouldn't hit a lass, but they don't know that do they?

We duck into the Swim Inn as the sirens power up round the corner. I did kind of hope that the redhead wouldn't phone the coppers but I guess she had to, no matter how much she wanted to ride my cock and let me wear her like a beard, and as Justin goes to the bar I go to the toilet to throw more coke up my nose. I'll probably end up going back round to the Frog later to see if she still fancies a ride.

13:38

Oh no dear boy, still hiding? Damn them! Best get a move on! The squatter in Alan's head had taken root firmly and was refusing to leave. Landlords rights or not. Alan was unable to shake him. To Alan, this invader sounded much like he might imagine Sherlock Holmes would talk, or a moustachioed hunter stalking the jungles for lions in old black and white movies he remembered from his childhood. It certainly wasn't his own voice or personality that was in there, but like him or not, the invader had carried him thus far. He had carried a trembling, snivelling Alan to Tinsley to kill a man, James, his name was. To sneak with stealth to where the man was crying, facing the railway lines, squatting, rocking in his blood stained shoes, whining to himself. He had pulled forward the mental strength to pull his arm around James' neck, to pull back and squeeze until the man passed out, to draw his knife across his still pulsing neck and watch the arcing blood shoot toward the sky like the sprinklers on a cricket pitch in summer, firing off in at an ever decreasing angle, then strip him naked and leave him in a pool of his own congealing blood. The strength the invader had summoned from Alan's weak, slim frame was almost superhuman, he had never even tolerated touching another human being, let alone the closeness he had experienced when he powerfully and almost cleanly snuffed out the young life of his supposed enemy. That was Sunday, a good four days ago, and the going for Alan had been somewhat slow over the weekend. He and his mental squatter had hidden well, kept moving as low key as possible, and when the roles were reversed he had sought out as well as he could, but just getting close to his prey a tad too late, and then having to retreat with haste. That's how it felt for him, like the movement of the tides. He could seek as well as his efforts would allow, get close enough to touch his intended target, then the roles would change and as quickly has his tide came in, it would be forced to withdraw. So as the latest instruction was that he was hiding, the moustachioed hunter decided to lift his tired frame from the bushes into which he had found himself. Extending his head like a wary turtle from it's shell he scanned the coast to ensure it was clear and emerged , brushing away debris and leaves, thankful that it wasn't what he used to call "sticky buds", small bobbles of green that he and his pals would often pelt at each other when he was growing up, as an unfortunate born victim Alan would invariably find himself coated from head to toe in the blasted things, whilst his so-called pals would be rolling around in fits of laughter at his ridiculous appearance, it wasn't a coincidence that he eventually found himself withdrawn and- *Sod the sticky buds old chap! Get a bloody move on! These rotters won't kill themselves!* Considering himself told he manoeuvred as nonchalantly as he could to avoid being overtly noticed by any members of the public. They had said that of course he should stay out of the main public areas, but also acknowledged that it would be impossible to conduct the proceedings without ever stumbling into unknowing members of the public, so the aim was to remain as low key as possible, keep conversations to a minimum, and that food was to be provided anyway so nobody should ever feel obliged to enter shops and the like. It felt to Alan that they really had thought of everything. The moustachioed hunter might guide him on his mission to whatever destiny he had laid before him, but he certainly wouldn't be able to muster up the power to force Alan to go against- *Steady there! We're in this together old boy! Let's just stick to the job at hand!*

He found himself apologising to his ubiquitous mind squatter, and shuffling further on, eventually reaching the pinnacle of one of the city's seven hills, and settling to perch on a wooden bench to recollect his thoughts. The vast grey city with belts of green certainly looked nothing like home anymore. No, it looked like a sprawling mass of hiding places, for both himself and his three remaining, well, contestants, he considered, for want of a better word. A vast game and hide and seek. Without the benefit of clues and constant location updates, somebody searching for Alan might consider it the equal of searching for a needle in a haystack, but the person searching for him did have the benefit of those things. So, on he moved.

13:45

Justin's looking wild eyed and replaying his belting of the scruffy fucker in the pork pie hat, complete with sound effects.

"Oh, hurruff hurruff long fucking word- BOOM! Get down you dirty fucking cunt!" I laugh at this 'cause I'm feeling brilliant right now, my woes of joblessness a distant memory and I'm definitely living in the moment. The coppers will no doubt be round there now, the students embellishing the story of their own destruction with glee, Justin will probably have smashed a bottle and held it to one of their throats, with murder in his eyes. I've done a roundhouse kick to the Knight in Shiting Armour's jaw, breaking it into a million pieces. These students are generally skint aren't they? One senses that there's a blame here, so there will defo be a fucking claim getting put in. In my mind I'm seeing him hobbling around with a walking stick, maybe a neck brace, the big fucking hero on campus, the fanny that took on ten thugs and lost, but at least he put up a brave fight. There's a part of me that senses the injustice in this, that I don't get to put forward my argument, I'm pretty good at arguments, debates, if you will. And I want to be able to say "Hey! Laddo! There were two of us! Get your fucking facts right yeah? You fannied it, that's all there is to it!" And I want him to be all like "Oh, um, well, the fundamental facts of the incident to which I refer are that you were entirely vicious in your destruction of myself and my acquaintances, and this is something to which I take great exception" and then I want to belt him again just because he's being entirely superfluous with his diction. Yep, for sure, I know big words too shit head. I don't know how long I was in my fantasy just then, but Justin's not here when I snap out of it. A quick panic scan of the pub places him between two young ladies in suits and blouses, clearly here on a late lunch, probably got to be back in the office for two o'clock, but now they've been sidetracked by the charms of a coked up pisshead with an arm around the shoulders of them both. They're clearly taken in by whatever he's saying to them because they're laughing, and it doesn't seem to me like they're doing it to humour him, like, laughing at him instead of with him, like some people seem to do. It occurs to me that it could just be my drug induced haze that makes it seem like that, so I try to scrutinize them from afar, to see if what I originally thought was wrong, like, were they taking the piss out of my mate, right in front of his face? Like, were they patronising him? I can't quite be sure, and Justin is smiling his big grin at me and beckoning me with his head so I put it out of my mind, and head over. "This fucker here ladies, this fucker here is a hero to the working man!" He's pointing at me with his bottle now, keeping it together really well considering what we've put down our necks and up our noses this last couple of hours. The girls are fucking lapping it up, and so am I, 'cause he's really doing a number on my ego, and he's going on "You know what he did? He stuck it to the fucking man yeah? He doesn't like his job? Does he stay there? Does he take it up the arse every day?" I start to interject here because in my head I feel they're gonna actually take this like do I actually physically get a cock up my arse, which I certainly do not! So I'm gonna say something but he's already beaten me to the next line "Does he FUCK!" he shouts and a few people turn and tut now, but we do not give one fuck. Who are the lairiest fuckers in the town this afternoon? Us, that's who, and fucking proud of it we are too! For sure, this coke is obscene.

13:59

Jumping jelly beans old boy, busy about the town isn't it? He hadn't meant to venture so close to the centre of the city, and felt a vast array of emotions as he turned onto the Moor shopping precinct into a wave of shoppers, and buskers, and people carrying clipboards trying to coerce the public to part with bank details to donate ever increasing amounts of money to charity. On one side of his were anti-BNP campaigners with sheets and sheets of petitions against legally inciting racial hatred, on the other were animal rights campaigners with sheets and sheets of petitions against using animals for testing make-up and such upon. Alan danced between people all vying for his attention. The moustachioed hunter worked his feet as if he were a boxer dodging jabs, his retained control of his own eyes, keeping them firmly fixed on the cracks, and seemed to navigate using pieces of ground-in chewing gum on the floor as he were navigating using the stars in the sky. He felt the city breathing him in, sucking the life out of his lungs, playing a rapidly increasing rhythm that his heart was happy to follow, the feet of the people around him melted away beneath the sweat pouring from his forehead into his eyes, stinging bile rose in his- *keep it together old chap, nearly there! Not long to go, don't go all flaccid on me now! We're relying on you!* And he turned a corner, and exhaled with his back to the wall, out of the flow of the river of humanity, a humanity he had never truly been a part of, never even wanted to be a part of. As a child he was more than happy to fade into the background, allow stronger, funnier, chattier, bigger kids to take the limelight, and on the other end of the spectrum he was ashamed to admit that he wished badness on the weaker, smellier, uglier, more poverty stricken kids, the bracket he fell most firmly into, not because he had ill feeling toward them, but because it would keep the attention from himself *I say chap, now really isn't the time for memories, move it damn you!* And he moved, guided through quieter back streets, towards Devonshire Green he was allowed to breath, his heart settled, and a calmness seeped into his mind. He knew exactly where he was destined, and the Botanic Gardens that were so often his utopia, where he could retreat from a reality of debt, poverty, hunger, somewhere he could get away from his own mind. At Devonshire Green he stopped a while to watch some young lads on the skating park, some were sitting in groups smoking and playing music with each other, others were more active and rolling around on their contraptions. A sadness crept into him, that served to remind him his childhood was a poor one, and a slight regret lingered that he hadn't allowed himself to open up more, to make friends, to be stronger person. These kids had friends. What the devil made them so different to him? If he ever made it through this, Alan was damn sure he would make a change. But that was a big if.

14:42

They were all pretty much the same distance away when the message had been delivered, so it was just a case of who he wanted to go for, if he played his cards right he could get two of them in this turn, leave it down to the inevitable one on one showdown. He fancied his chances against any of the three remaining, although he didn't have a clue who had killed who, other than the two he'd done. For all he knew the NHS glasses motherfucker with the farmer stink had nailed the other two and was hard as fuck, but it made no difference, he had to do what he had to do or he'd be just as open as they were come tomorrow, so he headed into town. He considered himself pretty cool about things, he hadn't panicked yet, just gone about the task at hand following the rules. He'd got himself into this shit, there was only him gonna get himself out of it, and if they demanded certain things of him, then certain things he would have to do. He cast his mind back to that room, the others all seemed so jittery, he sat there thinking *What the fuck is this shit man?* But he stayed cool, that's all mans had to do, stay cool. Don't be showing that you got weaknesses because people can smell it. They can pick up on it and manipulate it. So he kept the head down, listened to the others, paid attention without giving the image of paying attention. Worked them out. Like, the metal-head kid with the long hair, sat there drowning out the world with his rock music, not listening, just thinking he was there to maybe answer a couple questions, as if it was that easy to just respond to an advert, show up, win himself ten grand and go home with a hard on. Nah man. Shit's harder than that. It seemed like a paltry amount to offer up as a reward for what they had to do as he listened to their instructions. Like, man could go and open boxes with Noel Edmonds and be disappointed if you came away with ten grand, and while they explained the shit he was involved in it became increasingly clear that there was much more at stake than ten fuckin' G's. He had been the fourth to go through that door, and what he found behind it was just as clinical as the room he had come from. A massive empty room with a chair in the middle, another door at the opposite end of the room, a big mirror down the left side, no doubt a two-way so the organisers of this shit could watch him, see his reactions close up even though there were two blinking cameras watching him too. They had him from all angles. A woman's voice had instructed him to take a seat, she sounded foreign, Russian or something like that. He'd sat and waited, not bothering to look at the mirror, he reasoned it might just serve to antagonise whoever it was behind there, and he'd already figured out by then that it was a sinister deal. A few minutes later the door in front of him had opened, revealing a the small framed figure of an old boy, slightly balding, clad in tweed, bearing a dark wooden walking stick which appeared to be just for show, given that he strode in with an air of militarian authority. The old guy hadn't said much, just cast an inspecting eye over Daniel and silently judged him for what seemed like days. Daniel stared ahead, let the man do what he was doing without question, and if he was satisfied or not the man didn't let on, just turned on his heels and left the room, closing the door behind him. Almost immediately it swung open again, this time bringing with it two people, the big blonde motherfucker who'd brought him here, and a slender pale skinned girl, who looked no more than early twenties, dark brown hair pulled tight into a long pony tail, high forehead, pale green eyes and petite

features, but looked like she meant serious business. Daniel had then looked up in recognition at the blonde guy.
"Daniel, how are you doing?" he asked.
"Okay I guess"
"Nervous?"
"Course I am man, this shit-" He had paused at his swearing and looked at the girl. "Sorry. This stuff is a bit far out man, don't know what I got myself into do I?"
"Allow me to explain"
What he then told Daniel blew his mind, he knew that however he got out of this shit, if he got out of this shit, nothing was going to be the same again.

He'd been walking about ten minutes through the town, turned onto Devonshire Green, and stopped in his tracks. The NHS glasses motherfucker was right there, and the man was in plain view of the whole city.

14:50pm
From the relative darkness of the back of the Astra with its blacked-out windows, Christophe scrutinized the screen of his laptop. Tapping at the keyboard he thrashed out the events of the last few hours for his coded report to the old man. Hoxton. A man who, to Christophe, liked to think of himself as a typical English gentleman. He was certainly that, but only in the sense that he was full of breathless pomposity and carried himself with an arrogant stubbornness that was enforced by the fact that he was always correct. In his head. To give him his dues he was a very clever man, very wily, there was always something ticking over in his brain behind those busy eyes. He had installed

around him an able group of people who were as ruthless as they were discreet and efficient, none of them contributed anything less, or indeed more, than what was required of them. They had sneered at Christophe for the way he was brought into the operation, but never openly in front of Hoxton. It wasn't as issue for Christophe, he fully appreciated that he didn't have to be taken in as he was. Even back then he was made aware that they could have simply killed him and left his corpse to be robbed and stripped in the slums of Paris, turning ever blue until such a time that one of the local Arabs felt it necessary to report the stinking rotting corpse inconveniencing the immigrant children in a decrepit play area. A lesser man might have seen it as a real injustice that he wasn't permitted to simply continue with a life racked by the guilt of his inadvertent homicide without ever knowing that this particular group of people ever existed, let alone the type of people that they were. For Christophe however, it was a chance to wipe the slate clean, to end the life of Jean-Christophe Bergin, accidental murderer and sexual deviant, only son of Franck and Vanessa Bergin, and to give birth to Christophe Berg, ice cold killer and sexual deviant, son of nobody. Four years later Ada generally led the subtle flogging of him with their colleagues, expressing a wish to have done exactly that, and the threat of still doing that if he ever fucked them over. Hoxton had never baited him with such threats, as it was taken as a standard policy of his organisation that a deserved, painful and humiliating death would meet anybody who felt the twinge of ideas above ones station, and it was also unsaid but plainly obvious that anybody who thought otherwise was naive and unworthy of mercy anyway.

As he was ready to forward his report his eyes were drawn to the green illumination of his vibrating phone as it gently danced over the fabric of the back seat.

"Dietmann, how is it going?"

"Not so good. Have you checked the tracker?"

"Not recently, I'm about to send my report"

"Check it. Two of them are in the city centre and too close to each other, about three hundred metres from your current location, it appears that the seeker is ready to take his chance. Mr Hoxton requests that you persuade him to find somewhere more appropriate and advise us when it has happened"

"Ok, consider it done"

15:00

"Sir, today's edition of the local newspaper, very interesting developments" Dietmann was holding up a copy of newspaper called The Evening Star for Hoxton, a local interest publication that appeared, to Ada, to be revelling in the current activities in the city.

They were in the small control room, Ada and Hoxton had been discussing the potential city centre clash and were interrupted by the young German who had entered with the most recent public interest update. The Evening Star had kept most keenly abrest of what was happening in their own back garden. When the first body was discovered it had obviously been treated as a solitary tragedy, but as proceedings rolled on the killings drew more and more attention. This, of course, was very much intentional. The more of these events they created, the tighter the planning was, and adapted

to each location, in this case the English press were notorious in their sensationalising of even the most minor of occurrences, of creating their own reality for the pandering public, and if there were no stone cold facts, they would be imagined. Speculation was key. The media equivalent of throwing a mouse into a large room full of elephants and then closing the door to watch what happens. So as the front page of the first edition after the initial killing featured a memorial and a small piece berating the mystery man at large, surrounded by images of local gardeners holding aloft oversized leeks and carrots and beckoning the reader to join them on the page nine, the headlines and fillers became entirely based on what was happening, the families and loved ones of the protagonists in the event were asking why their lover, daughter, or son were doomed, why they were in the wrong place in the wrong time, how they would be remembered forever in the form of a bench or some such. Ada had intently watched the story take a life of its own, with a sense of self satisfaction at the titbits being fed to the press by sources within the police force, who in turn had been fed red herrings by "anonymous" sources from the public.
Hoxton sighed a little, if he was annoyed by what he read he gave very little away, the man was a ruthless creature. The tentacles of his influence seemed to know no end. Things happened for him almost instantly if he desired something. Ada had never known him to have anybody in his life that he could be mistaken for having emotion toward. No significant other. He had never displayed any evidence of having a sexual side to him, while herself, and Christophe would make sure they

had their needs tended to with whoever they wished and whenever they wished, Hoxton remained as good as asexual.

He scrutinized the newspaper, turning to absorb the pages on which the story appeared to continue, and once finished he folded it up and placed it on an empty stool between himself and Ada, and rose to look at Dietmann "Get Christiano for me" he instructed before he left the control room, leaving the two of them looking at each other .

"What has happened Dietmann? Is it anything to worry about?" she enquired of the German.

"I wouldn't wish to say Ada, take a look" he responded, bidding her to pick up the newspaper and see for herself, she did as she was bidden, and skimmed over the front page. The headline made a question of whether there were more than one killer, which was intriguing enough in itself, but upon reading further she saw why Dietmann found it so necessary to bring it to Hoxton's attention.

By David Harston

Forensics experts have today revealed that we may be looking at multiple killers in the case of The Sheffield Ripper after evidence discovered suggested that the victims throats were cut in varying angles. This reporter today has seen crucial reports that point to what could be vital proof that the murderer is not acting alone, which, if correct, means that Sheffield may have been descended upon by a gang of bloodthirsty ghouls who take great pleasure in killing, and observing their naked victims before taking their clothes as a trophy of their act of

random violence. It is also possible that these killings are what might be referred to as Rites Of Passage for younger members to attain themselves positions of prominence within the gang and prove themselves to their peers. Police sources confirm that they have not ruled out the possibility that the murders were commited by several perpetrators, rather than a singular vicious beast, and would certainly be looking into gangs working within the area, possibly of Eastern European origin.

This last speculation irked Ada in particular, who felt she'd read enough, she hadn't been in this country long but the racist views which were on display toward people with accents like her own were bordering on the obscene. The English were the most awful nationality she had ever encountered, parading with illusions of tolerance and live-and-let-live attitudes, yet were the epitome of intolerance as far as her opinion, and she felt it necessary to act. Not yet, however. This David Harston character could wait. For now. They had a task to complete.

15:04

Alan passed the skating park and aimed for a side road beside the high rise blocks of what the sign confirmed as "Luxury Self Contained Apartments" and nervously wandered along Broomhall Street, toward the main road that circled the outskirts of the city centre, if he could get to the other side of that road he reckoned he could get to the gardens untouched.

15:05

He watched the NHS glasses motherfucker duck down the quieter road, security cameras clung to the side of the flats on the right, nothing could happen here, the only safe thing to do would be to follow at distance. This fucker was a dead man.

15:06

"Those girls were fit as fuck mate" Justin's still going on about the business girls we met, Jenny and Kim, reckons we're taking them out later in the week, the optimist in me says we'll be balls deep by the weekend, the realist says we'll have forgotten all about them in a couple of hours' time. Where we're at right now is walking up West Street towards the Uni area, we've made big enough scenes here in town, so we're gonna go make dicks out of ourselves in the student bars instead. My jaw is fucking killing from grinding my teeth, and we've gone through a couple of grams each so far. The longer we go the more it occurs to me that it's been well over an hour since I had a piss, and that seems like a bit too long for me, because once I start drinking lager, I need a piss every twenty minutes or something, but then the coke is working itself through my body and I've been well and truly side-tracked by chatting shit with Justin. He's still gabbing about Jenny and Kim but I have to stop him a second.
"Pal, pal, I am fuckin' bustin' for a piss, let's go down here a bit, we can get back on the main road up there" and I'm pointing down a small road behind the takeaways on West Street. So on we go, down this little road, and I'm trying to find a suitable spot for unloading my bladder. There's steam coming out the back of one

of the chinkies, and usually I'd be giving it the starving diatribe but cocaine properly kills the appetite, and I stop by a big black wheelie bin and pull the little fella out so I can have a piss. Justin's stood keeping lookout for me, and I'm rocking on my feet, trying to keep balance, watching the yellow stream coming out of my cock with one eye closed. It's a nippy day so it's steaming up something rotten, right in my face. I squeeze off a last few sprinkles and tuck the little fella away, beckoning Justin along with me. We're still chatting shit and walking up and I cannot fucking believe it, but who the fuck do I see? It's only fucking Jean-Claude Van Lundgren! He can't see us because he's walking away from us and I'm grabbing Justin's arm, all excited, because I reckon together we can take the cunt.
"Mate, you know that big blonde cunt I was on about? That fucker that give it the big yap yap about shaggin' that bird from t'Frog? He's fuckin' there mate, cheeky big cunt!" And Justin's all over it, he knows the score. So we're following him with big plans. Normally I'm not that hot for fighting, but for sure, when I'm coked up I fancy taking on the world. This big nobhead is going down for the count!

15:10
Christophe was watching his palm computer, the dots were getting ever closer. Ahead of him he saw Daniel pass the end of the alley, he and Alan were playing very dangerously being so close to the centre, they had been told to keep it as low key as possible, so this was not ideal by any stretch of the imagination. The boy Daniel was considered reasonably intelligent, so Christophe

didn't feel he needed to intervene as he'd use his common sense and hold off anyway, but the word from above was that they felt he ought to, so he was obliging. As he turned the corner he saw Daniel dropping down some steps into the subway under the road, and followed him.

15:12

Not far now old chap, keep it up, nearly there. The moustachio'd hunter was quite correct, they had successfully navigated the city centre together, and the subway he had just negotiated was almost halfway to the gardens, only about a mile to go, after a small rundown working class area he would then have the luxury of getting through quiet, leafy streets surrounded by large old houses, with large driveways. He knew the area well, and could go a while before he crossed paths with another human being. Comforted by that knowledge, he afforded himself a breather and a rest on a small wall by a disused petrol station.

15:15

As he slowly ascended the steps from the subway he poked his head up to check the view. The NHS glasses motherfucker was there, plain as day, sitting there with his back to Daniel, and the rest of the city. He took a breath, looked around, and readied himself. He considered that things could quite easily go wrong here, the location was pretty close to town, and the traffic roared above his head so it wouldn't take much for man to be spotted. Part of him wanted to just get it done,

fuck the consequences, but the other part of him needed this to be deeper into the quieter area. A chase would mean that the route would be decided by the NHS glasses motherfucker. Fucks sake he thought. He pulled the knife out of his bag, and crept-
"Mr Jackson" he turned with a start to see Berg, the bulky European motherfucker, at the foot of the stairway, moving up toward Daniel, cool as hell, looking up at him. His heart thumped, they wouldn't have sent him if things were looking rosy. He took a couple of steps toward him, steadily, so as not to appear jumpy. Who knew what the man might do if he thought Daniel was gonna attack him?
"Fuck man, what have I done? I'm playin' by the rules!" he hissed in panic.
"I appreciate that Mr Jackson, but what you have planned just now places everything, in particular you, in jeopardy. I suggest you hang back, allow him to move on" the big cat was a calm man, just saying it like it was. Daniel took stock of what he was saying, the emphasis on the fact that if he wanted to go kill the NHS glasses motherfucker in plain view of the road, he might end up disappearing himself. He sighed.
"I wasn't gonna do the man here, I was gonna wait man" He protested, in vain as it turned out, because the man Berg looked pointedly at the knife in Daniels hand, he conceded the issue, kissed his teeth and began to open his bag to return the knife, and was interrupted by voices getting rapidly louder from the subway.

15:23

We've followed Jean-Claude Van Lundgren through this tunnel and are getting properly hyped up, the cunt is well getting it, no doubt about that. A flickering light in the ceiling of the subway is messing with my eyes, and the good job the council did of putting little mosaic squares along the wall to try and cheer the place up has been fucked up by local scrote-bags drawing dicks, and spray-painting their tags all over it. I mean, for sure, what's the point of trying to brighten a place up when the jackals are only gonna descend upon it and rip to bits anyway? What's that saying? Oh yeah, you can't polish a turd! Hah! I like that one. I might try and get it into conversation with Justin later, got a nice ring to it. We're chattering away, and we can't be far from the massive fucker now, probably this is a better place to go for him anyway, so we turn the corner and Jean-Claude Van Lundgren is right fucking there! Him and some black kid who's carrying the biggest knife I have ever seen in my life. Now I don't know what the fuck is happening 'cause Justin's powered in and smacked the big blonde cunt in the jaw, who's just standing there, and Justin's going off on one, like, he's properly fucked his fist up on the guys face, and we're looking at each other 'cause the black guy is taking a few steps toward us holding his knife up. This shit is fucked. Whatever we had planned has gone to shit now, and I've sobered up quick sharp. Justin is still shouting about his fist, and his eyes have filled up. Now I'd always bet on my boy to come out on top in a scrap, he's got some real power to him, but the way Lundgren has taken his punch like it was nothing has shit me right up. Add to that the fact that there's some mystery guy holding a cleaver, and it doesn't look like he's mugging our boy Lundgren, it looks more to me that the knife man is shitting it from him too. If I wanted to hedge my bets I'd say he wouldn't be well up for all three of us jumping the man mountain and cutting him to ribbons. No, if I was gonna hedge my bets I'd say quite the opposite, I'd say he'd side with the man mountain and make us poor cunts disappear. Now, it's all silent except for Justin whimpering, like, everybody's figuring everybody else out. The black guy's looking at Lundgren, who's looking at Justin, who's looking at his rapidly swelling fist. And I'm looking at all of them.

15:40

The situation was in danger of spiralling out of control here. Christophe assessed what was happening. For whatever reason the fuck monkey from the bar earlier had appeared with a companion, and felt it necessary to attack him, albeit without much conviction after the first failed attempt. He kept his stare firmly on the two gate crashers, and turned his head slightly, and pointed at Daniel behind him.
"Leave, and remember what I said" And the guy wasn't slow in following that instruction, Christophe heard his footsteps quickly fade away, and glanced over his shoulder briefly to ensure he was now alone with the two idiots.
"Now. What the hell do you think you're doing?" he directed this at the guy he met in the bar, whose face was contorting and shifting between confusion, fear, shock, and anticipation. His massively dilated eyes blinking away. He said nothing.
"I will ask again"

15:42

All our cocaine fuelled bravado has fucked right off. I don't know what has happened to my day any more. When I woke up this morning I really truly did not expect this, how could I? We've got some sort of hitman nobhead with his gun aiming right at us and asking us questions I can't answer, not because I don't know what he wants us to say, although I guess that would be right, it's just that, well, fucking hell, how many times does the average person get a gun aimed at him? I'd say not very often. And I can't get words out. I want to apologise, tell him we'll go, we won't say anything, and we'll just go home, but there's this voice in me telling me that if he's gonna carry a big hand cannon like the one he's got levelled at us, then he knows how to use it, and more importantly, he knows he's gonna need to use it, and will. I'm willing a message to Justin to run, I want him to hear my thoughts, I want us to run together, take our chances, see if we can get into plain view, back to Dev Green, CCTV and maybe even the police we were so keen to avoid only a few hours ago. Those hours feel like months ago. I feel sick as fuck.

15:44

Christophe felt the jolt in his hand as the silenced pistol fired a bullet into the forehead of one of the idiots, the one who had felt it necessary to punch him in the jaw. He had the gun aimed at the corpse's friend before it had even hit the ground, and pulled out his mobile. Without taking his eye from his target he spoke softly into the receiver, ensuring the idiot would not hear what he was saying. Things were very much fucked just now.

The tone emanating from Ada was one of fury, and contempt. She held him responsible for this, and she told him as much, he was being relieved of his duties and was to get rid of the witness, disappear, and await collection. Christophe knew what this meant. Relieved from his duties. Hoxton would not tolerate this. The gamblers would be all over him for answers, and if people were going to harass Hoxton, then Hoxton would almost certainly harass Christophe into an early grave. He believed the term was Shit Rolls Downhill. He needed a plan, and he needed it quickly.

15:56

"Gentlemen, things are in hand, do not worry, your bets are still very much alive, but we have hit what might officially be deemed, a snag" Hoxton was addressing the gamblers. There were eight of them in total. One for each of the original contestants. The way it worked was that until the final three, the gamblers who were "out" would be permitted to rebuy just once, on a remaining contestant, and at dramatically reduced odds. So far the four who had bet upon Tina, Ruby, James and Graham had all placed their rebuy on Daniel.
Ada watched from the corner of the room as Hoxton delivered his speech to the gamblers who knew better than to voice too much disdain, Hoxton held with him far more power than the eight gamblers combined. There had been grumblings but if the old man told them things were fine then they knew not to worry too much. After Hoxton had informed them he left the room, and Ada followed.
"What are your thoughts Ada?" If Hoxton asked a question like this he was genuinely interested in the

answer, but Ada still considered her response before speaking.
"Christophe has messed up sir, in my opinion, he was tasked with a simple request and now we are left with an unexpected corpse" The old man thought this over as they walked, and remained silent as they approached the control room. Before she opened the door to the room he paused, as if to say something, but then turned and walked away. He arrived at the door to his own personal room and turned to her.
"Perhaps you're right Ada. Deal with it" And he left it at that.

15:58

The Rose Garden was silent but for the mild rustle of the tips of the flowers colliding in the winter breeze. Alan loved the serenity of this place. In here he could believe anything was possible. The miracle of nature was truly on display and it enveloped him in a bubble where he was untouchable. The events over this last week had threatened to tip him over the edge. The revelations made to him in the bare room, after he was called into it, shook him to his core. Now he was away from the close shave by the subway, he allowed himself the chance to take stock. *Something about this seems fishy old boy! Why would Mr Berg be associating with the young coloured fellow? Is he feeding him information? That's darned unfair I must say... Keep it together, they don't know that you know!* He had grown to enjoy the company of his moustachioed hunter, and mused that it was a shame he hadn't come along sooner, a surprise even, considering how withdrawn he had been throughout his life. The moustachioed hunter, or

Algernon, as he had dubbed himself, he thought retrospectively, was entirely at fault for the position he was in. It was he that wouldn't let that newspaper advertisement go, it was he that dragged Alan's lumbering frame onto the bus, and it was also he that ensured Alan was still alive to be here, in the silent bliss of the rose garden.

That room, on the solitary chair, under the shadows of Mr Berg and his accomplice, the things they told him, and demanded of him.

"Mr Foster, you have been selected from a great number of possible players, we have followed you for months, you have been vetted, we know everything that there is to know about you, we know you better than you know yourself, and I know you will not feel inclined to interrupt me whilst I advise you of why you are here" he had threatened, his eyes had seeped with cold neutrality, he continued;

"What you are now a part of, you cannot become, how can I put this? Not a part of, any more. Unfortunately or otherwise, Mr Foster, you are with us until the end. You and your fellow players, the people you have seen enter this room, and those yet to enter it, and will play a little game of hide and seek. If we tell you to hide, you will hide, and if we tell you to seek, you seek. Now, Mr Foster, I appreciate that you may have questions, you may be wondering why all of this, secrecy, for a game of hide and seek? Why would we need to know everything about you? For nothing more than a children's game? I shall explain. You will need these items to assist you in your quest"

At that point his petite accomplice had revealed a back pack, and slowly unzipped it. Without word she pulled out a roll of cloth material, and unravelled it onto the floor in front of him. As she laid it flat his attention was drawn to the huge knife which lay upon it. It was pristine, almost freshly made, untouched. Next to the knife she placed a mobile telephone. Beside both she placed the bag itself.

"These are the tools of the game Mr Foster. These, and you. On the telephone you will find a map of the city. This map is your boundary. You may explore any area of the city within these boundaries. If you feel like you may want to venture outside of these boundaries, well, Mr Foster, my advice to you, is don't. This telephone is our communication with you. Your role will change approximately every twenty four hours, we will advise you when this role has changed. If you are allocated the role of seeker, you will be given the exact locations of those who are hiding for one hour. After that hour you are on your own, so you will need to travel quickly. Of course bear this in mind, Mr Foster, because if you are given the task of hiding, then you must stay on the move. Do not go home. I must stress this to you Mr Foster, do not go home. Now, the knife. Listen very carefully. This is how you will remove your fellow players from the game. In the event that you locate somebody that is hiding, you will cut their throat, you will bleed them dry, you will remove their every item of clothing, and you will place those items into the bag, and place them in prearranged locations for collection. Very shocking I know, Mr Foster, we are the scum of the Earth, but we are also now the people to whom you will answer. Do not ever feel inclined to inform any law enforcement. Your every move will be tracked, we know where you are at all times. We can hear you. Stay away from busy, metropolitan areas of the city. I do sincerely hope that you are listening carefully, because if you fail to adhere to any of these, guidelines, you may wake up dead." Mr Berg then laughed loudly "That is a little joke I allow myself Mr Foster. It is a contradiction in terms. Wake up dead. I'm sure the irony is not lost on you, in any way." They had, in no uncertain terms, made sure he knew who was in charge of his life from now, placed all the goods back into the bag, blindfolded him, and bundled him into a car.

That was two weeks ago. His old life was nothing. Nobody missed him, nobody would miss him. It dawned on him why he had been chosen for this. Alan was nothing. Not a name, not even a number. His was a pitiful existence in which little occurred except he turned oxygen into carbon dioxide. He wasted air, and space. He- *Don't be thinking like that old chap, you're a super bloke, we've done some amazing things recently, if we get through this we'll join a club or something! Make some use out of our damn lives eh?* He sadly conceded the issue, and watched the sun set behind the statue of Pan, Spirit Of The Woods. The guards would be around soon enough to eject him, so he made his way to the Woodland Garden to lay low. With any luck he could grab some sleep now that he was alone in his haven, but he also had some serious thinking to do. There was that issue of the near miss he had experienced, and how best to deal with it.

16:24

We've been walking for twenty odd minutes, I haven't said a word to him, and he hasn't said anything other than to tell me when jump, and how fucking high. This cunt killed Justin, left my boy's body there to fucking rot, but not before taking everything out of his pockets, his cash, his fucking coke and his phone. I don't have a scooby what the plan is, and I'm not about to ask any time soon, the cunt can go fuck. He can kill me if he wants. For sure he's made me very fucking aware that even though the gun's away, if I fancy my chances he'll fuck me up and if I go shouting my gob off he'll fuck me up. I'm on the loser of a lifetime here. Fucking cocaine. If I'd kept that shit out of my nose I certainly would not be trying to catch up with some bodybuilder hitman nobhead and trying to jump him. Admittedly I'd probably be slouched in some corner with sick down my front, but my boy would be alive. Fucks sake. I don't have it in me to formulate any plans just now, I'm just walking beside him, into student country. I don't know where he's taking us, or why, but my guess he's fucked up himself, the little tinny ranting from some bird at the other end of his mobile, it can't have been his wife. He was looking all shifty at me while he was talking, even though he was talking some other language to her, it was defo his boss or something, and my guess is that me and Justin had stumbled onto something nasty. Now this bulky fucker is dragging me along somewhere, I reckon he's on the run. From who, I haven't a clue, but my guess is also that he needs me for something. I dunno what. It can't be leverage, what worth am I to him? Fuck all.

The sun's pretty much gone down and dusk's settling in, I wonder if he knows he knows what he's doing. He doesn't strike me as the local type, and we're still trudging until we come up to an old Victorian house and we're standing at the door, I've been in these kinds of house before. Student houses. Used to belong to doctors and judges back in the day, back when this area was rife with cash. Now they've all been snapped up by foreign landlords, who've allowed them to get properly run down, and they've split it into, like, nine or ten bedrooms, one big living room that stinks of the mountain of tab ends and half smoked spliffs in the plethora of ashtrays, a kitchen piled to the roof with takeaway boxes and pots, and a brown (that used to be white) bathroom with shit all up the shower curtain. I don't profess to be the cleanest of blokes, but some of the stuff I've seen in these houses would blow your mind. Who this particular shit hole belongs to I don't know, but this fella here seems to be putting some faith in them. I'm kicking my feet against the wall in a gentle rhythm, like I used to do when I was younger and waiting for a bus with my mum, it used to annoy the fuck out of her, and it's getting on this fucker's tits too by the looks of it. Whoever he's here for isn't around and neither of us is talking because for one I'm numb, I saw one of my best mates shot in the face right in front of me, no warning, no nothing. He's not talking to me much because I reckon he's panicking. Hasn't a clue what he's gonna do, which suits me, because if he drops his guard I'm taking the cunt right out. Kill my mate? Yeah, get fucking ready pal.

16:49

"Ada, Christophe was not at the rendezvous, and is unresponsive to our attempts at contact, and I have several reasons to believe he has gone to ground, will I inform Mr Hoxton?"

"No Dietmann, continue in your efforts, we will not bother him until it is absolutely necessary. What of the tracker?"
"He has disposed of it, we found it approximately half a kilometre from the scene of his fuck up"
"What are your thoughts Dietmann?"
"My thoughts are that he has no intention of seeing any of us again, but that he cannot have travelled too far, his car is still parked in the city centre"
"Any news of the witnesses?"
"This is another issue Ada. The corpse of the civilian that Christophe shot has been discovered by a member of the public and the police currently have the location locked down. Our source informs us that only one body was discovered. It appears Christophe is either moving with the witness, or has released him"
"Why would he keep him alive, do you think?"
"Of this I am unsure Ada, I do not know what use the witness could be to aiding his cause"
"He is not an imbecile Dietmann, I'm sure he has a plan, of course this alters the situation somewhat, I shall inform Mr Hoxton myself, please continue to attempt to contact him, and await further instructions"
"As you wish Ada"

What the hell did Christophe think he was going to achieve by preserving the life of one of the civilian witnesses? Ada racked her brains to come to a conclusion. This was a question Hoxton would no doubt ask, sometimes he asked questions because he was genuinely interested in knowing what her opinion was. Sometimes though, she felt he asked questions simply to see what kind of answer she might give, as though she were being put through an interview process under the guise of a conversation. Nothing was ever simple, but he was the boss, so she must respect his ways and procedures.

At his door she readied herself for a brief moment, knocked firmly, and waited until she was beckoned into the small room. It was a reasonably neutral room, as decorated as a temporary workspace might need to be. A large wooden desk in front of his oversized leather chair. The man had no requirements for technology as his underlings were his technology, if he needed to know something then that information was gathered on his behalf, and fed back to him. The only piece of machinery he would ever make use of was his mobile telephone, not because he needed for people to be in touch with him, but because he needed to be able to contact any of them at any time.

"Ada, to what do I owe this pleasure?"

"Sir, we have a development of undoubted importance"

"Do tell"

"Christophe failed to make the rendezvous, sir, and has now gone to ground, the civilian witness is missing, presumed alive and in the company of Christophe but as yet unconfirmed. This piece of information came about as our source informs us that only one corpse was discovered at the scene and the police have the area locked down as we speak. Dietmann is constantly attempting communication with him, but as yet he had been unsuccessful, sir"

"And what of his vehicle?"

"Still parked where he left it, sir, I believe we are to presume that he is still within the area, and will more than likely attempt to tamper with the game, he has allowed Daniel to go free already, we know this much

from the audio recordings, but that may not be the case should he encounter any of the participants in the near future"
"If you were in my position what would you do Ada?"
"I would send me to find him personally, sir"
"And what makes you think you can find him any sooner than the rest of the team?"
"Because, sir, I have taken the liberty of requesting a pattern of his whereabouts throughout the operation, I will endeavour to revisit anywhere he has spent extended periods of time, I would undertake my task with the utmost of efficiency and discretion, and, as you are well aware of my opinion of Christophe, you will also be aware that I will personally enjoy destroying the man who has so flagrantly abused your trust, sir"
Hoxton watched his hands as he considered this.
"And who do you believe may have the balls to step up and control the operation Ada?"
"Dietmann, of course, sir"
He looked up and a glimmer of pleasure twinkled across his eyes.
"Ada, you are a credit to this organisation, do what is necessary, advise Dietmann that the operation is to continue despite this minor setback, and I do not want to see your face again until you return with Christophe's treacherous Gallic head in your hands"

17:11

In the rapidly descending dark, Alan lay in the shadows of the trees. The breeze had picked up as the late afternoon threatened to turn into evening, and a chill arrived in the air now the winter sun wasn't providing a smidgen of heat on the clear October day. On his back, in the dirt and the leaves he stared though the branches reaching out above him, to the steadily darkening sky, watching the events of earlier in his mind's eye. He remembered sitting on the wall of the disused petrol station, taking a breather, and hadn't been there more than a few minutes before he heard a dreadful ruckus happening from the subway he had just come from, and from his new squatted position behind the wall, he saw the heads of the young coloured fellow, Daniel, he believed, and Mr Berg, having a moment together, then Mr Berg sent Daniel on his way. As he kept his head below the eyeline of the wall he had heard him run by, not even two metres from Alan. For a few minutes he thought he heard more people pass him, and eventually became sure that it was safe to get on the move. Silently and rapidly he made his way through the streets deeper into the suburbs, the noise of traffic subsiding behind him, his paranoia building as he felt curtains twitching in the large houses that overlooked him, a woman pulling her daughter from the children's seat in the back of her car seemed to hold her closer to her frame than she might have if Alan hadn't been there, her hand pulling the child's head to her neck, sheltering her from the murderous paedophile that had descending upon their leafy area, the paradise that would usually be safe from people like him but now felt as vulnerable as everybody else, no amount of CCTV, and large electric gates could help them feel safe. As he passed a closed driveway he had leapt with a start as a guard dog snarled at the sound of his feet, it's jaws eagerly reaching out under the few inches of clearing between the floor and the foot of the black iron to try to rip apart whoever this intruder to its owners abode might be. Doing the job it was trained for.

Alan closed his eyes, and exhaled deeply, he desperately wanted to sleep, but his mind could not wind down, Algernon had been quiet, seemingly allowing him time to reflect, and now it was awash with paranoia, and fear, disgust at his own actions, however self-preserving those actions were. He considered that the young man he had killed would just as easily have killed Alan, that one of them that had to die, but what was to say that James would have survived any longer than Alan? He could have sliced his neck, then become dead meat himself within a few hours. He mind was so noisy, that he barely registered the measured, tiptoed footsteps that approached him, rustling through the fallen leaves and moist soil.

17:20

They were in her bedroom. Nobody had said a word for the last 30 minutes. The idiot was acting sheepishly around the girl. Christophe stood by the window watching the road below them, cars passed sporadically, none of them appeared anything like suspicious to his eyes, although his attention was caught briefly by a solitary character hanging around the telephone kiosk across the road who, after having been using the thing for a few minutes, waited around until a car pulled up beside them and a swift exchange was done. Christophe assumed drugs, perhaps marijuana. He mused to himself that if they wanted cocaine he had a great deal for them, having picked up about seven grams at less than cost price earlier in the day, it had been a steal. He smirked to himself. The

idiot had not cheered up any since they met again, the guy looked physically sick, staring off with a stupid look across his face, as if he could not comprehend what he had got involved in. It had been a regrettable few hours, Christophe should be back in his car right now, tracking the players, but no. He felt a great sense of injustice about what was going on, after all, was it not they who instructed him to intervene and obstruct Daniel in what he had planned to do? Not only that, it was they who had instructed Daniel to do what they intended to obstruct! Now he was on the run. He could not be sure if he had acted too rashly in taking the idiot prisoner and running, perhaps they would have let the matter go if he had gone in, explained himself, but then Ada would have reprimanded him for fucking the girl before the end of the operation, getting himself involved with civilians whilst he was supposed to be remaining anonymous, and Hoxton put a great deal of faith in her opinion. Maybe the bitch was giving the old man head, swallowing his pompous cock in exchange for the job she had. Christophe felt his fists clench involuntarily. He turned to the pair behind him, and looked at the girl.
"Earlier in the bar, he wanted to fuck you so bad" he gestured toward the idiot with his gun, he had yet to even ask his name. "I saw you looking at him in the same way, why do you not fuck now? Let me watch you act on those impulses you had?" a sinister smile developed across his face. The girl, Jess, trembled with fear. It was a shame that the circumstances in which they met this time was one of danger for everybody involved. The idiot looked at her with sadness, and then at Christophe with hatred.

"I've got an idea pal, why don't we watch you go and fuck yourself?" he offered. Christophe smiled, approached the idiot, and drew his face closer to his own.
"I see that you are developing a pair of balls now that you have an audience, but be sure, my friend, I will not hesitate to give you a slow and painful death for my own pleasure. Who knows? Maybe I will personally fuck your anus until you bleed to death? You will not be given the luxury of an instant end such as the one your friend came to. Remember him?" The idiot lunged, and was met at the forehead by the butt of Christophe's gun. He was out cold. Christophe turned to the girl.
"Shall we fuck?"

17:34

He lay on his back, looking up at the sky through the trees and the ever decreasing dirty light of dusk, choking back the tears, struggling against weight of what was supposed to be his prey, stinking dirty hands snaking themselves over his mouth and throat, he was utterly convinced that this was it. The end. It shouldn't have happened like this. He had him, there was no way he should have done this. Man was supposed to be a pussy. Clearly not. No, the man had surprised him. NHS glasses motherfucker, with his wonky haircut and that foul smelling wax jacket. Man looked like a psycho but the sort of psycho that would sit with an inane grin on his face whilst he talked to himself and slapped his own forehead repeatedly. No, he felt he should not be in this position right now. The guy was supposed to be easy pickings. He had watched him, from the thick

coverage of a giant redwood, he looked like he was trying to grab some sleep in the scant undergrowth beneath the trees. That was the then, whereas the now had Daniel prone, on his back, the guy sitting on his chest, hands clawing at his face and neck. The knife had skittered away from them so he was content to try to, do what? Choke him? It certainly felt like it, but the man was crying as he did it, weeping quietly, talking to himself. He seemed to be summoning a power that belied his skinny malnourished frame. As he leaned over him, his foul breath fogged over Daniel's face, making him gag under the grimy digits that were crawling all over his face and into his eyes. The man leant closer in, attempting to look right into his eyes, the grip of his hands got ever tighter around his jaw, allowing him to breath finally, Daniel stopped struggling, and held his stare.
"Well dear boy, it seems that you are well and truly jiggered eh? Why, in my day, negro boys were good as nothing but slaves and playthings!" The man was talking in some piece of shit fake accent, Daniel knew he didn't speak like that, he had heard him with his own ears, and the shit he was saying, he was an absolute fruitcake. He struggled against him again.
"Whoa there! You're a lively one old chap! Be careful, you'll do yourself a bloody mischief! Why, a chap might get to thinking you didn't want to die! Well, tough titty toenails!" He let out a hoot, leaned further into Daniel's face and roared "Because I'm in charge now old bean!" Daniel opened his eyes at the point the NHS glasses motherfucker slammed his forehead into his nose with a sickening crunch and sent him spiralling into unconsciousness.

17:48

My head is pounding. The last thing I saw was the boy Lundgren smash me with his pistol. Now I'm laid out on the floor at the end of the bed, looking at the ceiling, I can hear her, Jess, muffled and crying. There are two pairs of feet intertwined above my head, I know which ones are hers because they're the naked ones. They're also about five sizes smaller than the boats at the bottom of his legs. I don't say anything because I don't want the cunt to know I'm awake, I haven't moved a muscle. The thing is, I really need to move right now because from her noises, it doesn't sound like she wants it. The dirty fucking rapist cunt is taking what he wants. My eyes feel heavy and my brain groggy. I need to move. I need to destroy this meathead fucker before he does any more damage to either of us. He's speaking French at her. You can tell he probably pulls that shit all the time, makes a girl feel like she's the only one he's ever wanted, talks that romantic crap in her ear as he's wriggling away on top of her, gives her the whole performance. A line clicks in my head that Justin used on those girls earlier, Kim and Jenny, when he talked about having the techniques and all that, he pointed to me and said that I didn't have any skills, that I didn't need it when I had four inches and a fast arse. It cracked me up that. Fucking, Justin. What a top cunt he was. Her crying's doing my head in. I have to help her, this isn't right, it's never right, if a girl doesn't want to fuck you, you have to hold your hands up, say fair enough, I tried, I failed, I'll try to find somebody who'll sort me out. I'd never do what he's doing to her right now. He has to be stopped. I don't know how the fuck he appeared in our lives, but he needs removing from it quick sharp, and it seems I'm the only one who can do anything about it. He sounds like he's building up to a climax, so I don't have much time, I roll away from the bed and silently get to my feet, my head is killing me, like the crack I took to it is combining with the ale I've supped to create a cacophony of pain that's playing a drum and bass beat in my skull. I'm wobbling over them, looking down at him going hell for leather on top of her, she's got her eyes closed and I'm praying she keeps them shut, and doesn't give the game away, I need to move fast. I can't see the gun anywhere, so I'm reckoning he's got it under the pillow, keeping it close like. I remember the look on his face when Justin belted him, like it was nothing, so I can't take any chances with cracking him with anything light, but I don't want to hurt her at the same time, Jess, the poor cow. I scan the room, and the boy Lundgren is in a world of his own. Bile rises in my throat when I suddenly remember him threatening to fuck me until I bled to death, he's a class A weirdo this one, and for sure I totally believe that he'd do it too. No chance pal, not on my fucking watch! So I'm still scanning the room and down on the floor Jess has dumped a pair of heavy looking stiletto shoes, flashy looking pair they are too, maybe expensive, but I'm not about to start asking if she minds if I ruin them on the rapist cunt's skull. In my head I'm wondering if I should say something cool to get his attention, like something like *Hey, shithead, rape this you cunt!* before I smash his brains in, but knowing my luck, he'll have shot me in the head before I can even get my words out, so instead I belt him full force in the side of the head with the stiletto. Blood spatters out across Jess' face and she starts screaming and struggling underneath him, it hasn't knocked him out but he's stunned, like a boxer who's about to go down, and he's pulled himself off of her and wrestling himself up on his elbows. His face is streaming with sticky dark blood, it's dripping onto Jess who's fighting him off her, screaming blue fucking murder at him, calling him all the cunts under the sun, punching at his chest and trying to push him onto the floor but he's a big guy and she's tiny so he's going nowhere. His arm reaches under the pillow beneath her head and I reckon that's where he's keeping the gun so I fly at him with the shoe and crack him again, this time it's right in the middle of his face and his nose explodes across his face. He's out for the count now. Jess is spitting at him, pulling at his hair and wailing like a banshee at the blonde lump laid on his back on the floor with his expensive trousers round his ankles and his ever more flaccid cock dangling pathetically between his legs. That's the weird thing about cocks, in my experience, being the owner of one, they do the trick when they're stiff as fuck, but they look like floppy pink slugs when they're on the wane, for sure that's why women are better to look at than blokes, cocks are ugly as you like. So the shoe falls from my hand and I'm watching her, she's well within her rights to smash him to a pulp, but I don't reckon it's helping her out any, so I step up behind her and put my hands on her shoulders, like, try to let her know I'm here for her, I don't have a clue what to say to her, after what she's been through how can I? She falls to her knees over him, coated in his blood, and her dry retching is the only thing I can hear, until a faint buzzing starts to emit from the lifeless lump of the boy

Lundgren, which, unless I'm very much mistaken, is the familiar vibration of a mobile phone. I locate the source, hoping it's Justin's phone but it's not. It's the boy Lundgren's own phone, and there's no name flashing up, it just says Private Number. I answer it.

18:18

The door opened, revealing a dishevelled looking, but reasonably handsome man, a bruise rapidly forming around a deep red gash on his forehead. His eyes looked so tired, but at the same time he exuded an aura of defiance toward Ada, like he was running on fumes, but had taken enough shit today. He looked like he was preparing to offer his hand to Ada, but paused to take a look at them, covered in a light crust of blood, and visibly shaking. He looked at her apologetically. Ada made the first move.

"Thomas? I presume?"

"Tom, yeah"

"Are you going to invite me in?"

Tom looked warily at her, and then back over his shoulder, before stepping back and opening the door to encourage her to enter. Ada cautiously glanced around her surroundings and stood inside the house. It was an old building, she cast her eyes over the interior of the hallway, which was decorated with posters of movies and musicians that concealed the predominantly brownish yellow wallpaper, some sort of throwback design from nineteen seventy nine, but Ada was in no mood to judge. As Tom closed the door behind her she turned to face him and spoke.

"I believe we have a mutual acquaintance, Mr Tom"

"You could say that, yeah"

"Show me to him"
Tom's eyebrows raised involuntarily at her forward approach, let out a weary chuckle, and shook his head before sheepishly edging past her in order to guide the way, taking the effort to avoid contact, or brushing her with any of the several patches of blood about his person. He started up the stairs and beckoned her to follow. The stairwell was darkened but the theme of popular culture posters, some frayed and curled at the edges from being taken down and put back up, moved around and the like. More than likely the yellow brown sunburnt wallpaper was much fresher beneath those shrines to Robert De Niro, and Beatrice Dalle from movies that were made over twenty years ago and worshipped by each new generation of those who attended university. Tom led her past two doors, one from which hung a chalked upon sign instructing people that the room would be occupied by somebody named Lauren, the second door was left slightly ajar and appeared to be unoccupied in any way. Tom paused at the third door on the right and looked at her.
"It's a fuckin' mess, and she's been through some shit, be easy on her yeah? Please?"
Ada looked at him neutrally and bid him to open the door with her hand, a silent order which he obeyed. He disappeared into the room slowly, and she approached the open doorway. The scene before her was as bloody as it was unexpected.
The small room was decorated in a lot fresher and basic a manner than the parts of the house she had already visited, a large mirror hung above a selection of shoes and boots, the majority of the furniture and linens were variations on white and pink combinations. What

seemed out of place, however, was a semi naked young woman sitting cross legged with her back to the headboard, whose face, neck and chest were coated in blood, with clear streams from her eyes from where she had clearly been crying, the sheets that she sat upon were flecked dramatically with gore, and a large bay window housed the bound and gagged body of Christophe, staring at her with misplaced relief through his ice blue eyes. His trousers hung around his ankles and his flaccid cock sat weakly between his legs. For a man who boasted so many lovers, it was a remarkably uninspiring piece of limp meat which dangled from him. For a brief moment she felt a flutter of relief herself at never having succumbed to his charms, and was snapped back to reality when faced with muffled yells of whatever from the Frenchman.
"Christophe, my my, what have you got yourself into?" she asked coyly as she crouched before him and held his face in her hands.
More gagged calls that appeared to be begging to her conscience.
"Do you know how long I have waited to have you like this?" she looked with disgust at his cock "Well, not like this" as she viciously flicked the end of his member with her index finger "But, well, you know" Ada ripped the taped gag from Christophe's face, inciting a pained howl from the Frenchman.
"Ada, you fucking crazy bitch, I have done nothing wrong, I have only done that which I was ordered" He looked away from her and to the girl on the bed, Ada followed his gaze, the girl wouldn't look at him "I simply allowed myself a little pleasure along the way" he sneered at her. The girl quietly broke down in tears,

and the man known as Tom approached her to comfort her, but without the closeness of somebody who knew her well, he simply laid a hand on her shoulder and gently squeezed it.
"In what way did you allow yourself pleasure? Christophe?" Ada enquired curiously, almost cautiously, she was not sure she wanted to know his answer, based on the clues around the scene she had entered. He did not answer, merely looked down at his cock.
"Christophe? What did-"
"He fuckin' raped her, yeah? Fuckin', knocked me out, and raped her at gun point! That's not allowing himself pleasure, that's taking fuckin' liber-"
"Mr Tom! Please! Allow him to answer my question, I wish to hear this from his own filthy mouth" she interrupted without averting her stare from Christophe's own eyes, and continued as she brought her face closer to his. "So, Christophe, tell me, what did you do?"
He brought his eyes to hers, and stared deep into her eyes, and spoke in a low growl.
"I fucked her, she has already willingly allowed me to enter her, she has proved herself to be a slut. A slut will never say no" Ada felt a sadness rise within herself as Christophe confirmed what she had feared, she looked over her shoulder at the pair by the bed and addressed Tom.
"Please, take her and clean her up, I need to be alone with him" He did as he was told, gently lifting the girl from the bed and to her feet. The shirt she wore hung down past her buttocks and covered her privates, for which Ada was happy, the girl would be feeling enough shame as it was, she did not need it amplifying. She

watched them leave the room, slowly closing the door. The second she heard the sound of the locking mechanism click into the hole she turned to Christophe. "Just me and you now Christophe, how about I punish you suitably?"

18:36

This day had gone from bad to worse. In all aspects of his life he had had everything under control up to a point, and he knew exactly when that control was lost forever. Paris. But he had slowly regained some semblance of order to his life and the stupid fucking civilians spoiled everything. Sure, he could have kept himself to himself and gone about his job in the shadows, but in Barcelona he had done exactly the same thing as he had here and there were no repercussions, they knew what kind of a man he was, they almost expected him to behave as he did, but they were all under the spell of that old bastard Hoxton, and now Christophe realised that they were waiting for him to slip up all along. Ada, Christiano, Dietmann, that bastard Hoxton, they were setting him up for a fall. He had spoiled their game in Paris by killing her. A participant. The girl on who most of the money had been placed. Her name was Adeline. The sole reason he ever found out these people existed. Of course, his own libido and curiosity guided him after her, but she was by far the most beautiful thing he had ever laid eyes on, and he was a slave to his eyes. He had probably surprised them by lasting this long without taking his eye off the ball. No doubt the fuckers had been even betting on him to last this long, running a pool on his survival.

So here he was, trussed up like a prize turkey, Ada circling him like a velociraptor with her knife.
"So you think you can go around treating women like this Christophe? You think this is acceptable behaviour of a man in your position?"
He didn't think about his answer long before he spat out at her.
"Let me loose Ada, I will give you the exact same thing that I gave to the slut"
"I see you hold no desire to continue living then yes?"
"Fuck you"
"Never in one million years Christophe"
Christophe, resigned to his fate, held up his head and stared firmly at Ada, teeth clenched, breathing heavily through his nose, pulled in vain with his fingertips at the tape around his wrists. He expected her to cut his throat, in some moronic and ironic gesture. It was how they had dealt with everything in the past. As he prepared to keep his honour by keeping his mouth shut, take his punishment, Ada came right into his face once again, and held the knife to his neck. The pressure slowly increased, and he felt ready to meet his devil, he closed his eyes, whispered short prayers to himself in French, and smiled as the knife suddenly withdrew from his skin. He opened his eyes to view Ada's wicked grin.
"Not just yet my sweet"
She reached down to his cock and balls with her left hand, gently stroked at his testicles until she felt the blood surge into his shaft. She slowly worked at it, pulling it to its full glory.
"Ada, I do not understand, what is going on?"
"This"

A blinding pain tore across his abdomen and up through his chest into his brain, it shot down his legs to his toes. His body shook in agony, and shocked confusion as he saw Ada hold up a stiff piece of flesh with a sagging bleeding flap of skin that she had torn from his body, two grey eggs dropped from the flap as the realisation hit him that those eggs were his balls. The bitch had ripped off his cock and testicles. She had aroused him to his limit and cut off his manhood. Christophe felt himself weaken as he watched an increasing dark red pool build around his crotch. Vomit spewed from his mouth down his own front, over his crimson crotch, the acidic bile sending further shocks to his already overloaded nerves, he felt his head lolling around, and his eyelids losing control, by now he hoped to die sooner rather than later, just get it done with, see if there really was an afterlife, and what it might be like, maybe there were sluts to fuck in hell, maybe the devil had an ironic infinity lined up for him, whereby he would be fucked until his cock was raw, and then continue to fuck him until it fell off. He had to laugh. If he didn't laugh he would cry, and that would show weakness. His eyes closed, and reopened as he looked to Ada.
"You crazy fucking-" was all he could slur at her before she had pulled out a pistol from her belt and shot him in the face.

19:00

Bloody hell! Of all the damned and blasted luck! The jammy little scoundrel! Algernon spoke as Alan's body had been running for the last thirty minutes without stopping. His heart pounded, the taste of blood in his mouth had failed to go away, sweat poured into his eyes, stinging them to the point where they were squinted, a blurred slit his only means of negotiating the streets, the traffic, occasional humans. The night had fallen and he concentrated on his own shadow under the street lights, stretched out before him, then succumbing to his chase and disappearing underneath and behind him, only to reappear before him and continuing on the same cycle. He had run through side streets and alleyways, and found himself en route to Hillsborough, the very limit of the boundaries that had been set for them. Algernon had formulated a plan to circle the those boundaries, avoid confrontation, and Alan was forced to go along with the plan. He was no longer in control, it had been coming for a long time, now he had willingly begun to dissipate into the background, let a more experienced hand take charge. It had almost come to instant fruition in the near-past, in the woods, against the coloured fellow. They had him at their mercy, unconscious, naked, and about to tear open his neck. Algernon had been entirely instrumental in getting them to that point, Alan would have folded under the pressure, he would have laid there, closed his eyes, and simply allowed the fellow to cut his throat without a fight. He had become too tired for this, so tired he was delirious, certainly delirious enough to allow an imaginary friend to take over his mind and body and perform all manner of criminal activities. And now Algernon was carrying him as fast as he could.

They did have him at their mercy, and would have carried out their brutal task had it not been for being caught in the blinding beam of a security guard's torch, a holler to enquire as to what he thought he was doing, and then a chase. He was so close. He had held up the coloured boy's head, blood still streaming from his smashed nose, down onto his sporadic tight curls of hair that scattered across the centre of his dark chest, and pooling into his "innie" belly button. He had the knife to his throat. He pressed in, the tip had pierced his skin. Then the light of the torch, it shone directly into their eyes, blinded them, they dropped the young man's head to the floor and stood up tall. The guard shouting at them, demanding they stop, but Algernon had them away like cat, through the trees, batting branches away like they were nothing, running through blankets of Camellias and Rhododendrons in the Asian themed gardens, the flowers that Alan had previously coveted so badly, on into the Mediterranean themed area, and over the perimeter wall. Algernon was playing it over and over in Alan's head as they ran. Alan's eyes concentrated on the shadows whilst Algernon's concentrated on what went wrong, made contingencies for next time. They both wondered what would happen about the coloured chap.

Surely those rotters will make sure we don't get caught old chap! They could end up with egg all over their faces! It'll be a bloody outrage no doubt about that!

19:08

His eyes opened. A bright neon tube light hovered over him. The buzzing of it burned into his ears. Became the only thing he could hear. He was aware that he was naked other than a thin cloth gown. He tried to sniff up what he took to be snot and a blinding pain thrashed his skull, forcing into his mind the last thing he remembered before he woke up here. The racist NHS glasses motherfucker talking in his new fucked up accent, ramming his nut into Daniel's nose. But what had happened after that? How was he here? Alive? Was he even alive? His hands clawed at the linen beneath him, it did feel real, he clutched a handful of it taut and shouted out, no real words, only a throaty roar, his back arching to the ceiling, his wide eyes focussed on the heart monitor he was hooked up to.

A man and a woman hurried from nowhere to appear at the side of his bed, she was in white, he was all in green, he tried to calm Daniel down whilst she attempted to get to his eyes with a small torch. The voices faded in and out behind his screaming. All that noise and none of it made any sense. Who were they? Were they part of this? Was he back in that building where it all started? In a public hospital? And if so, did that make him any safer? So many questions he couldn't ask because every one would inevitably lead to their batting it back with another question that would lead him no closer to knowing. He screams subsided, bringing with it the echoes of the voices of the people by his bed. They wanted his name, he said nothing. They asked if he was okay and he said nothing. His jaw ground his teeth into his skull, he let them poke and prod at him without argument, the only evidence that he was alive being his heartbeat, his clenching fists pulling at the linen, and his changing pupils when they were subjected to the torch beam. They silently molested him until they gave up the ghost and retreated back to the nowhere they came from.

Shortly after they left him alone, Daniel rose unsteadily to his paper-slippered feet, the gown flapped around his front leaving his rear uncovered. His head felt heavy and dazed. A tannoy requested that a Dr McQueen attend some ward with an animal's name in paediatrics as a matter of urgency. Daniel pulled monitor pads from his chest, an extended bleep cried out to anybody that would listen that he had died. He wished that were true. They had made sure he knew that if he was ever caught, they would find him, and kill him. They said they had contacts, fingers in pies. After what he'd been through he had no reason to even consider doubting that. The incessant bleep continued to scream monotonously behind him as he stuck his head through the curtain that surrounded his bed, through blurred vision Daniel saw so many people headed his way in response to the sounds, he silently appreciated that if it were a film they'd probably be struggling over each other in slow motion, papers flying all over, the theme from Chariots of Fire playing ironically. At the front were the man and woman who'd previously inspected his body, behind them two policemen, then a bunch of other doctors and nurses, men with cameras. He was definitely in a public hospital, they wouldn't have so many people around. Daniel tried to make a getaway, limping fruitlessly along the corridor as the chasing pack caught up with him with ease. He kicked and cried out as he was manhandled back to his bed. Flashes from cameras blinked at him, voices drowned each other out like he was at his own film premiere, asking how he felt, why he ran, who he was, telling him to calm down. In the corner of his eye as they lowered him back to the bed he saw the glint of a needle, and felt a prick in his hand, and found himself falling deeper and deeper into unconsciousness, the world slowed down, like a vinyl record spinning round a player that had just been switched off, and Daniel succumbed to them once again, there was no way out.

19:24

For sure I'm in some sort of fucking nightmare. The bird that came round after I answered the boy's mobile is calling the shots now. She's got me all over the bedroom pulling the sheets off the bed and wiping the walls. The boy is still there looking at me with his head resting on his shoulder, glassy dead eyes that seem to follow me as I scurry round the room with my bin bag. She definitely did a number on him, his dick's been cut off and there's a dirty great hole in his face from where she shot him dead. Turns out his name is, was, Christophe. I only know that because she called him it, for sure she didn't tell me, no matter what I say to her she won't answer any of my questions. Needs to get laid I reckon that girl, she's really fit too, in any other circumstance I'd put myself forward as the man for that particular job but she just keeps barking orders then getting back on her mobile to whoever, then disappears to go and check on Jess. She's calmed down a bit more now she's been cleaned up. I sat outside the bathroom listening to hear crying in the shower, properly broke my heart it did. Can't imagine what that shit could ever feel like, now she's in the spare room alone with her thoughts. When the foreign bird told me I had to get the room cleaned up Jess looked horrified, was going on about how she wasn't leaving my side, but the bird told her she didn't want to go in there. Told her she'd made the fucker pay for what he did. From the look of him she wasn't fucking wrong. She was brutal with him, not the kind of girl you want to get on the wrong side of, that's for damn sure. I don't have a clue what she's got planned for us. To be honest I'm not sure I want to know anymore, the way this day has gone I'd half expect me tied to a fucking conveyor belt slowly running toward a circular saw while some villain tells me what his intricate plan is, while they dangle Jess over some fucking piranha tank. My head is fucked.

I've never seen a dead body before, other than my peaceful looking blue lipped Auntie Sue after she gave in to the Big C and I went into the chapel of rest to give my mum some moral support, now since quitting my job this morning I've seen one of my best mates shot in front of me, and some dirty rapist cunt sat in front of me with no cock and half of his face missing. I wish I'd just got on with it this morning, bent over and taken whatever they wanted to give to me. For sure, there's a lot to be said for the quiet life. What's a few wankers shouting facelessly secure at you down the phone compared to this fucking horror show that my life's become? It really does get put it into perspective when you face what I've faced already, and what I'm currently facing. I've ended up putting a bin bag over Christophe's head, he was freaking me out. The girl comes back in, this time she's got two mates and they're in balaclavas. One of them's carrying a suitcase which I'm pretty sure they're intending to fit Christophe into, the thing is, it's a big case, but nowhere near big enough to fold him into, no matter how many folds they want to do. They're not gonna get him rolled up like you do with trousers and towels when you need to get more than you should into your case before you fly off to Tenerife or some such, and they're daft if they think they will. They push past me, pull the bed away from the body so as to make some space, and set the case down. The girl looks at me and tells me to leave the room, go and sit with Jess, which I'm more than happy to do. As I leave the room I turn to see the girl's two mates pulling some clear plastic from the case, which is fair enough, but I'm thinking it's a bit late, like, the horse has bolted on the keeping the place clean front, then I quickly change my mind as they pull two of the biggest hacksaws I've ever seen from it too. It seems they have a much better plan for getting his body into that case than trying a bit of corpse origami. Fucking hell. These guys are mental.

19:46

Whilst Lukas and Yannick were making easy work of Christophe, Ada had her trophy, but now had to consider the matter of what to do with the witnesses. She knew what Hoxton would suggest, and for the most part she tend to agree that they needed to disappear, but Tom had done an incredible job of subduing Christophe, and she felt an out of character sadness toward the girl. Her own life growing up in Budapest had not been a happy one on the whole, and she had been witness to a great many crimes against women. Although it had never been an issue she felt to have a personal issue with, certainly not one that she would risk her life to defend against, she nevertheless held a great belief that now she was in a position to help a woman against whom a man she held in the highest contempt had committed an unmentionable sin, it was maybe her duty to offer that help. Mr Hoxton would undoubtedly reprimand her for putting the operation in

jeopardy by allowing them to live this long, but she had to make a quick decision, if she killed one she would have to kill the other, Lukas and Yannick had only brought one piece of kit with them so this exercise could end up being a great deal more time consuming. If Mr Hoxton wanted them dead he could order it at a later time, but for now Ada felt it necessary to take them with her. She left the guys to it and entered the room that held the civilians, who were engaged in some sort of get-to-know-you conversation, something which Ada felt somewhat strange given the events of the past few hours, although Ada supposed that there was a chance they had never even met. This address was one which was on her list of possible hideouts as Christophe had spent several hours here overnight recently, so the chances were that he had dragged the hostage, Tom, along. Although he was not stupid, Christophe was predictable. The civilians looked at her expectantly.
"We will leave this place now, my colleagues will finish up" she addressed them both then turned to the girl "Please ensure that you have provisions for the next few hours"
"Why? Where are you taking us?" Tom enquired, his tone verging on the confrontational.
"This, I cannot say, but rest assured that it is how it will be, my only advice to you is that you do not make trouble, for me, or yourself"
"But we haven't done anything wrong, none of this shit makes any sense"
"In which case, Mr Tom, you will simply have to trust me, come"
The civilians warily rose from the unmade bed, Jess looked at Tom apprehensively, fear almost, Ada made

no attempt to put her at ease, she had far too much to deal with. She addressed the girl once more.
"Get your coat, we are leaving now"
"But, my housemates, what if they come home?"
"Again, this I cannot say, but the faster we leave the less chance that there will be a problem"
She was starting to tire of the pair, they asked too many questions, and posed a great danger to proceedings if they did not begin to follow simple instructions, she pulled out her gun. Tom rolled his eyes and sighed, instinctively placing his arm around the newly petrified Jess.
"This was not my intention and I do not wish to end your lives, but if you do not follow my instructions I will be forced to, now, move"
The questions immediately stopped and they did as they were bidden, Jess physically flinched as she passed the end of Ada's gun, Tom appeared beaten as he trudged past her. She followed them down the stairs and out of the door, concealing the pistol as they stepped out into public. She opened the back seat of her Lexus to allow them into the car, climbing into the front seat herself. Two young locals on bicycles circled the car giving it an appreciative whistle, clearly having never seen such a luxury automobile in the area before. She bore them no mind and powered up the car. Ada glanced into her rear view mirror at Tom, who was the more mentally stable of the pair right now.
"As I said, I do not wish to kill either of you, if that were the case then believe me that it would already be so, do not attempt to do anything stupid and we will all be friends"
"Where are you taking us?" he asked her.

"Somewhere" she responded mysteriously.
"Why should we believe you won't kill us?" the girl, Jess, had opened her mouth, she had remained quiet throughout the ordeal, and was now finding her voice.
"Why should you not?"
They quietened down and allowed her to drive in silence. The blacked-out windows clouding their view as the city turned into countryside. Ada looked them in the rear windows occasionally, Tom had appeared resigned to whatever fate he had before him, his eyes looked heavy. Jess was wired, and constantly peering through the windows to see where they were going.

Eventually the farmhouse rolled into view as the driveway crunched under the wheels of the Lexus. Both of her passengers became jumpy and eager to take in their destination.
"Where are we?" Asked Jess
"We are somewhere" replied Ada, bringing the conversation to a close.
As the car ground to a halt Ada turned to them, pistol in hand
"You will wait here, I will return"
Before they could respond she had gone, slamming the door behind her, leaving her passengers to speculate upon their fate. Let them speculate she thought to herself, for now she had a trophy to present.

20:32

Things have been awfully quiet old boy Alan hoped that Algernon was referring to the amount of the human traffic passing through Hillsborough Park, but he knew in his heart of hearts that he was bringing their attention to the lack of contact since the incident. Alan truly hoped that it was a case of if he didn't hear anything then nothing was wrong, but was expecting the sugar to hit the fan. Algernon however had different aspirations entirely, *If the blighters want to bring a war then so be it! We're soldiers now old boy! Get your bloody head out of the trench and face them head on!* Alan felt this to be a good idea in theory, but they were only one man, against forces that at least one of them had never even dreamt to believe existed, let alone come into contact with, and even further from the realms of possibility would be taking a fight to. Algernon was by now a very permanent fixture rattling around his head, bringing with him uncontrollable urges to buck against his own nature. Although Algernon would invariably choose fight over flight, Alan had argued himself into the darkest corner of the park, his back hunched against the angles of a wall, trees overhanging to provide coverage from the helicopters he imagined would be out searching for him. Algernon's plan to cover the limits that had been laid out for them was still the agreed way going forward, but Alan needed rest, he couldn't take another day without sleep. I only need a few hours' sleep, just some respite from all of this, for Christ's sake- *Behave yourself old boy! In my day I could go for weeks without a kip!*- But this isn't your day Algernon, it's my body- *Quite on the contrary sir! This IS my day, it's OUR day, and we're going to take the bloody lot on! Sleep is for queers and the dead!*- Just a few hours Algernon- *Well you can bloody leave me out of that then! I'll be back later you damned poof!* And at that Alan's mind felt clearer, emptier, which was all he could have asked for, a time for his brain to shut

down, no thoughts of what the future might hold. There were still four of them left, and by the time morning came he should be back to seeking. The morning seemed so very far away. As his eyes grew heavy he fell into pleasant dreams of growing up with his parents, of time spent alone in his small box bedroom in their terraced house, retreating into fantasy worlds where he was a member of the Famous Five, getting into implausible adventures in the company of travelling funfairs and jewellery thieves. These adventures became the basis of summer afternoon playtimes with his so called pals, and his dream descended into nightmares, as his rose tinted memory became him on the floor, his face becoming their punch bag, tearing at his second hand clothes, lurching over him, their cruel jibes becoming a melted vision of faces circling, his brain rattling with an endless stream of "Smellan Foster, Smellan Foster" over and over and over and over and over and over and over and-
"Oscar! Oscar!" A woman's voice ripped him from his shivering sweating nightmare, a dog barked and the patter of its feet crept up to him with haste, as it arrived he tried to deflect it's playful pouncing at his body as it attempted to lick his face, the woman called for her pet again and appeared- *A damned dog! Needs sorting good and proper*- Algernon, no!
It was too late, as Alan stood away from the spaniel, the echo of its yelp rang around the park at an earsplitting pitch as Algernon crushed it's oesophagus beneath his battered shoe, the more pressure he applied the gurgled whine gave way to a crack when it's neck broke.
"Oscar?" A worried voice emitted from the small silhouette that suddenly became more apprehensive in

its approach toward the darkened corner "Oscar?" she stepped closer and closer to the corner until she saw the glistening twitching corpse of her beloved pet spaniel beneath the foot of what looked like a smiling man in a dark jacket wearing glasses holding a large knife. The woman screamed. Then ran.

21:02

It's been a while now, the foreign bird has been inside the house for ages. There's a beefy looking fucker been standing at the door watching the car, making sure we don't disappear like. Not that we'd try. I'm knackered, and to be honest, I'm getting a bit intrigued about what we've got ourselves involved in here. I'm trying to side-track Jess, she's panicked like nowt right. Soon as the bird left us alone she was pulling at the door handles, front and back, both sides. Not happening. Then the beefy fucker arrived and I pulled her back to the seat, tried to calm her down, get her chatting like. For sure she's a smart girl, been working at the Frog and Parrot for extra spends whilst she studies art history, this is what I'm getting out of her like, trying to keep both our minds off of proceedings. Her dad's dead and her mum lives with her new fella in Chesterfield, they're not too broke or anything, her dad had his own business doing cars up before he kicked it, so they sold it off and got Jess away to do her degree. She's a properly sweet girl, and I'm feeling guilty as fuck for my dirty fantasies earlier. She tried to justify about how she knew Christophe but I stopped her before she could start it, didn't want to pull her back into the reality of what she's experienced. No, she'll have plenty of time for regrets when, if, we get out of this. So she's 20, good few years younger than me, so now I'm feeling even more protective of her. I've seen my mate shot dead today, and it's understandably knocked me for six, but for some reason I'm having these feelings toward her like I'd die today if it makes sure she's safe. I don't want to die like, I'm just saying, I would. She's been through hell and back, but she's one of the sweetest girls I've ever met, and I'm a cunt. I know I am. I'm an obnoxious gobshite. And I've wasted my own mind. I know it's not too late to change but I don't think I want to. I like being the confident brash dickhead, I'm smart enough to argue and hard enough to fight and that's how I like it. But right now I don't feel worthy of being in this girl's company, let alone being her only hope of getting out of this alive, so if it means ridding the world of a cunt like me to make sure she still gets to breath, then so be it. I'm in. I've been telling her how I quit my job, told her about how I stuck it to Chris, our glorious fucking leader, I tried to inject some humour into it, but she didn't look like she'd laugh at anything today, I also consider that maybe humiliating somebody isn't everybody's cup of funny, maybe you just have to be a cunt to appreciate it as the joke it is. I want us to be somewhere else, getting to know each other, me maybe brushing the lock of ginger that's fallen down over her eye, smiling at her as she thanks me for it. I reach up to do it anyway, but not with half as much tenderness as I'd like to, now is definitely not the time. As I pull my hand away from her face I see movement through the window over her shoulder, the door to the house has swung open and the light casts the foreign bird's shadow right over the driveway between us and her, for sure in that light she looks about fifteen feet tall, even

though she's only about five foot. Jess catches that I've spotted something and turns round, all jumpy like. Getting ready for whatever's going to happen. She grabs my hand, squeezes it tight and I get this weird turning feeling in my guts. I give her a squeeze back and wait. The bird gets to the car and opens our door, the beefy fucker stays by the main entrance, he's not worried about how our hostess handles herself for sure, she could probably wring my neck before I've even had a dream of taking her on. Just in case though, she's still holding her gun, but doesn't point it at us, just holds it loose by her side.
"Come with me" she says, still no closer to being anything like friendly, though I can tell she's got a soft spot for Jess. Birds sticking together and all that I reckon. We follow her tentatively, Jess kind of hides behind me while we walk to the house. I squeeze her hand out of support and we edge further toward our fate.
"Tom, I'm scared" she says, breaks my heart it does.
"Me an'all lass, you'll be alright, I won't let owt happen to you, I promise" I whisper back, the foreign bird's probably heard me but I don't give a fuck, and now I've made that promise, I'm bound to keep it. I might be a cunt but I do have some degree of honour.

In the house we're met by a silence I wasn't expecting, some sort of music plays in a room somewhere, I know I've heard the song before but I can't place it. Probably been on an advert. Our hostess marches further on ahead of us and looks over her shoulder to check we're still there. The beefy fucker has followed us in and closed the door. Taken away any chance of us just walking out of here scot free. No, we're definitely in something shitty, and we're in deep. We pass one door and there's voices, all men from what I can tell, the music louder at this door, I still can't place the tune though. Our hostess has stopped at a door further up and beckons us to speed up, which we obligingly do, as we approach her she knocks at the door once and enters, the door stays open and we shuffle closer to it. The room is pretty bare, not much to it. A great big wooden desk with a few newspapers on it. There's an old boy sat behind it, totally dwarfed by his chair. He's staring at us and there's something about him. He doesn't look like he could fight at all but I don't think he needs to. I think he could kill you with his eyes if he wanted, pulls the Jedi mind shit and gets you to do his- Fucking hell! I've just noticed the boy Christophe's fucking head sat on a table in the corner! No body, no nothing, where his head finishes is his neck, and from there it's just table! Brutal. Fucking brutal. Jess notices it too because she's grabbed hold of my arm and starts to whimper. The old boy looks like he's about to talk but something needs said, it'll send her fucking wappy. "Excuse me, sir, my friend's been through a bit of shit at the hands of your boy there" I point at the head "Any chance you could, I dunno, turn it round or summat?"

21:27

"Are you scared? Do you know the perpetrator, is that why you won't answer our questions? We can only help you if you help us. Let's start with your name."
They had been dancing the same dance since they brought him back round, out of unconsciousness, they asked the same questions every time and every time he rebuffed them with silence. Simply stared at the ceiling.

He was no more safe here than out there, hiding in bushes away from the public, they had told him they knew everything and who was he to doubt that? This cop looking at him from the chair at the side of the bed could be working for them. Testing him. He could say one word and get his head blown off. Even if he was safe here. What was to say they'd believe a word he said? He'd killed two people, he had blood on his hands, so even if he could do anything to take them down, he'd be going with them. Silence was golden.
"Who are you protecting?"
Nothing.
"Why are you protecting them?"
Nothing.
"Why won't you tell us your name?"
Nothing.
"What sort of trouble are you in? They can't get to you in here"
Nothing.
The cop let out a loud exasperated sigh, got to his feet and stomped out of the cubicle. Daniel heard muttered voices of the same guy talking to somebody else. His tone sounded calm, his faceless colleague was much the same. His eyes remained on the ceiling, expecting them to try an old tag team of good cop, bad cop, and the colleague to come in shouting the odds at him, spitting coffee into his face. This didn't happen. Both men entered the cubicle together. Out of the corner of his eye he noticed the new guy was a lot taller than the other one. Appeared more domineering, bulkier. They stood watching him; the atmosphere edged itself ever more uncomfortable. It felt to Daniel like a silent stand-off, a battle of wits to see who'd crack first. His

continued to stare up, focussing on a thin crack that ran the length of the room. He trained his mind to wander, take his mind away from the stand-off, and he considered how long it had been since the ceiling was painted. His eyes followed the crack as it ran from above his head along his body past his feet, then back again, repeating the action until his eye line was obscured by the face of the taller cop stepping into view. The man was smiling at him as they held each other's gaze. Daniel felt his eyes water as they soundlessly sized each other up. The smile the man was displaying unnerved him, like he knew something, Daniel had been holding his cards close to his chest in his refusal to respond but the man seemed to know exactly what those cards were. His smiling eyes bore into him with knowing delight.
"Well done Mr Jackson"
Daniels mouth dropped slack at the revelation. His eyes narrowed in confusion as he tried to make out what the man was all about.
"What the fuck?"
The man's smile broadened, he held his arms aloft beside his body.
"Ahhh, at last! He speaks! Hallelujah!"
"Who are you?"
"I am your salvation Mr Jackson" The man spoke with a neutral accent, but Daniel picked out undertones of the North East, perhaps Newcastle or somewhere like that.
"I don't-"
"You don't understand, I know, I know, but you don't need to. You've proved yourself excellent at following

instructions. There are two poor souls who will testify to that."
The man stifled a chuckle and continued.
"I feel I must apologise for my religious choices of phrasing. I'm not a man of God, it's simply a coincidence. So Mr Jackson, as I have said, you have a proven record of following instructions, but have found yourself in a rather sticky situation. You know by now that we have a remarkable influence, however, outside forces are also at play"
"What you talkin' about?"
"What I'm talking about, Mr Jackson, is the army of photographers, and journalists gathered both in the hospital and outside within the grounds who you will find to have a lot of time for you"
"So?"
"You really are a man of few words aren't you? If you couldn't tell, I like to hover at the other end of the spectrum, I find it helps to make my point a lot clearer if I explain myself fully. You may call me Mr Charles, and I have a plan"

Part 3 - On The Wall Of A Gallery

Sarah Simpson
(ITV News Northern Correspondent)

Friday 12th March 2010

"I'm outside Leeds Crown Court where the jury have today delivered a guilty verdict in the case of the Crown versus Alan Foster. Foster, dubbed The Sheffield Ripper, wreaked havoc over a two week period back in October, murdering six people at random in cold blood, and also a dog, between October sixteenth and November second two thousand and nine. The jury took less than an hour to deliberate and come to their guilty verdict.
Now, what seemed to be an open and shut case was blown apart when Foster was deemed unsuitable for trial after psychiatrists diagnosed him with Dissociative Identity Disorder, also known as Multiple Personality Disorder. The details of the illness are unclear but it did ensure that the trial was put on hold whilst extensive testing on Foster's psyche was carried out. Judge Michael Fisher passed down a life sentence with no chance of parole, advising that Foster was indeed a danger to society. Behind me of course you can see the crowd of protesters that have been a permanent fixture throughout the trial, who believe Alan Foster to be a victim of an injustice, given his mental state, and believe that his human rights have been taken away from him by a system that has ignored his illness and tried him as a fully functioning human being.
On the other hand, however, are the protesters who believe in justice for Alan Foster's victims. These two groups have clashed on several occasions as the trial

has gone on, sparking a national debate about whether a man who had murdered six people in such a clinical fashion had the right to even be allowed anything other than a full trial and the hands of the Crown.

The death toll could have been much more had Foster not been caught after two people escaped his clutches in a single night. First of all he allowed Daniel Jackson, of course, to escape when Foster was interrupted by a security guard in the Sheffield Botanical Gardens on October twenty-ninth, clearly not satisfied Foster then travelled several miles across the city and killed Oscar, a springer spaniel, and gave chase to Oscar's owner, twenty four year old Laura McCoy, who evaded capture by running into a main road and stopping traffic. Viewers will be well versed in many aspects of the case, as the story has remained front page news for several months and will no doubt continue as the human rights debate goes on.
Foster's victims will now be remembered in a memorial service at Sheffield Cathedral on Sunday. The six victims, Graham Capper, Ruby Spenner, Lisa Wallett, James Crosby, Geoffrey Whittaker, and Thomas Ferguson, will each have a candle lit, and words spoken by each of their respective families and loved ones. As the news was released tributes poured in for those who perished at the hands of the man that the media has dubbed The Sheffield Ripper. David Capper, uncle of Graham made a statement earlier today, he said "*Our family can rest assured that the man who took Graham from us so early in his life is now behind bars where he belongs. Nothing can ever bring him back to us, but there lies some comfort in knowing that the streets are safer and that nobody else will have to go through what*

we and the families of the other victims have been through this last few months." Such is the emotion that has surrounded this case, when Foster was driven away from court, protesters broke police cordons in an attempt to get to him, and four arrests were made. So as one chapter closes in this controversial case, another will undoubtedly open as the debate rages on, and I for one expect us to hear about Alan Foster for a long time yet. Sarah Simpson, reporting for ITV News, outside Leeds Crown Court."

Terry Collins

Sunday 10th November 2009

You 'eard? They've got somebody for it ant they? They've only gone and got somebody for it! Dirty looking fucker he is an'all. You can see it in his eyes. Have you seen t'pictures of him int Sun today? You can see it in his eyes he's a slimy fucker. If it's not him that's done it I'll eat my fuckin' balls on toast! Wi' brown sauce an'all! Took the bobbies long enough to get him really dint it? His picture's been all over t'news for a week. You know? That one they took off a CCTV? Yeah, got him ont same camera as that young black lad who got away, you know the one? Course you do, he's never off the chuffin telly anymore! Our lass says she saw him on Loose fuckin' Women on Monday! Loose fuckin' Women! Yeah, saw him all quiet and that, saying how he's havin' nightmares about it, sez he sees the fella every time he shuts his eyes! Now, I'm not bein' funny right, but he looks an hard nut yeah? There's no fuckin' way that kid's havin' nightmares about it. Our Tina reckons it dunt matter how hard you are, nearly gettin' killed by a serial killer could knock the best of folk for six, but still, yeah, nightmares? Pull t'other one pal! I bet he's gettin' ten grand for every "nightmare" he has an'all! See, am not thick me right? That bastard is milkin' it for all it's worth. Now, that young lass, you know the other one? Her whose dog got killed? Seen her once, and that were ont news like, just a picture of her when they talked about her, she's not out there shovin' her mug all over everythin' she can get it on. You know the fella though, now I'm not bein' funny, but I reckon he'll have his own telly show eventually, you know like that fuckin' Jordan bird, big tits one? Our Tina fuckin' can't get enough of her, she never does fuck all that Jordan bird, but our lass goes mad for her. I've sat through one of 'em, you know when I was laid up when I pulled me back? Couldn't come out to darts could I? Well, I had to sit through one of them fuckin' documentaries. Well, I say documentary but in my book a documentary is Richard Attenborough tellin' me about polar bears or lions or summat. Or, I'll tell you what I do like, war documentaries, that kind of thing. But Jordan prancin' about is not my cup of tea. Nice tits though, no doubt about that! Anyway, what was I on about? Oh yeah, so that kid'll probably have his own telly show before long. You don't chuck your face ont telly as much as he has if you aren't after summat long term. Him that did it, summat Foster, can't remember now, it'll come to me, but him that did it. You can see it in his eyes, he's a wrong un. Nowt surer than that. I were sayin' this to our Kev when they showed it ont telly this mornin', he's got the eyes of a rapist, or a paedo or summat like that, he's got to be ont sex register, can't believe they never had him as suspect before now. Definitely, I wunt be surprised if he'd killed more than six folk. You can see it in his eyes. I reckon the bobbies have dropped a bollock on this one, it'll come out, I'm tellin' ya, the Sun are all over that kinda stuff, they'll be asking the questions we're all askin', they're good at that The Sun, they represent the working man, they know how we think, they stand up for us, for our opinions. Yeah, The Sun will be asking how they managed to let him get away with it for this long, they'll uncover his shady history like they always do, then they'll ask why he were allowed ont streets, I know they'll do that 'cause that's exactly what I'd do. Told ya, they're like the newspaper version of me mate. You know where you stand with The Sun, just like you do with me. If I ant got time for ya I won't have nowt to do with ya, an' if I don't like ya, you know for a fact I'm gonna meck sure you know about it! Meck no bones about it mate, I'm a straight john bull man me. Your round is it? Pint of heavy for me pal.

Cheers. Now, where was I? Yes! Yes! This fuckin' nutcase they've caught for them murders, where were you when you heard about it? I were sat in me armchair yesterday mornin', plate of bacon an' eggs on me knee, brew ont coffee table, our Kev laid ont sofa in his kecks. You've got to remember the details mate, it's all about the details! It's one of them times we're gonna remember forever. You know like when Diana kicked it? I remember exactly where I were. Bed. Oh aye, I'd been on nights and only been in bed an hour, then our lass comes in to the bedroom in floods o' tears, an' I do mean floods. The lads weren't old at all, so they're bawling their eyes out 'cause they know their mammy's upset. Took me an hour to calm her down and she tells me why she's in such a state. Yep, that's where I were. Chuffin' bed. I'll not go into where I were when that beardy fuckin' Arab sorted them twin towers out, I've made me point. So this slimy shit that's been out murderin', surprised me a bit it did, I actually thought it were Pakis that did it, I'll not lie, I were surprised when the fella that did it showed up white ont telly. All grubby as fuck he were, little beady eyes peeking through his thick fuck-off jam jar specs, his hair all over the shop. Looked like he'd been hiding for weeks, looked like a fuckin' tramp. They showed his picture ont telly like, matched it up wi' that one from CCTV, but when they showed him gettin' into t'bobby car he were covered wi' a blanket, they always do that dunt they? But yeah, white as they come he were, though I suppose when they are white they always look like him dunt they? Lonely fella no doubt, pissed his bed when he were little, probably gets knocked back a lot when he tries it on wi' birds, probably just chucks a tablet in their drink and fucks 'em when they knock him back anyway! Yeah, he's definitely a shady character, you can see it in his eyes.

Daisy Beckford

Taken from internet blog: The Many Personalities of Justice

Saturday 13th March 2010

Here are some numbers for you. Six murders. Six life sentences. One man. Two personalities. Zero justice. The simple mathematics behind a gross miscarriage of justice that has occurred this week. A gross miscarriage that I am currently campaigning against, and would appreciate with the utmost of sincerity, if you could please sign my petition for a fairer trial for those with mental illness. Allow me to elaborate please, dear reader.

Alan Foster, a local man, was yesterday found guilty of six murders committed in Sheffield last year. Regular readers of my blogs will know this has been a situation that I have kept a close eye from start to finish, and into which I have put my proverbial two pence worth on more than one occasion, and with this latest twist in the tail, I shall continue to do the same. I am not so self-unaware that I cannot see that my critics may have a point when they accuse me of self-righteousness and melodrama, but this is the beauty of the internet. We can all have a voice. If my critics do not wish to hear mine then they can simply not listen. I do not write to convert anybody's opinion, but I do try to educate with my words. As for melodrama, I am trying to make a difference, was Gandhi being melodramatic? Were the suffragettes being melodramatic? We can only make a difference in life if we try. It is easy to take a step back with the idea that one person cannot make change happen, but if everybody takes that stance then what change can we make? None. Now that I have got that minor gripe off my chest I will continue with my point.

On paper, without knowing anything other than the man murdered six people in cold blood, Alan Foster deserves every minute of his sentence. Any sane man that had snuffed out six lives would deserve the punishment that was cast down upon them. Any sane person would deserve it. But herein lies my issue. Alan Foster was declared to be suffering from a form of Dissociative Identity Disorder. Multiple personalities. Alan Foster is not a sane man. Throughout his trial his defence was that his hypothetical car was being driven by an alter ego named Algernon. I do not believe that Alan Foster knew that he had committed a single crime. The things we know about his disorder are that sufferers have experienced a lack of childhood nurturing and social support, and psychological trauma, more often than not at the hands of parents. This trauma can affect how the child then develops, or fails to develop integration skills, greatly increasingly their imaginative states as the awareness, memories and emotion toward any traumatic experiences are forced deeper and deeper into the subconscious, fetching to the foreground dissociation as a coping mechanism during stressful times. Other contributing factors have been reported as experiencing loss of somebody, or something at an early age. Now, I do not profess to be an expert in this particular field, but I have done my research. Now, take the above information and place the template of common reports made surrounding

Dissociation Identity Disorder over the life of Alan Foster.
Born in July 1960, Alan Foster grew up an only child in Heeley, Sheffield. The son of a father who died in an accident when stealing a motorcycle, and a prostitute mother who plied her trade in the family home. He would often spend days alone in his bedroom reading books and retreating into a fantasy world. This bedroom was situated directly next to his mother's, so his life would be encroached upon by a continuous loop of strange men entering his life through his ears and his innocent mind being corrupted by the actions of his mother. When he was not in his room he was bullied mercilessly by his peers, several of whom were called as witnesses throughout the trial to say as much themselves. As he grew older his mother became increasingly dependent upon him as she succumbed to cirrhosis of the liver set off by Hepatitis C, and rather than seek care from elsewhere Alan found it more comfortable to his own mind to become her sole carer. After his mother died in 2001 Alan continued to live in the family home, in as much as it could be deemed a family home any more. Reports have been provided as to his living conditions as the case has gone on, and they are that his home became a hovel where he found solace completing jigsaw after jigsaw.
One of the defining images of this particular case is the one, and I am sure that you have seen it, of his bedroom, the floor covered entirely in completed jigsaws, and an amass of violent pornographic photographs covering the walls. A total juxtaposition of imagery. Alan Foster is a man whose mind has been tainted, pulled out of all shaped, ripped apart, by his

upbringing, so much so that he retreats into it and allows this character Algernon to take control of his actions, his speech. It allows Alan to not take and make decisions. It allows his body to be used as a puppet by an alter ego. The fact that he remembers the occasions when he is taken control of is why the courts have allowed him to be tried as a fully functioning person. One of the major symptoms of Dissociative Identity Disorder is a lack of memory when alter egos take over, and the courts have found themselves siding with the popular opinion that, because Alan Foster will appear to have arguments with himself, or Algernon, that he does not conform to the regular diagnoses. It is common belief in the media (about whom I have made my feelings very clear on several occasions, now is not the time) that he is attempting to play the courts for a fool, that he is a very clever man who has manipulated the likes of myself, and his supporters into believing his lies. If this is the case then the man is indeed a very calculated, and sly person, but considering other factors in this story, I find it very difficult to attach any weight whatsoever to his being mentally stable, and I will continue to campaign for a fair trial. I will continue to appear outside any future court appearances he makes. And I will continue to ask you, dear reader, for your signature. Please do not let Alan Foster suffer at the hands of a justice system that will allow him to rot in prison, a system that will let him down again and again. I will not let him down, and I will not rest until he is given a fair chance. Thank you for your time today.

COMMENTS
PAGE Next 1 2 3 4 5 6 Last

New Thread Reply to this thread

Most Recent

Reply 79
13/03/10
18:04
Sender: Anonymous User 35
dont talk shit u fucking silly bitch u don't have a clue wot the famlys r goin thru. You shud be ashamed of yourself!!!!!!!!!!!

Reply 78
13/03/10
18:02
Sender: Man At Arms
Well said Daisy, another superb blog, while I do not agree entirely with some of your points you make them well and I applaud you for your efforts. Keep up the good work, you know I'm a big fan of yours.
@Anonymous User 33: Another faceless troll, another eloquent argument. You people are the sick ones.

Reply 77
13/03/10
18:01
Sender: Anonymous User 34
There are six peoples families who would disagree with you. Get a grip.

Reply 76
13/03/10
17:53
Sender: Anonymous User 33
I hope you get cancer and aids and die in a gutter you silly cunt I hope you diiiiiiiiiiiiiiiiiiiiiiiiiiiiiiiiiiiiiiiiiiiiiiiiiiiiiiiiiiiiiiiiieeeeeeeeeeeeeeeeeeeeeeeeeeeeeee

Reply 75
13/03/10
17:45
Sender: WoWFan
My brother has Asperger's Syndrome so I know where you're coming from with the mental illness argument, if he did anything like The Sheffield Ripper did, he would have a pretty strong case against a full trial. I wish him all the luck in the world. You are one brave lady though. Well said.

Reply 74
13/03/10
17:23
Sender: Anonymous User 32
WOW! I can't believe this actually works! I lost 3 stones in 2 weeks! You can too, simply click here!!

Reply 73
13/03/10
17:20
Sender: DaisyB
Thanks for all your words of support guys, please please click on my petition site here and we can try to get as many signatures as we can. You know he deserves a fair trial. @Anonymous User 31: I have passed your ip details to the police, they WILL find you.

Reply 72
13/03/10
16:53
Sender: Anonymous User 31
u r da scum ov da earth, I only cum on ere 2 see wot da fuk u was on about wen my bro sed u was tapped. he aint wrong bitch, you are delushional. I ope sumting happens 2 u like wot happend 2 dem families. den u will no real pain. u best lay low cos if I see u in sheff I will kill u bitch, no kiddin, I will actually kill u!!

Reply 71
13/03/10
16:45
Sender: McLovin
Daisy you are an inspiration to everybody that wants to go out and change the world. I agree with you 100% and I hope the petition is a success. Alan Foster might not be innocent but that's not the point. He deserves justice as much as his victims. I am behind you all the way. Go girl!

Reply 70
13/03/10
16:37
Sender: Jesusfreak
You are deluded if you think you will make a difference. The commandments said "Thou Shalt Not Kill", it can't be twisted and changed to suit the need of some self-righteous idiot who feels like she needs to protest against anything and everything. I know it goes against your socialist agenda to just keep quiet and let it happen, but you make me SICK to the stomach that you feel like everything on God's planet is yours to put right. Some things are beyond redemption, just deal with it. If he had been sane you would still be out on the streets waving banners against him. You and your misplaced righteous self-importance will ALWAYS lose, just deal with it.

Mr Isaac Charles

Friday 22nd January 2010

You do not get into this game if you have an appreciation for morality, believe me. There is absolutely no place in this industry for emotion. No place for attachment to anything. Believe me, I represent some people whose actions would mortify the working fellow. But therein lies the beauty of it. The working fellow, and his wife will devour every word of what's written about the people I represent. They clamour for it like Africans around a bag of grain that has been tossed from the back of a moving aid truck, or a stinking filthy well in the middle of nowhere, somewhere they have travelled weeks to get to, only to kill themselves with what they find there. Those Africans are also, I suppose, a kind of metaphor for the people I represent. They will go to hell and back for a little piece of notoriety, only to kill their own reputation when they find the vultures circling at the end of the line. Yes, believe me, you see the harlot who rather coarsely described her nights of passion with the married international footballer in the red-topped newspaper? The same harlot who had pictures of his team-mate's penis on her mobile telephone? And the very same harlot who was found dead from an overdose of sleeping pills? Yes. She was one of mine. She was simultaneously loathed and loved by the readership of that newspaper. I am the fisherman. They are the fish. And she was the bait.
You see the children's television presenter who was photographed snorting cocaine in a nightclub toilet and

was fired from his job, and enjoyed a successful stint on Celebrity What-have-You? You'll know the one, relegated to late night gambling programmes but still made a fortune with his ghost written autobiography, a fortune which was then frittered away on the powder he coveted so much? Indeed, I still took my slice. And the current flavour of the month?
The young gentleman who murdered two people and survived an attack himself, by a deranged lunatic with a Victorian lion hunter alter-ego who has found himself the hate figure *de jour*? The one who has since appeared on every chat show, and in every lifestyle magazine since? The very same young gentleman who is in talks with regards releasing a topical rap album to coincide with the inevitable guilty charge of his unfortunate attacker. And believe me, he will be found guilty. Yes, all of it, my work. Oh, quite correct, you have picked up that I said his attacker was unfortunate. You are quite astute. You display good listening skills. I like that. Oh, but I shall get to it later, all good things come to those who wait. My client, is doing very well on the circuit right now. He has been something of a challenge, given the circumstances in which he was thrust upon me by a very good friend of mine who, to you, shall remain nameless. Oh yes, a challenge indeed. What one must do is send certain aspects of his character to the metaphorical recycle bin, take the time to right click and empty said recycle bin of course, obviously one would not want any nasty surprises surfacing in the future. Airbrush his character so that blemishes can only be viewed in high definition, and even then you may have to really look for them if you do not know that they are there. Speaking of

airbrushing, this time next year your daughter may well have a copy of his official calendar hanging from her wall alongside her posters of pubescent man-boys and cartoon mice. Oh, this project is marvellously entertaining, and lucrative for all involved, of course. He has been a tremendous sport, although he didn't have a difficult choice, given his alternative, but still, he has taken proceedings well within his stride. Believe me, he has been very easy to work alongside. Now, in all fairness, the building up, getting him out there into the public domain has been child's play, why, I could do that for anybody. I could do that for you! What has made the task all the more interesting is that running almost parallel to my client's meteoric rise to prominence, is the simply hilarious destruction of another man's life. I did tell you, do not ever get into this game if you ever feel guilt. Believe me, the things I have seen could drive a man to the point of hanging there from the strongest light fitting in his house. The trick is to not dwell. Move on. Detach yourself from the task at hand. For the most part my job is to build you up. Make you more palatable, make your story more interesting. Nobody is interested in a dullard. If you have fellated a postman you are nothing. If you have fellated the next big thing you are the next big thing. Every now and then an opportunity drops into my lap, one which allows me to systematically strip away every aspect of a person's life, take them away piece by piece. More often than not these opportunities are handed to me by my very good friend, who, once again, shall remain nameless. Naughty naughty! You shan't loosen these lips. Believe me, I grasp these opportunities with both hands and I ensure I do the most professional of

jobs. On this occasion I was tasked with a most curious of gentlemen. I found in my possession some remarkable tools to work with. Audio recordings of him having fantastic conversations with himself, which formed the basis of the destruction. When a gentleman has such dramatic foibles, one can make the other pieces of the jigsaw fall into place almost effortlessly! Speaking of jigsaws, well, you've seen the news, you know to whom I refer. As with the positive aspects of my job, the trick is to exaggerate. If you were found with a gram of cocaine, you may as well tell the news it was five. Notoriety is key. So what if there were only three jigsaws in your abode, I'm going to ensure they find a hundred. Give them hints that you need things to occupy your tiny mind. Violent pornography? Oh, that's simply set decoration. Give me unrestricted access to any man's home and I'll have him hung, drawn and quartered by the baying mob by the end of the week. There's always a local teenager who'll daub faeces all over his window in the shape of words declaring him a paedophile for the right kind of money then the mob will do the rest. Plant the seed and watch it grow! Of course, your opinion of me may sour even further when I reveal that sometimes I do this for sport, to entertain myself when times are, shall we say, quiet?
You'll know what I'm talking about when I tell you about the quiet polite heterosexual musician, rather shy in front of the cameras, his output is rather bland in all honesty, so much so that it rather offended me. Get enough people to sell their stories to various newspapers and the rumour mill will transform into a perpetual motion machine. I think I've said enough about that though, you get the point that I am trying to

make. One is not forced to be a violent man to be a dangerous man. Oh, believe me, Isaac Charles is a name that is both vilified and revered in the same sentence. You do not have to like me to respect me. I do not have to be your friend to be your hero. But by Christ, do not make an enemy of me.

Friday 30th October 2009

Her eyes opened as she woke with a start, scanned the room as the familiarity seeped into her body, a wave rolled across her as reality set in. She looked at the clock above the bedroom door. 4am. She'd had three hours of fevered broken sleep. Even that was a struggle. Since she and Tom had been forced to part company Jess felt no safety. The Ada woman had attempted to provide a degree of comfort but there was only so much she could do for her, given that the company she kept would suggest that she had killed dozens of people on their behalf. Being comforted by Ada would probably stir the same emotion as being hugged with barbed wire, or kissed with the end of a broken bottle. They had made no secret of the fact that she was still a prisoner and it shit her up no end. She needed Tom. Badly. She always considered herself a strong person, somebody who would tackle life her own way and never suffer fools easily, had always had an answer for anything, never taken life too seriously and tried not to worry about things she couldn't affect too much. Just now though, this was something she couldn't affect and she was going out of her mind with worry. The old man had responded to Tom asking him to turn, his- she couldn't bring herself to even think his name- head around so as not to face them silently. He had seemed to be having a conversation with his eyes with Ada, who pulled Jess' arm and led her out of the room. She'd felt like making a scene, clinging to Tom, her hero, she really did not want to leave the room without him. She didn't want to live her life without him by her side ever. They'd had a spark when he came to the pub with his violent thug friend. She felt it. She knew that he'd felt it too. She was gutted when things kicked off and they had to make a hasty exit. She knew she'd see him again though. She just wished, she so wished that it had been under different circumstances. Not these ones. Her old life felt so far away.

At Derek's tutorials, being told that her essay on the influence of Surrealism on the modern world shone an entirely new light on his opinion of the matter, going home and chilling out in the communal lounge with the lads. Jonny, and his daft curly hair that he let her straighten when they were stoned one time. Paul, who would take every opportunity to wave his pierced bell end about the place. When they would take the gentle mickey out of Man Boob Rob and his big red body warmer, saying it would be a good name for a band, "Man Boob Rob and his Big Red Body Warmer" which was a running joke amongst them. Rob knew it was done out of affection so there were never any hard feelings, apart from when he got off his tits on mushrooms and had a major paranoia trip, even then he apologised the day after. Those small things that she never realised she would miss.

Now she was here alone in a dark room on a small bed with crunching thin springs. It seemed strange, considering the grandeur of its surroundings. A painting on the wall she knew to be a copy the Henri Matisse painting "Music", it had to be a copy because the original hung on a wall in a gallery in Chicago. She smiled a bittersweet smile, she was such a geek, doing her homework when she was here, locked in this room in this house, somewhere on the outskirts of the city. She wondered what had happened to Tom. Had they killed him? She hoped to God he was alive, somewhere, she hoped to God they'd just put him in another room, leaving them both to stew separately so that they couldn't cook up some scheme together or get any stories straight. Even if they did get left together and escaped they probably wouldn't get far, and what was to say that these people weren't connected to the police? Tom. He was brash and bold and really didn't give a toss who anybody was, that was part of his charm. When she'd heard him take exception to Grub in the Frog and Parrot, listening to him attempt to sound more intellectual by using so many more words than he needed to. But that was just Grub, he had been floating around the university for years. She'd last heard that he was homeless and got by on crashing at whoever's place that he could. She'd seen him huddled in a doorway after one student night at a club in the town. Jonny and Paul got talking to him and invited him back to theirs for the night. He stayed for four days. And when Tom took exception she knew the kind of guy he was. Smart but he never allowed it to become him. He was his own man. What he had done for her had almost certainly increased her estimations of him to almost through the roof. Her hero. He stood up to the old man, the man she knew these people worked for. Neither she, nor Tom had an idea as to what they were up to. Tom had explained when they were alone in the car what he had witnessed, and why he had been dragged along to her house by, him. She felt a lump in her throat as he told her about his friend, mounds of water building up above the dams of his bottom eyelids, those dams bursting and allowing two wet snakes to slither down his cheeks when he blinked, laughing at himself being so emotional and daft, wiping his eyes dry with the back of his sleeve.

So what he knew then she knew, and it wasn't a great deal. Nothing they could ever hold against these people. The only thing they could ever testify to is that they had seen their faces. So why were they still holding them? The only man who had done any harm in all of this was, him. He was the one who had shot Tom's friend Justin, he was the one who had kept them hostage at gun point and- everything else. Ada had come and cleaned things up on behalf the old man. God, when Tom stood up to him, even though he appeared to be the boss of everything, he knew he'd got nothing to lose. It was like he was asking the question to himself, what else could they do to him? When they took her the look in his eyes said "It'll be okay, do as they say" so she did, she gave in to their demands without question, the trust she put in that look from Tom was enough to ensure that.

That was last night, when Jess had spent all night crying to herself, trying to take her mind off things by reciting the words to her favourite song over and over again.

A kiss, before midnight, is all I ask of you, hold me tight, make me safe, tell me what I need to do...

It was still dark outside when she awoke, she looked at the clock again, 4:16, she was wide awake, sitting up she cast her gaze to the video camera recording her movements, spent a few unblinking minutes staring into its lens, willing whoever it was that was watching her to rescue her, take her away from this

room, this house, this life. A door clicked further down the corridor. Fingers of fear made their way up her spine, taking with each step a shiver of anticipation as footsteps slowly increased in volume, almost certainly approaching her door. Somebody had been watching her intently. Seen her awake and looking back at them. The footsteps sounded heavy, almost laboured. The slice of light under the door that cut through the darkness of the room became hindered by two shadows. Somebody's feet. Paused at her door. A muffled jangling of keys being pulled from a pocket. The shadows stopped moving. Jess pulled the sheets further up her body and watched the door in anticipation. The clicking of metal in the keyhole and a crunch as the lock slid back into it's mechanism. Again the shadows stayed behind the cover of the thick dark wood, fearsome in it's stillness. her breathe heavied as her heartbeat picked up in it's pace. It felt to her as though it would crash through her ribcage, tear through the fabric of her t-shirt and bounce around on the wooden floor, blood squirting from the ventricles. The handle squeaked into life as it was pressed down by the mystery hand on the other side of the door, and the slice of light began a chase vertically up between the frame and the door, becoming a cascade into the room, shaded only by the silhouette of the person that stood there. Jess inhaled sharply as the realisation hit her as to who was there.
"I'd like a word with you" he said, as he stepped deeper into the room.

Vincent Sharpe and Tyler Williams
Telephone transcript

Thursday 27th May 2010

Vincent: So what are Endemol saying?
Tyler: They won't touch it.
Vincent: Any reason?
Tyler: Too soon.
Vincent: What? Too soon? We leave it any longer and it'll be old news.
Tyler: Vinnie, seriously? Old news? People are still making fuckin' films about Ted Bundy, serial killers sell, they just think the wounds are still a little raw.
Vincent: So I have to sit on this for how long? It's a fuckin' masterpiece!
Tyler: A year?
Vincent: A year?! A fuckin' year?! Can't we just take it out of the country? The French go mad for stuff like this, have you tried Canal Plus?
Tyler: I'll get Felicity onto it.
Vincent: So you haven't already tried? Fuckin' hell Tyler, what the fuck do I pay you for?
Tyler: You know exactly what you pay me for Vinnie, don't be an arsehole.
Vincent: Okay, I'm sorry, I just don't want to have to come up with all the ways we can get sell this thing. You're the agent, you sell it.
Tyler: Well, we're still in talks with Tiger Aspect, they haven't said no yet.
Vincent: Yet? Jesus Tyler, be a little more fuckin' positive yeah? I mean, come on, make me think we

might have a chance here. You could be telling me they haven't said yes yet.
Tyler: Well, yeah, but given that most of the production companies aren't touching it, we need to be realistic.
Vincent: I am being realistic, these fuckin' idiots can't see a work of art when they see it.
Tyler: Vinnie, are you not listening to me? They're saying it's a fuckin' good script, they just don't wanna risk a public backlash by glamourizing things so soon
Vincent: Tyler! Have they even read it? There's no glamour there! It's as a real as a documentary! It's more like Ken Loach than Quentin Tarantino!
Tyler: I know this Vinnie, I know this. But still, the Shipman film caused a shitload of trouble when they made that.
Vincent: Exactly! And that was years after he killed people! There are always gonna be the victim brigade ready to jump on the back of any controversial piece of work!
Tyler: Vinnie-
Vincent: You saw what they did to Stew Lee when he did that Jerry Springer Opera, you can't get a little edgy nowadays without some cunt taking exception, that's just life.
Tyler: I can't believe we're having this conversation, five companies say no, we still have plenty more to go to.
Vincent: I might just make it myself, get some funding together, and direct it myself, that seems to be the only way.
Tyler: You?

Vincent: Yeah me, why did you say it like that? You don't think I could do it? You saying I don't have the skills?
Tyler: Okay, when was the last time you directed a four part drama series?
Vincent: Are you being facetious?
Tyler: No, Vinnie, I'm not. I told you, let's be realistic, everything you do turns to gold, they know this, but the subject matter is a little near the knuckle right now. Let's sit on it for a while, wait for the dust to settle. Alan Foster's corpse is still warm, his victims corpses are still warm.
Vincent: Yeah, and we wait, some other cunt will get their version of the story out before I do mine.
Tyler: Are you kidding? You're the most cutting edge writer this country has produced for years, they could put a hundred versions out and there's only one guy walking away with the BAFTA.
Vincent: Get your tongue out of my arse Tyler.
Tyler: You can be a real fuckin' dick sometimes Vinnie, you know that?
Vincent: Yeah I fuckin' know that. You get fuckin' nowhere by being nice.
Tyler: Yeah but we've known each other years, I don't think I need to be taking your shit still, we're a fuckin' team
Vincent: Yeah, you're right. I just want to get this made so fuckin' much. This is the best story this country's had in a long time. I mean come on, fuckin' schizophrenic serial killer-
Tyler: The guy had multiple personalities, not schizophrenia, there's a difference mate.

Vincent: Potato potahto, the man on the street doesn't know the difference. Now he's dead we can tell them he was anything.
Tyler: Point taken, but still, a little historical accuracy for the purposes of pitching this thing won't go amiss.
Vincent: Anyway, we're on a whole other avenue of conversation here Tyler, who else are we gonna pitch it to?
Tyler: Well, Steve Harrison at the Beeb says it might do well on BBC4.
Vincent: BBC4? Seriously? That guy's an arsehole, never liked me since I took The Dangerous Stranger to Sky One. No, fuck BBC4. I'd rather it didn't get made than put it on that seven viewer piece of shit.
Tyler: Well, shit, Vinnie, he didn't even say yes yet, like I say, he just said it might do well on that channel.
Vincent: And like I say, it's not going on that channel even if they did want it. No, fuck it, take it to the French, I told you, they love this kind of stuff.
Tyler: Okay Vinnie, I'll get on it. Listen, I'm just about to go into a meeting with Suzie Harper, I'll keep you posted yeah?
Vincent: Okay Tyler, be sure you do. Later mate.
Tyler: Bye.

Alan

Wednesday 17th March 2010

"Well dear boy, we're in a right old pickle here aren't we? Oh well, make the most of it I suppose eh?- Algernon, this isn't a laughing matter- Who's laughing chap?- Oh shut up! Shut up! This is all your fault!- Well, if you hadn't been such a wimp you wouldn't need me around eh? You'd be home alone, member in hand!- Algernon behave, please-"
"Oi! Killer! Shat your fackin' marf! Talkin' bollocks all the fackin' time! I'm tryin' to do a shit here, my fackin' arsehole can't do the business if you're fackin' yappin'!" The voice from the next cell down echoed through the halls, Alan's neighbour had been very vocal in his disdain toward him. He'd not left Alan alone since he got here. Made it very clear that his card was marked. The situation frightened and confused Alan, although Algernon hadn't had any such fears. He was well and truly in his element, the smell of sweat in the place aroused a carnal side to his character that had remained long dormant.
"Oh dear boy, all this talk of your arsehole is giving this old stag a stiff one, do continue!" he teased the lag in the next cell.
"You what? I'll fackin' rip your fackin' 'ead off you fackin' faggot!" The incredulous reply came.
"Oh you flirtatious scamp, I shall- Algernon, please, don't upset him- Upset him? I shall UPSET HIS BLOODY INSIDES WITH MY MEMBER!" he howled into the corridor.

"You're fackin' nats you fackin' cant!" the more subdued response, the neighbour in the next cell. The thug in him more than a little threatened by the convicted serial killer biting back. He clearly wasn't used to being stood up to, but there was a chance he simply didn't want to get into this whilst he was in the process of emptying his bowels.

Alan's mind was not his own anymore. The things he had been subjected to over the past few months were a blur of events. He remembered being caught, trying to explain what had happened, but Algernon interrupted every conversation, made people think that Alan was mad, crazy, mentally ill. He didn't feel mentally ill, he was just sharing his body with a moustachioed Victorian lion hunter. He knew that sounded crazy. But he felt no less normal, he felt no more different than he ever had. But the things they said to him, the questions they asked him. The newspapers digging up his past. The abuse he got being taken to and from court. Why did they not believe him when he told them the truth? About the waiting room? About Mr Berg? They brushed it all under the carpet, *nothing* he said was taken seriously. Algernon didn't make things any better, interrupting him mid-flow all the time. The police interview, trying to tell them what they wanted to hear but Algernon stepping and declaring them all a bunch of crooked scallywags stood only to make things worse.

Every step of the way he did nothing but tell the truth. And all they did was raise their eyebrows, write in their books, make their judgments. The doctors were no better. In the clinic, strapped to the gurney, alone in the cold. Algernon made more than enough noise for both of them. Alan retreating to a place in his mind where he was safe. A happier place. But then their questions brought him out of those happy memories through the wicked times, his mother screaming, drunk at the strangers that came to their house. An endless conga line of uncles, new dads, friends of the family, all of them in and out within an hour, the noises that came from his mother's room, evil wicked awful screams, swear words, the sounds of wet flesh slapping against wet flesh like a butcher constantly slamming a heavy steak onto his work surface. Their questions made constant reference to it. How did it make him feel? What did it feel like to hear his mother being used by these filthy bastards? He knew how it felt. He felt helpless. Sick. He wanted to kill each and every one of them. But he was innocent. No, they said he wasn't. But he was. Because he wanted to kill each and every one of them then it meant to them that he had killed six people as a substitute for the men that had paid his mother for sex. He told them. He had killed one person. James Crosby. They wanted to know about people called Graham and Ruby and Geoffrey and Thomas. No, he said, Geoffrey and Thomas were alive the last time he knew. *They must have done it. They must have killed them and blamed me!* But no, they didn't believe him. And God, the courts! The solicitors in their capes and wigs throwing accusation after accusation at him, Algernon answering for both of them. Laughter echoing from the gallery each time he spoke, which only served to antagonise him, so then he would bellow out that they should close their bloody cake holes or be faced with a stiff punishment. Again, this only served to make things worse. Alan remembered a time where he was grateful for Algernon in his head, but not anymore. He had done this. Alan was innocent. Algernon was the guilty one! But how could they differentiate? He saw their point. He would try to stay calm, answer their questions as truthfully as he could, but then they'd ask the same ones again and again, and he could hear the insinuation dripping from their tongues. They weren't listening to a word he said. They'd made their minds up. The jury were sitting there, nodding with every point the prosecution appeared happy to have made. The woman who owned the dog that Algernon killed, in tears, pointing his way when they asked if the man who had so cruelly taken away her beloved Oscar was visible to her in the court that day, the way they built up her relationship with her dog, made the jury well aware that the dog was her only remaining link to her fiancé who died whilst serving in Afghanistan, how he'd bought it for her as a birthday present when they first moved in together, that Alan had destroyed her life. But it wasn't Alan, it was Algernon who had done it. The worst day was when he took the stand. The young coloured man. Daniel. The bloody celebrity. He made Alan's brain itch, how he could tell all those lies? He had sworn on the bible! They had to be responsible for him too. Why though? What made him so special? When he told his lies and started to cry his crocodile tears, telling the court he had never heard of Mr Berg, he had never met Alan in all his life, he used to go to the Botanical Gardens because his grandma used to take him there when he was younger, before she died of course, that's how it was such an important place to him, how he didn't think he could ever return there because the memories were now too painful.

Everything they said in that court was built up to hurt Alan, to make him look like a bad man. He wasn't a bad man, but they twisted and manipulated every answer.
"So, you admit that you intended to kill Mr Daniel Jackson?"
"Yes but they made me do it, they told me-"
"And these are the voices are they Mr Foster? The voices tell you-"
"No! Mr Berg!"
"This is the Mr Berg that nobody seems to have heard of?"
"Yes, but he knows him too! He was supposed to kill me too, it was the rules!"
"So it's one man's word against another's, well, with respect Mr Foster, Daniel Jackson has never murdered a dog and chased down members of the public"
And Algernon would spoil everything.
"Oh behave you rotter, you'll get a ruddy good thump if you don't close your lips!" and the people in the court would stifle their laughter, and the prosecutor would look knowingly at the jury, and they'd make their notes, and Alan would take another step toward the end of his life.

Tom

Friday 30th October 2009

All I'm thinking is that this is for her. If I don't do this then it's all fucked. For sure it's already fucked, but this is damage limitation. And I'm supposed to be thinking that this is a lifeline? What world do these people actually live in? I mean, seriously? What fuckin' planet can you possibly live on to to think that this behaviour is normal? Am I supposed to be grateful for what they're asking of me? I guess I should be asking the old fella that put me up to it, instead of myself, but still, it doesn't hurt to have a little internal venting. For sure, ranting at myself helps to keep her alive. Ranting at them kills her. I've been made very certain of the rules. As he sat there dictating to me what I had to do it was very obvious that he was used to giving orders, that sureness that I was gonna do everything he said, and I was gonna behave myself, that's something that comes with experience that, you can't learn that in school. So it's early morning, still properly dark outside, and the digital clock reads 5:07. The beefy fucker still hasn't told me his name, still hasn't said a word to me. Just sits and drives. A weird looking satnav type bit of kit's on the dashboard, three little green flashing dots move about on the screen and he's guiding us toward one of them.

After I asked him to move or turn the head round he got that bird Ada to take Jess from the room, not that she wanted to go, but I gave her the most reassuring look I could. Not that I knew where she was taking her, she could have been taking her to a back garden where

there was a firing squad waiting to pepper her with bullets, but in the back of my mind I was thinking that if they didn't have plans for us we'd already be in an unmarked grave, so I chanced it and tried to reassure her and she left without a struggle. So then it was just me and the old boy, and I'm trying to scrutinize his face without appearing to scrutinize his face, get it in my head for in case some sort of miracle happens and I find myself in a position to be recalling it. His weathered face reminds me of an elderly turtle or something like that, like Michelangelo or Donatello got old, and retired from being ninjas, and he's got these wild eyebrows that curl up away from his forehead like a Saturday night slag's fake eyelashes, pure white though, with a go-faster stripe of black through them. I'm not sure whether his hair's a toupee or something like that because it seems really thick for how old he looks, and it's slicked in a smart side-parting that you can tell he really likes to look after, so maybe it's his real hair, like, he takes proper pride in it. What's the most striking thing about him though, is his eyes. They're sneaky as fuck. Now I like to think I'm pretty intelligent, but the bloke looks like he's always thinking, like he's always one step ahead of you. It's at that point that I realised he's been doing the same as me. He knows I'm trying to memorise his face, he's either doing the same or taking the piss by mimicking. The sneaky fucker!
"Tell me, young man, how the hell you came to be standing here before me?"
"Do you want the long version or the short one?"
"Take a seat, indulge me, choose which version you wish to tell me"

And that was that, I had big designs on giving him the short version but he's stopping me every few minutes to ask me why I did or said whatever it was I did or said, so it turned into an all-nighter, and it felt more like a job interview than anything else. Ada came in after about an hour of me telling him everything I know, fetched a tray with a decanter of brandy and a couple of glasses. He didn't even look at her, just stared at me whilst I'm still telling the story and she's pouring two hefty servings of booze, then leaving the room. I hesitated around whether to take a drink or not but he sensed it and gave me the go ahead.

At the end of me giving him the skinny on how I came to be stood there, prisoner to a bunch of mysterious dickheads who act far harder than they need to he sighed and looked into his hands, the only kind of noise was the music coming from a few rooms down, the blokes in there had gone quiet. All this silence, all the time, and the 'speak when you're spoken to' ethos that just makes for a very uncomfortable time, I don't think I would ever want to work with these people to be honest, for sure, I know my own mind and usually I like to speak it, and this environment would not make for a happy Tom.

"So, if you were in my position what do you think you would do?" that's what he asked me! Seriously, the guy asked me what I'd do! Well, what could I say? I'd let me go pal! I'd pack me and the beautiful red headed angel I came with, back into a car and I'd drop us off at home! I didn't say that. I said

"With respect, sir, I don't think that anything I ask you to do would happen, I genuinely don't know what being

in your position entails, my only concern is the girl I came with"
"Very chivalrous indeed. Okay, allow me to clarify. If you were in a position whereby you were in the middle of something very important and two flies appeared, to irritate and possibly jeopardise that something?"
"Swat them?"
"Yes, I suppose you would. But herein lies my quandary. You see, the owner of that head" and he pointed to the rapist cunt Christophe staring out with his dead eyes "was somewhat important to proceedings until he so carelessly rocked the boat. I understand that you did what you felt you had to, you displayed the courage to act selflessly for the greater good of your young friend, but now I am left with various tasks which need undertaking, and I require somebody to undertake these" Then he stared at me expectantly, and it took all of a second for the penny to drop exactly who he expected to do these various tasks.

So I'm left here in the passenger seat whilst the beefy fucker glares at the satnav tracker thing and powers the car alongside another. I look at the back seat window and a little girl waves at me, she's up on her knees on the seat, entertaining herself at the same time as her young mum talks into a mobile. The innocent little smile she's displaying compels me to give her a little wave back, and she's giggling, turning to tug at her mum's sleeve to boast about how she got somebody to wave back at her. The mum ignores her, and the car turns off and we leave the little girl to her solitary delight.
"Any idea where we're heading pal?" I chance my arm with a query, see if he's playing the game.

"Yes" and his eyes glance into the mirror, checking the traffic behind him as he pulls into the right lane and indicates right, pausing at a junction.
"Any chance you might tell me?"
"You will find out"
I'm reckoning this guy's Spanish or something, thinking he probably doesn't know a great deal of English, maybe that's why he's being such chatty bastard.
"Okay, well, let me know in good time fella, I feel sick as fuck about this"
And he swerves the car to a halt at the kerb, just turns his head to me and studies me quietly.
"You will be fine, think about your friend, would you rather she lived or a stranger that you have never met?"
"Point taken, but it still doesn't mean it's gonna be any easier"
"Are you ready?"
"What? Now?"
"We are here. Come"
“Any chance I could ask you something?”
“Quickly”
“Can I have one of these before we go?”
And I’m holding up a bag of Justin’s coke, waving it hopefully. For a second I see a knowing, almost smiling, twinkle in his eye, but then they glaze over again as he goes stony faced. Then he sighs.
“Quickly”
How mint is that? So I’m on it like a tramp on a pasty and hoovering two fat lines up off the back of a Shirley Bassey CD case, mad as fuck that this big beefy Spanish loves Shirley Bassey, but I don’t say anything, a rush jumps through my body which crackles to my brain and I’m already feeling on top of the world. Okay

Mr Beefy, whatever you're cooking up, I'm in! I hold up the bag to offer, which he declines, but I'd have to say it's begrudgingly.
"No worries, but cheers"
He gets out of the car and waits for me to follow him. We're at a dead end in the road that looks like it turns into a footpath. My shadow stretches to the end of the road and into the small entrance to the path. The shape of my head dances over the leaves that overhang at either side of the wall, then it becomes my shoulders and body as the light's coverage is hindered and me and Mr Beefy enter the pathway. The sky's the strange kind of blue it gets when it's early dawn, like, this blue is never anywhere else apart from in the sky at dawn. I like it when it starts to go orange as the sun comes up, in the distance like, when it looks like photos that losers send in to the local weatherman to show on the telly. A real claim to fame. The same people write in to the telly pages to give their opinion on an outrageous storyline on Hollyoaks or something. Or at worst, the kind of people that send in hilarious stories to a lifestyle magazine about when their toddler said something cute. Usually punctuated with exclamation marks! After! Every! Sentence!

I digress, we're walking down the path and all I can see is the shape of the beefy fucker crunching down the path, he's keeping some real pace and I find myself taking a couple of skips to keep up. From behind you can see the edges of his nut glowing as he's looking down at the satnav tracking thing he's brought with us. Now I know from experience his vision will be fucked in this darkness if he keeps staring at the thing whilst he walks, he's gonna be seeing that glow for a while yet.

The path opens up and we've found ourselves on an open playing field, even in the dark you can see it's a vast expanse of grass, several football pitches, the outline of some goalposts in front of that blue, and a darker blue cloud moving behind it. He stops in his tracks and holds an arm in front of my chest to hold me as I walk up alongside him. For a split second I'm tempted to crack him on the side of the head and get out of here but that passes as quickly as it arrived. I'm here for her and her alone. I'm not even fucking here for myself anymore. I'm not harbouring any big hero fantasies, the only fantasies I'm harbouring are of getting into my bed and sleeping for a week.

At the side of him I'm watching the satnav tracker thing, we're right on top of one of the green dots here. I can feel the inevitable getting closer. Now I know I'm coked up, and yeah, I smashed the boy Christophe's head in because of what he did. This fucker that we're after hasn't done anything to me and mine, but what can I say? My hands are tied. I have to do it.

A rustle sounds in a bush behind us and we turn round to face it.

"Thomas Ferguson, come out, the game is over" this is the beefy fucker talking to nobody, and the response from nobody is predictable; nothing. He has another go. "Mr Ferguson, I know why you are here and who told you to do what you are doing. Do not worry. We need to talk" and this time the nobody he was talking to appears from the bushes we're looking at. I can't tell what he looks like until he gets closer. The guy looks positively feral, this long lank wet hair hangs down over his face, a long leather Matrix-film jacket covers

his body, and yet again one of the people these guys are involved with is carrying a giant knife in his hand. This is fucking mad. He's holding the knife toward us and wave it slowly, warding us off like.
"Who are you? Where's Mr Berg?" as he gets closer I can see some hair growth around his lip and his chin, for whatever reason I'm thrown back to that Johnny Long-Word cunt from the pub yesterday, I think it's the lack of full growth on there. Like, patches on his cheeks and all wispy instead of a full Brian Blessed sort of beard. Then something else clicks, this boy's called Thomas the same as me. I always had a weirdness around people with the same name as me. Like, when somebody called Tom ever phoned me up at work, and I'd have to be using his name all the time, and he was calling me Tom, like "Okay Tom, how can I help you Tom?- well Tom, you can help me by doing this for me Tom- No problems Tom" and it got to a point where I had a freakish phobia of people called Tom with all the Tom overkill, and now I've got to help snuff a Tom out. Fucking coke. This puts an even more surreal spin on proceedings, and the Mr Beefy is holding up his hands as if to calm the boy down. The knife's staying put though as he flicks his greasy hair out of his eyes and looks straight at me while he guides the tip of the knife my way.
"I said who the fuck are you? I don't know you!" he screams, dancing from one foot to the other out of nervousness.
"Hey! Pal! Put your fuckin' knife down yeah? I don't know you either, I'm as clueless as-" and the knife goes clattering as the Mr Beefy knocks the other Tom right out whilst he wasn't looking. His body drops to the

floor and I'm fucking gobsmacked, the sound of his big shovel hand meeting the other Tom's head was loud as fuck! Now there's no time to be gobsmacked 'cause he's down by the lifeless body we've got in front of us and he raises his head to me.

"Now is the time you save your friend" and he holds the handle of the knife my way "Cut his throat".

Daniel

Saturday 1st May 2010

"Danny! I haven't heard from you in time bro! I'm gonna 'llow it 'cause you're the big celebrity now but hit me back yeah? Don't forget your roots man, s'all I'm sayin', don't forget your boys"
He clicked the phone shut. A pang of guilt rocked him. Leon's answer machine message was reminding him of a time he could barely remember. He'd only been in the public eye a short time but he couldn't imagine going back now. Man was a celebrity now. He'd been sculpted so dramatically by Mr Charles and his people that he couldn't even remember who he used to be, let alone where he came from. His thoughts were no longer his own, he knew that much. Mr Charles had been behind him at every turn, pulling his strings like the big flamboyant puppet master that he was. Every time Daniel made an appearance on TV Mr Charles was there, answering questions for him. If he felt himself about to answer something, he'd feel a hand on his knee as if to stop him, then he'd hear that voice in his ear answering the question on his behalf. The statements when the court case was going on, all made by Mr Charles, they'd been cited as being synonymous with each other in a lot of the media. His life had been under the spotlight for months, and whenever he read anything about it, he knew exactly which part was the brainchild of Mr Charles, and what was real, in that one hundred per cent of it was the brainchild of Mr Charles. Nothing was real. Everything was fabricated. This was probably the main reason for the man being at his side

all of the time, so that he wouldn't trip himself up by trying to remember the lies that he had so intricately woven around Daniel's being. The interviews had been strictly arranged that all questions were vetted prior to meetings, so his days were the same as the last, they melted into weeks which melted into months as his brain became accustomed to answering the same lies, finding himself reading an interview he'd never taken part in. His life story written and rewritten by Mr Charles and his merry band of followers. Kiss and Tell exposés with girls from Hollyoaks that he'd never even met, let alone "spent three steamy nights in a country hideaway" with, it seemed the whole world was a puppet of one Isaac Charles. There was always the underlying guilt he felt toward Alan Foster as his plight. The media obviously couldn't mention one without the other, given the circumstances surrounding Daniel's own rise to fame, the reason for him being in this five-star hotel hot tub with two of a reasonably successful girl-band made famous by a reality style talent contest.

He never once for a moment thought that the plan would work. How could the country clamour so much for the "one that got away"? He couldn't remember ever having given it much thought before, but he considered that this must be one fucked up country if near-miss victims of a supposed serial killer could be built into celebrities in their own right simply by exposing them to the public so much that they begin to form opinions of him, and if the man-behind-the-man is a master manipulator then their opinions will be decided for them, a country with so many sheep and so few shepherds only have a limited amount of opinions to form. The man Foster was a fruit cake though, a racist schizophrenic motherfucker who was unhinged enough as it was without putting a knife in the man's hand and pointing him in the direction of seven throats and saying "cut those", but it could so easily have gone the other way. He knew that. If the knife had been in the other hand and Daniel was the one who was almost caught killing the NHS glasses motherfucker, then Mr Charles would have been destroying his life instead. He'd be the one rotting in the ground in an unmarked grave so that the public couldn't find it and de-face it, or dig him up and take bones or his skull as trophies of the notorious "Sheffield Ripper" like they had tried to do since his death last month. The papers called them Ghouls. No, he was under no illusion as to how fortunate he had been to be in this position, that things could have been very fucking different. What was weird was the lack of communication from anybody that he'd met when this started. The big man, Berg, or the old boy, or the small woman with the tight arse and tighter pony tail, none of them had ever contacted him, even though they must have arranged for Mr Charles to do his stuff. Like they had faded into the background, maybe not even in the country anymore. Like they had just said to Mr Charles "Him, work your magic on him" and disappeared in a puff of smoke. Daniel wasn't complaining though, his bank balance was healthier than it had ever been, five figure amounts had been rolling in regularly and he considered himself set for life. No, he didn't have any worries for a long time yet.

Ada

Friday 30th October 2009

She remembered thinking earlier in the week that if all went well she would be home by today. Now all had not gone well and she was still here in this city. The plan had changed dramatically and they had all had to think on their feet. The game was over, that much was true. Mr Hoxton had called her into his study after he'd done with Tom and they discussed things at length. He'd called Isaac Charles last night, the second they'd heard about Daniel being taken into the civilian hospital, and that aspect was under way but there were so many other loose ends which needed tying up, such as the three players still roaming the streets, the two civilians she had brought in, and the eight drunken gamblers holed up in a room without a clue as to what was going on. Were they to find out then Hoxton would have one hell of a problem on his hands, and Ada was sure it would only end one way, like it had done in Moscow.

"Ada, you have displayed a concerning amount of empathy to the civilians over the last twenty four hours. Tell me, do I have cause for concern?" To give him his dues, the man generally would give people a chance to explain themselves. Christophe might still be alive if he had remembered that fact. As it was, he remained dead and headless and had been buried in several pieces. So with his question he offered her the opportunity to say her piece.

"Sir, as you are well aware, the girl was placed under severe distress at the hands of Christophe, and her

companion showed great strength of character to defend her against him. I saw something in both of them that I felt would be of some assistance to us"
"And if you could put a name on that something Ada?"
"It is difficult to say, sir, perhaps the best word would be Loyalty?"
"I see"
Then the old man became quiet and his brow furrowed, his mind working quietly as she sat, accustomed to these silences, until he spoke again at last.
"Ada, I trust you infinitely, I have made no secret of your value to my organisation, but I am uneasy about this. I have placed Tom in a position which will test this loyalty which you believe you saw in him, should he fail in that test then I shall have no option other than to hold you responsible. If you wish to take back your belief in them both then please tell me now, and the necessary shall be done"

She saw this coming, she knew he would put the decision back on her shoulders, give her enough rope to hang herself, and test her. Indecision was seen as weakness, so her hands were tied. She could not go back on her choice even if she wanted to. Hoxton would send Tom with Cristiano to track down the two players who held no importance to the plan, and make their pieces fit into this very messy jigsaw. They would be instructed to leave Alan Foster alone, he had become a very loose cannon and would be dealt with separately. If Tom failed to fulfil the tasks that had been laid at his door then there would also be a grave alongside Christophe, and in it would be three more bodies, and this year's event would continue in its path toward being the messiest yet.

"No, sir, I stand by my word, and I will take full responsibility for what I have done. If he fails to prove me correct then I shall kill them both myself, and then I will accept whatever punishment you deem necessary, whatever that may be, sir"
"So be it Ada, I shall allow him to continue with Cristiano, and if he succeeds in proving your faith in his character, then he may well become useful in future endeavours"
"And what of the girl, sir?"
"I will speak with her personally Ada, I have other plans for her"
"Very well, sir"

The conversation turned to the gamblers, and the touchy subject of the failed event due to one of Hoxton's employees. The cost of this failure would of course run into millions. The reimbursements of failed bets. The fee of Isaac Charles alone was seven figures. She knew what he was thinking, and she knew that he knew what she was thinking, and she also knew that he wanted her to tell him what he was thinking.
"Lukas and Yannick are still in the country, sir"
"Indeed they are Ada, indeed they are"
"Would you like me to make the call sir?"
Hoxton watched his hands a little more until his eyes flickered a touch. As he exhaled loudly a tiny fleck of spittle shot from his mouth and came to rest on the face of his gold watch. Ada watched the fleck intently as the second hand ticked past behind it, the briefest of moments where the black of the hand became magnified under the speck, and her attention shot back to her employer as he looked at her.

"Yes. Do it. Let's ensure this whole mess is cleaned up by the end of the day Ada"

Frankie Francis

Friday 30th October 2009

This is one fucked up position I'm in, I'm tellin' ya. I'm laying here, four holes in my fuckin' stomach, no fuckin' way outta this, I shoulda fuckin' known. She hasn't even finished, she got to me first, I can hear tha cries of fear all around me, mixed up with agony as tha little whispers of her gun spittin' bullets around tha room hit their targets. Bobby White's a few feet away from me, he got hit in tha throat, his hands are reaching up to tha ceiling, clawing at nothing, the guy's number is up, I'm tellin' ya, there aint no coming back from a shot in tha throat, not in my experience anyway. I'm slowly bleedin' to death here, I'm tellin' ya. Ya life can't flash before ya eyes if you slowly bleed to death from four bullets in ya stomach, no, it don't do no flashin'. Yeah, ya can take that time ya take ta bleed to death ta have a little reflect on ya life, but there aint no fuckin' flashin' goin' on. And if ya given that time ta reflect on ya life, ya better pick the good parts. Take it from me, ya don't know when tha big final pump of blood around ya heart's gonna happen, so pick tha good times. Pick tha time ya first got your fingers in a girl's pussy, pick tha time ya took a hit of ya first joint and got sick but the feelin' was unreal. Yeah, pick a time ya gonna want to remember, one that'll make ya smile. Like ya old mama pickin' ya up when ya graze ya fuckin' knee when ya fall from ya Chopper. Yeah, those tha times ya wanna be rememberin'. As the voice of experience I'm tellin' ya, do not pick tha time ya sold ya soul to the Devil and became a fuckin' badass gangster at the cost of ya own fuckin' father. Do not pick tha time ya watched ya wife and kid shot down in a hail of bullets waiting in tha car outside tha fuckin' Walmart because ya fucked with the wrong guy and he thought you were in that car but you weren't, because ya'd gone to pick up some fuckin' diapers. Do not pick tha time he looked you in the eye and laughed when he saw what he'd done. Didn't even point tha gun at you because he knew he'd just taken everything that meant anythin' to ya. Do not pick tha time you sat in total darkness cookin' up a fucked up plan for revenge. Feel free to pick the time ya stood outside the motherfucker's house watching it burn to the ground with half his fuckin' family in there, laughing at his fuckin' teenage daughter beggin' you to help her through tha window before the flames swallowed her up. I'm tellin' ya, pick tha fuckin times that'll make ya smile. Then, when ya done gettin' ya smile, ya can take the time to reflect on decisions ya made, like the one where the fuckin' devil came callin' again and put a great big proposition your way, and you fell over ya'self to take advantage of it. When half the fuckin' New York Police Department is after ya blood, ya take whatever chances you can. So ya fly ta tha fuckin' UK and ya sit ya'self in some fuckin' farmhouse and ya put almost a mil on the outcome of some poor fuckin' saps who gotta kill each other. Yeah, big boo hoo, some good people gonna die for the entertainment of some bad people. Nah, none of these people were ever that good. They all earned their places in tha game. Take the motherfucker I got my money on. Fuckin' Geoffrey. Piece a shit that he is. The shit he's done would make ya eyes water. I aint gonna go inta it, I don't have tha time, in case your attention wandered

any, I'm dyin' here, but take it from me, yeah, me, the guy is a piece a shit.
Back in the room I can feel the blood against my back, not all of it is mine. Bobby White's gone. Gave in to the pain ya know? I mean, once ya got a hole in ya neck ya, and that hole aint ya fuckin' mouth, then ya in trouble aint ya? Nah, Bobby's outta the game. Some fuckin' mysterious prick who went by the name a Jagger, that poor asshole musta died instantly, from my spot on the floor, I can see his face lookin' at me, his eyes still open, across the wooden flooring which is seperated by tiny oceans of blood, between the heads and feet of the rest of 'em, two holes in his forehead, his fuckin' brains slowly drippin' out. Yeah, take the time to reflect on those decisions that led ya to the unfortunate time where you're slipping away, unable to appreciate exactly how much blood you're losing. When ya start to lose the feeling in your hands, that's when ya should be thinkin' about those decisions, like how ya let ya fuckin' cock do the talkin', got caught with a hooker who just happened to be fifteen, so even if ya don't wanna join the fun times that are gonna happen, then you don't got a great deal a choice anyway. When a tiny little Russki bitch appears from nowhere. That fuckin' bitch. Came in all fuckin' coy and shit, like she does, played me for a fuckin' idiot. Made it sound like easy fuckin' money. She comes in now and then and pours more bourbon down our fuckin' necks, loosens our ties, plays us some calming piece of shit music that I don't even fuckin' like! Gives us regular updates on the lie of tha land with this game, how my boy, the fuckin' pederast motherfucker, is still alive. After every day that passes I'm thinkin' I could actually do this, my fuckin' filthy

piece of shit horse is gonna actually survive! So ya kinda get to be the competition when ya horse is still runnin', an' when there's this much money at stake there ain't no time to be makin' pals with any a these motherfuckers so ya don't take tha time to be playin' getting to know ya. Then, when ya can't feel ya fuckin' legs anymore, so ya feel like a swiss fuckin' roll with a head, take tha time ta remember when that same little bitch comes in one last time, smiling when she walks through the door, take the time, I'm tellin' ya, because hindsight is a great thing when ya bleedin' to death, take tha time ta think that behind that fuckin' smile, the eyes are scannin' the room, placin' every single one of us. When ya think back ya can see the bitch plannin' every shot she's gonna fire, ya consider that if ya'd been a little less fuckin' drunk ya coulda maybe took tha bitch out before she even got a single shot off, ya consider that if ya'd taken tha time ta get ta know Harry Hyde then mighta been sitting in another part of the room when she comes in, maybe get behind the motherfucker, play dead, maybe sneak out when she leaves tha room. Then ya take inta account the fact that we're in the middle a fuckin' nowhere and ya realise ya fucked. As ya body goes numb and all ya got is ya fuckin' eyes an' ears ya stop reflectin', ya watch tha room, ya listen to the groanin' comin' from all tha motherfuckers that didn't die either, but all in their own fuckin' moments of reflection. Ya realise that none of us motherfuckers is any different to anybody else, we all played the big hard ass when in our zones of comfort, but when we all bleedin' to death we're just as vulnerable as tha next man. As ya ears fail an' ya just watching whatevers in front a ya eyes, and ya can make out two motherfuckers choppin' up bodies an' makin' their way to you, that's when ya know ya fucked, an' ya know that that's a certainty as the shadow leans over ya, pulls out a fuckin' cleaver from their bag, an' whips that fuckin' cleaver right down onta ya nec-

The Memorial

Sunday 14th March 2010

Sarah Simpson (ITV News correspondent): It has been an emotional day in Sheffield today. Thousands gathered around the grounds of Sheffield Cathedral to mark the memorial of the victims of Alan Foster, who undertook a calculated and vicious killing spree in and around the city late last year, and was found guilty last week. The six victims' families each took turns to give tribute to their respective loved ones on a day where Sheffield was united in its agony. The day started at nine o'clock this morning, when a silent parade started at Meersbrook park where the first victim, Graham Capper was discovered by local woman Ethel McAvoy, and then gathered crowds of supports as the parade moved slowly into the city, up through The Moor shopping precinct, and then up to the Cathedral for eleven o'clock. Some viewers may find the following footage extremely emotional and upsetting.
Maureen Capper (Graham Capper's Mother): Graham will forever be in our hearts, never away from our thoughts. He was a beautiful person who never asked anything of anybody, and always went out of his way to help others. Please look after him God, please look after our baby boy.
John Capper (Graham Capper's father): Dear God, our Graham is yours now, take care of him, keep him out of trouble, please. He wasn't perfect but he was ours, and he was the glue that held our lives together, I will miss you son, so, so much. You'll never know

anymore how much we love you. You'll be the best scrum half in Heaven my boy. Show them how it's done. We, your mum and me, we love you, forever. Sleep well son.
Tina Wallett (Lisa's Mother): She were the best mammy in the world to little Kelsey, Jordan, Crystal, and Jonty, always made sure they were clothed and fed. Lisa was no angel in life, but in death she will be the most beautiful angel in Heaven. Lisa, we all miss you. Please, watch over us and look after us and make sure we're safe.
Kelsey (Lisa Wallett's daughter): Dear God, please look after my mam, please make sure she is safe and happy, please-
Sarah Simpson: At this point Lisa Wallett's nine year old daughter broke down in tears and was led away by her grandmother, who continued little Kelsey's heartfelt plea.
Tina Wallett: Please make my mam the happiest mam in heaven. Let her look down and be smiling and proud of her children. Amen.
Gina Harrison (Ruby Spenner's partner): Before Ruby, I never knew that love at first sight could ever truly exist. I thought it was something only found in films and love songs. Ruby made my life complete, we were two pieces of a single jigsaw, we were two halves of the same person. My life will never be the same again, I'll never know a love like the one I have with you Ruby, the world is a worse place without you, and will be a worse place until the day I die. Sweet dreams my angel face, I will see you again one day.
Sarah Simpson: As the day went on the emotions were raised for each one of the speakers in the cathedral, but

it wasn't as peaceful as it should have been, as the protesters who have been ever present as this particular story has unfolded, still picketing against the fact that Alan Foster was given a full trial when they believe he wasn't fit to stand, given that he suffers from Dissociative Identity Disorder, or Multiple Personality Disorder, and it is felt that he should be sectioned under the mental health act. I spoke to one of the protesters.

Daisy Beckford (Protester): Alan Foster is far from innocent, but that isn't the point, the point is that this country has failed him, it has failed yet another lost soul who has succumbed to mental illness.

Sarah Simpson: But do you believe that the memorial service paying tribute to his victims is the right place to be protesting?

Daisy Beckford: I have sympathy for the victims, of course I do, but we cannot allow the circus to continue under the impression that it is right to try a man with severe mental issues in the same manner than a man who is entirely sane.

Sarah Simpson: That doesn't answer my question, do you believe this a proper place to be making your point when surrounded by the grief of six families at the hands of the man you are protesting for?

Daisy Beckford: It is always the right time to change the world, no matter how controversial it might be.

Sarah Simpson: The longer the day went, the more emotions were threatening to boil over, which culminated in the son of Geoffrey Whittaker attacking several protesters and being arrested and taken away only minutes after his tribute to his father.

Stephen Whittaker (Geoffrey Whittaker's Son): Dad was a quiet man, who kept himself to himself, always

happy to help and a founding member of the local youth club, he surrounded himself with the community's children to keep himself young, and provide support whenever they needed it. Dad would never have hurt a fly, and it hurts so much knowing he's been taken from us. Please sleep well Dad, rest in peace big man.
Sarah Simpson: After the service I spoke to Daniel Jackson, the man who would have been Alan Foster's seventh victim, and also a man who has remained synonymous with this case
Daniel Jackson: My heart goes out to the families of the victims, there's this part of me that wishes I could change places with all of the other victims, I'd change places with any of them if only so that their family can go without the grief for just a minute. I count my lucky stars every single day that I got away from him, and I vow to make the most of every second that I'm breathing. God bless everybody that has come out to pay tribute today. God bless you all.
Sarah Simpson: So as the sun sets in Sheffield, six families have paid tribute to their loved ones, and this is a day that they shall remember for as long as they live, as will I, and they will hope that this service finally closes the door on the issue, takes the spotlight from their lives, and allows them to grieve in peace. Sarah Simpson, reporting for ITV News, in Sheffield.

Isaac Charles (ii)

Thursday 1st April 2010

What a wicked web one weaves! How marvellous! Things have become awfully good fun of late. The wicked multiple personalitied witch is dead! And on April Fool's Day too! What an exciting coincidence, you really could not make it up! Facebook will be awash with disbelief! Phase one is well and truly complete. My protégé is revelling in his role of media darling, they can't get enough of him! Sometimes I find myself in awe of how quickly and easily he has taken to the task, but then of course I remember myself and it passes. Everything passes. Oh, yes, believe me, everything passes, what's the old adage? Oh yes, Today's news is tomorrow's chip shop paper. However crass the saying is, it still speaks volumes, the sentiment still stands. Today he is the darling of the media, tomorrow he'll be cast aside, and I shall cut him loose, distance myself from him, and he will want to find himself joining forces in a "Celebrity" dating/swapping/eating, delete as appropriate, programme with the soap actress who quit her role as the busty barmaid in the hopes of finding proper work in more credible television dramas, then when that has dried up he will attain his money for keeping up the lifestyle he has become accustomed to so easily and happily, by working the nightclub circuit, answering the inane questions of drunkards, taking up the local whores on their offers of fellatio between the bottle bins that reside out the back. Yes, he'll find himself desperately grasping for more of the limelight, like a heroin addict crying into their sleeping bag by the doors of a now defunct well known high street store, chewed coffee cup in hand, shivering and trying to save up enough spare change to purchase another hit. And when the nightclub scene have tired of him he will continue his downward spiral and probably die. Believe me, this is the cycle I have witnessed so very many times, this is something I have instigated so very many times.

The trick is to quit whilst you are ahead, much in the way that creators of popular television shows cannot seem to get a grasp of, oh yes believe me, the most popular program will continue until it's audience have long since tired, and, much like the celebrity, it will become a jaded parody of itself. The trick is to raise the subject to the peak of their potential, and to recognise when their star is on the wane, and cut them loose. Believe me, my protégé is acting in a carbon copy manner of the last one, you know the one? Yes, the man who won forty-odd million pounds on the lottery but had a somewhat controversial crime record, given that he was on the sex offender's register, that same man who faced the red-tops with creditable fearlessness, who appeared in magazines attempting to justify exposing himself to schoolchildren, then found himself beaten to death by a mob of vigilante parents? He might still be alive had he not been advised by a certain individual, who shall remain nameless, oh okay, I shall take the credit, yes, it was me. I've said it before and I shall say it again in the future, without doubt, do not get into this business if you have any appreciation whatsoever, for the concept of morality. I suppose you could dub me the Robin Hood of Public Relations. I took from the rich paedophile, and then I gave him to the public, I convinced him it was a good idea to tell the world about what he had done, to try to show a more human side to your average every day paedophile, and the public did the rest. I simply love the public. So very easily manipulated, like one giant ball of plasticine with a billion faces. Oh my, I seem to have digressed somewhat, where was I? Oh, yes, one Daniel Jackson, a man who continues to be the flavour of the month. Not for long dear boy! The cutting loose of Daniel will be a delicate matter, given the circumstances in which he came to be in my circle of gravity. Understandably he may be a little, upset, when I advise him that I will no longer represent him, then he may wish to loosen his own lips with regards certain truths, and refresh the country's zeal for his activities, yes, one must anticipate the inevitable. Once his light begins to fade he will wish to change his story, start to, remember, certain aspects of the story that we have together worked so hard at weaving into the annals of time. He may, as a bona fide celebrity, begin to believe that he is untouchable, that everything he does is in the public eye so he is somehow safe from that which he is hiding. I believe the popular phrasing is "Too big for his boots", indeed, he will develop an ego which he cannot control, ask people if they know who he is when he is turned away from parties, probably tell them that he will have their jobs by the time morning comes. So, as his story begins its end, it is time to bring the curtain down gracefully, he has served his purpose, and earned his stripes. By the time you read about him again you will be reading his obituary after he is found overdosed with a needle in his arm, that, on the surface appears to be yet another celebrity who gave in to the pressures of being in the public eye, beneath the surface, well, one wouldn't wish to incriminate oneself. You will be passing the time of day with your neighbour by casually describing the whole thing as a terrible tragedy, but you will not give it a great deal more thought. You will have the children to pick up from school. You will have the bed sheets to bring in from hanging in the garden because the rain has started to fall. The electricity bill now has a red border, and your dog has developed a stomach ulcer so that will be another outgoing you need to cater for. My point is that every matter in your life will be more pressing than the poor corpse of a once-famous chancer who just happened to be in the right place, at the right time. And do you know what? The next one that comes along, he'll be mine too!

Alan (ii)

Thursday April 1st 2010

Three weeks had passed since they had found themselves here, and Alan was still no easier about what was happening to them. Algernon had, of course, made terrible enemies for them, amongst both the inmates, and the guards. His propensity for speaking Alan's mind had led to several altercations, with varying results. When he felt at his strongest Alan would avoid the confrontation, apologise and move on under the intense scrutiny of the dozens of pairs of eyes of his fellow inmates, physically flinching at the slightest movement from any of them, but none of them ever lashed out because when he was forced into the background he would find himself battling with guards after Algernon had bitten the throat out of one of the other cons who had taken it upon himself to provide a little vigilante action against the newest serial killer in Wakefield. After that occasion he spent a week in solitary confinement, with nobody but Algernon for company, and he became steadily more unsteady in his own mind. He had long since given up the hope of losing Algernon, and on some days he would fight back, in the fear of being pushed so far out of the picture that Alan would never be allowed speak his own mind again. Only the most hardened of prisoners would go anywhere near him, for despite his appearance, in Algernon he had created a fearless personality, fearsome even.

Although he was segregated with the rest of the violent criminals, who had all in their own way hurt people in the past, their true colours would inevitably come to the fore when faced with somebody who would fight back and face them down. Algernon was so volatile, one minute he was cheery, talkative, and attempting to pick Alan's mood up, but then he could turn, and his retorts were as hurtful as his fists, and he loved to talk with his fists, and occasionally, his member. A young gang member who had stabbed several enemies in an attack on rival grounds and found himself playing the big man in prison, had found himself as the object of Algernon's attentions since he had attempted to steal the food from Alan's tray.

"Oh dear, young fellow, awfully sorry to let you down, but unless that food is returned to my tray post-haste then you may well find yourself raped!" Algernon had bellowed into the young man's face, attracting the attentions and amusement of the others in the canteen.

"Yeah? You think you gonna put your fuckin' dick in me? Yeah? Fuck you man, man's a pussy'ole" he had replied, his face contorted in disgust at the very idea, and started to walk away with the sandwich he had graciously stolen from Alan's tray. Algernon had stood them up, and followed the young man.

"Oh, you are going to WISH I was a pussy hole young chap!" and commenced smashing the lad's face into the corner of a table, the cons sitting around the table all retreating from the sprays of blood that emanated from his rapidly opening face, with cries requesting for him to calm down. Inside their head, Alan watched on in horror as Algernon pulled their penis out of their pants and commenced ripping down the underwear of his prey. It was only at that point that the guards stepped in amid calls that they were about to do something very disturbing to the young man's anus. They dragged, a guard holding each limb, with both hands, the struggling serial killer back to his cell, his erect penis poking out of his lowered trousers, stiffly directed toward the floor.

Today, the bruised, scabbed and stitched up swollen face of the young man appeared again, and this time was far from the bold young spirit who felt himself to be tough enough to tackle an old hand like Algernon. No, the lad this time was almost apologetic in his manner, standing to one side whilst the bringer of his pain silently strolled past, watching him through his one good eye, the other sealed up and purple from where it connected with the corner of the table several times. Algernon had been quiet today, he was almost satisfied that Alan had become a feared member of the prison community, however much ridicule he would receive behind his back it rarely happened to his face. Some of the harder men still called him Schizo when they were referring to him in the room, and on the occasions when Algernon spoke up, it became a battle of words rather than fists, clearly neither Algernon, nor the con he was arguing with fancied any clear cut chances to come out on top, so they respected each other's space, and the banter would fizzle out with neither reputation tarnished. So today Algernon had indeed remained subdued, and Alan had been handed a rare opportunity to explore the freedom of his own mind, and had chosen to feed it in the library. Pulling down an old Enid Blyton book from the shelf he allowed himself a smile at the title Five Go Adventuring Again, he remembered it well. More memories of his younger self, happier ones, came rushing into his mind. He took himself to a quiet corner of the library and opened it up. It was an old book and that familiar smell of yellowed pages fluttered under his nose, bringing with it a sense of normality, of being away from these walls that kept him away from that changed life he had promised himself. The smell ignited memories of the Botanical Gardens, simply in its association to freedom. His eyes followed the story ravenously, tearing the words from the page and absorbing them with his imagination, he loved the simple writing style that Enid purveyed, allowed him to create his own world. He reflected sadly that this was what got him into trouble in the first place. He wished he was a stronger person, somebody who dealt with life head on rather than dodging everything, from everyday people, to paying bills, to having his hair cut. He wished he had been able to make friends, to look people in the eye, but he wasn't. He was a coward who avoid confrontation. He was a coward who created and developed an alter ego to deal with things on his behalf, an alter ego that had become the immediate opposite to his own self, somebody brash, and confrontational, who would use threats of violence, often sexual, combined with actions of violence, often sexual, to get his own way. He spoke their minds with wicked glee, and he had brought them here. Alan saw a brighter light in the future. Perhaps he could make something of himself, get an education? The book before him opened up so many potential changes to his life, he liked to fantasise like this when Algernon was on his quiet days. In his free mind he saw himself walking out of here in however many years a changed man, an articulate and educated man. Whilst his mind's eye was wandering, his eye ball failed to register the

shadow that danced over his shoulder, casting a minor increase in darkness. He was floating in a happy fantasy, one where he was an upstanding member of society, not the useless piece of sh... He hesitated to even think the swear word... Not the useless piece of rubbish he had become. As his mind was being licked by these fantasies, he scarcely registered the knife slide into his back, aided by the firm hand on his shoulder pulling him onto it. He looked down to see the end of it piercing the fabric of his prison clothes as it had made its way through his entire body, and looked over his shoulder to see his attacker. The young man, a monster with his swollen eye, his purple and green bruised face, the crusted clotted blood that bordered his cuts, and from the corner of his mangled face his good eye was spiked with pure malice and hatred. Alan simply smiled at him and peacefully watched the blood soak into his sweater, he coughed, waking up Algernon.
"Oh my, I leave you alone for one blasted minute and you allow some scamp to do this?- Shut up Algernon, please, just shut up, you've caused enough..."
And they faded away, holding onto a Famous Five adventure story, in a happy place.

David Harston BA (Hons)

Monday 5th April 2010

And so it ends. I remember the start of all of this. Less than six months ago I wrote my first article on what would become one of the biggest stories of the last decade, terrorist action notwithstanding. Now I'm on the shortlist for a major journalism award, and working on an acceptance speech, you know? Just in case. Six months. Life moves so fast. It's something of an irony that I find out about my place on the shortlist a few days after my last article on Alan Foster. I've followed the story from start to finish, and voiced my opinion at every opportunity. I dug the deepest, I spent the most money on gaining information through my "connections", I deserve my place on that shortlist and nobody can ever take that away from me.
The nationals got a hold of it far too late to offer what they could call comprehensive coverage from start to finish. I was there from the start, when Graham Capper showed up dead and naked, I remember sitting at my computer, puzzling over how to tackle it. I chose to take the sensitive route, play it safe, but as the bodies mounted up the easier it was to speculate, to build drama into my stories instead of the neutral exercises in fact giving. There were no facts. Alan Foster left nothing except naked corpses that had bled dry. There was no weapon found. They never found the clothes. It has long since been accepted that he burned them. In fact, witnesses and the fact that he was a fruitcake aside, there was no real proof. The courts gave him all the rope he needed to hang himself, and boy did he

hang himself. From my spot in the press box I found myself cringing at the crap that came out of his mouth, you know, where the hairs go up at the back of your neck out of embarrassment? Well, they were consistently up, and I mean *all the time.* So whilst I'm speculating I'm gaining more and more of a, fan base? Following? My number of twitter followers had climbed to well over ten thousand, people have been clamouring to hear what I have to say. My "connections" will forever remain anonymous, but they will have to take huge credit for the information that came my way, even if I cannot mention them in my speech, I must make sure I thank her, I mean, them, personally. Without them I would have nothing written, I'd still be writing fluff pieces about the victims, through a lack of actual knowledge. Yeah, I'd be known as the go-to guy if you want to pay tribute to somebody in the local press, the walking obituary, yeah right. No, no such fears for me, I can tell you that. I'm the rock 'n' roll journo of The Star, the man who invented breaking news, a pioneer! Yeah, you'll have read some of my stories by now, the day I broke it that we were looking at multiple killers, that was the edition that broke sales records, and I wasn't wrong was I? Just because it was the same hand, it doesn't mean that it wasn't still two different people that committed the crimes does it? Technically accurate I think. I have the front page framed in my apartment, pretty damn proud of myself for that one. Yeah, I speculated Eastern Europeans, but didn't we all? They're the new fall guys nowadays. My "connection" came to me shortly after that front page, it proved that I'd moved to a whole new arena in the role of Field Journalist, people were coming to me. Nobody else, me. It meant I didn't have to go scrabbling through bins looking for scraps of evidence, well, not so much, anymore. She, they, seemed to know things, I mean, I would never ask how the information came about, but the things they told me about seemed so much closer to what the truth could be, guiding me toward what the truth actually was. You know I was the first to break it that they'd caught somebody? You know I was there when they caught him? Yeah I was, both myself and Steve, my photographer. I guess my "connection" was feeding the police the same information that they were feeding me, but who am I to complain? I only have to take it to the bobbies anyway.

The body that was found in the subway, shot in the face, you remember the one? Well, everybody else was tying it to the Foster case because Alan Foster was on camera shortly before. I was the first to declare them totally unrelated, you know how? Yeah, because I was the one who dug deep enough and discovered that Justin Heaton was a cocaine dealer who had it in him to attack several people in a bar only a few hours earlier, the man was trouble, he more than likely made several enemies, not least Thomas Whitfield, the man that the police are still searching for in connection with his murder. It's insane to think that however much publicity they throw at it, not one person has seen Whitfield since 28th October last year. My guess? He's probably dead himself. So, I declared the cases totally unrelated, and guess what? Everybody followed suit. One step ahead of the game at every turn, that's how you do it!

I'm sitting in front of my PC once again, this time no longer trying to find a new angle on how to hook the readership, no, this time I'm trying to write my acceptance speech, you know? Just in case. I'm thinking I should thank my parents first of all, they'd love that, yeah, but I'm not going in for any of that God shit, everybody that wins an award sticks a plug in for God, nah, not me, I'm gonna try to make it different. Maybe thank Alan Foster for giving me such a great story to work on. Now, yeah, I'm thinking it might be a bit in bad taste, but hey, we're all journalists, they'll get the irony I'm sure. We all have the same desire for that one story that'll break us into the big time, I was just lucky that mine came so early in my career. That'll go in, definitely, they'll appreciate that. What probably won't go in, is the fact that whoever the highest bidder is, will be my next employer, if I win this award I can take my pick. I'm not gonna sit here in Sheffield wasting my talents, my career, my life. No, I'm already looking at flats in London, Kensington maybe. I do remember thinking that the world could be my oyster, well mate, it most certainly fucking is!

Jess (ii)

Friday 30th October 2009

He hadn't moved for close to a minute, just watched her, the air whistling through his nose became the only thing either of them could hear, his breath made heavier from his walk from what she assumed to be the surveillance room to hers. Her fingers gripped the bedclothes tighter to her body and she let out an involuntary whimper, her eyes felt like they were drying out from the lack of blinking, she couldn't take the chance that something would happen if she did blink. Without Tom she felt like she was nothing, that they could do anything they wanted to her and that there was simply nothing she could do about it, and even if he was here, they could still do whatever they wanted, but she'd feel safe, less alone. The old man cleared his throat and took a step to her.
"You and your young friend are in a bit of a pickle, wouldn't you say?"
She said nothing to him -she didn't know what to say- and watched him edge another step closer, for some reason he seemed less than the crime lord that he appeared to be when he was in his element, sitting behind his huge desk, in his huge chair. Here, he appeared frail, more vulnerable. The eyes were still shifty, but in the broken light of the room she could see his sagging skin hanging loose from his skull, his wrinkles created deep heavy shadows that cracked their way across his greying face. He looked like he could very much be at home covered in a dust sheet in some old forgotten room in a Victorian mansion converted

into a tourist attraction. But he wasn't, he was here, and her thoughts had taken long enough for him to elaborate on his statement.
"Yes, I do suppose it was a rhetorical question, and your tear stained face tells me your answer anyhow. As I have told you, I would like to have a word with you, may I?"
He was requesting her permission to take a seat on the small chest beside her bed. The human side he was displaying was almost unnerving Jess, her heart jolted in her chest as she felt herself nodding quietly which acted as the permission he had asked for. Leaning on his walking stick he made a laboured effort to lower himself onto the chest. In a momentary flash of good nature, Jess found herself climbing out of the bed to assist him in his endeavours, which he accepted with good grace.
"Thank you, young lady"
Shifting on his backside he made himself more comfortable and turned to her.
"How are you feeling?" the question threw her somewhat, so far the man had been cold, calculated and commanding, she had expected him to immediately bark orders at her. How was she feeling though? Scared? Alone? Fucking really angry? All of the above? Yes, all of the above. But how could she answer that? He obviously knew how she was feeling, he'd no doubt had women in this position before, probably asked them the same question, before drilling a bullet into their head and then instructing one of his underlings to bury the evidence. He watched her expectantly.
"Seriously?" she attempted incredulity but it came across as broken and weak, she realised she'd done

nothing but cry for hours, and hadn't used her voice since, when? In the car with Tom probably.
"I don't ask questions without sincerity young lady, I find it difficult to waste my words, so yes, seriously, and be as honest as you can please"
She thought about it for a moment, and decided to chance it, tell him the truth, get it out there, however much it hurt.
"Okay, since you asked, I'm scared, I need Tom. He makes me feel safe. You took him away so I feel scared, and angry. And in pain. Your, friend, raped me, him being dead doesn't change what he did, and how I feel about it, it's not going to wipe any memory of his grubby hands all over me. I won't ask if you've ever been raped at gunpoint sir, but believe me, it's not very nice" she'd felt her voice raising in volume and more emotional so she stopped, and took a breath. The old man blurred in her vision behind the tears that were welling up. And to think she thought she'd cried herself dry. He handed her a handkerchief which she accepted and dabbed at her eyes with.
"And for another thing, all Tom did was answer your friend's telephone, as far as I can tell he helped you to catch him, why are we being treated like-?"
The old man held his hand up to halt her spiel.
"One thing at a time please, we shall get to your friend in due course. I do feel obliged to tell you that the man you refer to as my friend is no such thing. He was an employee who, how can I put it? Who bit the hand that fed him, and will no longer be around to cause pain to anybody, not, I suppose, that that would be a great deal of comfort to yourself, but still"
He went quiet, as if in thought, then looked back at her.

"So you need your friend Tom? Allow me the liberty of asking you something else, it's something of a morality question"
The man didn't seem to tire of asking questions, but at least he was being civil, almost human.
"Okay?"
"Would you kill somebody to protect somebody you loved?"
"What?"
"I don't believe I spoke a foreign language, please answer the question"
"But, no, I wouldn't"
"What if that person you were asked to kill was a convicted paedophile? Or somebody who had desecrated graves for his own amusement? What if that person had suffocated his own whore of a mother in order to be free of the anger she caused? What then? Could you find it in yourself to do it? To save the one you love?"
"I don't know"
"No, I don't suppose you do, until a proposal was placed before you, you do not know what you would do"
"Exactly" Jess wondered where this was going, and in her head it was going to a place where blood would be shed, where she'd be forced to kill somebody, for who? Tom? She didn't love him though, although, she felt she could, given time, or opportunity, but why would they ask her to kill somebody for Tom? Surely it would be the other way around?
"Your friend Tom, he answered in the positive, he admitted that yes, he would kill somebody, to save you. How do you feel about that?"

She felt a flutter in her chest, a rush of something, a new emotion to throw in with the rest of the ones already flushing around her body, her eyes flickered, and a slight curl of a smile tickled her lips, replaced quickly with the reality of what she had been told, and a fear for Tom and his safety.
"What has he done? Where is he?"
"I am the one asking questions just now young lady, so please, answer mine"
"I don't understand, you're asking how it makes me feel to hear that he's going to kill a paedophile to save my life? On what planet is that a question any normal person could answer? What kind of people are you?"
She instantly regretted the outburst but the old man was going round in circles with his questions, and his *How does it make you feel?* shit. She just wanted him to get to the point.
"Evidently, very bad people, we do bad things to other bad people, that is about as much as you need to know just now, young lady"
"But Tom and I aren't bad people, we're just human, we've probably made mistakes, as many as the next person, why do we need to be involved?"
"Collateral damage is to be expected. Of course you haven't a clue what has been going on, and you may never find out"
He sighed, obviously aggravated at her failure to play the game.
"Clearly you are a fiery young woman, I suppose your red hair is very apt. Okay, allow me to change tack here. Your life depends on Tom returning here after having killed two people. One of those people is a paedophile at large, with any number of possible

victims, who we have photographic evidence of, masturbating in front of a seven year old girl. The other spends his time in cemeteries, smoking drugs and pulling down gravestones, urinating onto the very same gravestones. This is a man who has no respect for anything, not even the eternal resting places of children, wives, grand-parents, would you say that they deserved to die before you? I can stop this, but it will be at the cost of yourself and Tom, now, who deserves to die? The kiddie fiddler and the grave desecrator, or two people who happened to be in the wrong place at the wrong time?"
She thought about this, what did a person have to do to deserve to die? She always considered herself a liberal kind of person, the idea of capital punishment was an argument she often avoided, the same as religion, people felt too strongly about things nowadays. But then she found herself thinking about it too much, the point of them deserving to die wasn't the issue, it was about saving her own skin, but the old man was discussing morality, was it a test?
"Kill them. Kill them both" she finally declared.
The old man allowed a glimmer of a smile, and looked deep into her eyes.
"I thought so. Mankind will always claim the moral high ground above anything else, but when it really boils down to it, it's dog eat dog isn't it?"
His roundabout way of getting to his point irked Jess to a point of irritation, and her mind flashed back to Tom in the bar yesterday, and maybe it was the fact that he was here, alone, looking as vulnerable as he did, but part of her forgot the kind of man that he actually was. She took a chance.

"Can I ask you something?"
"Go ahead"
"You said you don't like to waste your words, but just now you made a really big meal of making that point, is it intentional or do you not even realise you're doing it?"
"I beg your pardon?"
"Am I speaking a foreign language?"
He appeared confused at the balls she was displaying, this was a man who seemed to have never been spoken to like this before. His mind appeared to be juggling a variety of possible retorts, but fell flat, and simply began to applaud her.
"Touché, young woman, genuinely, touché. I like you, you're a ballsy little vixen aren't you?"

Extract from Two Minds, a screenplay by Vincent Sharpe

18. Int. A pub. Evening
A GROUP OF YOUNG MEN are gathered in a bar, they appear to be celebrating something. In the corner of the bar, seated alone, is ALAN, he grips his glass of juice tight. A bead of sweat rolls down his forehead and drops onto his glasses. He looks from his shivering left hand which sits on his lap, and over the rim of his glasses to the YOUNG MEN. The noise grows louder and louder in his head, his head becomes ever more sweaty, and his left hand clenches tight. ALAN stares even firmer at the men and suddenly stands.

ALAN
(As ALGERNON)
Oh will you bloody idiots be quiet?! Can't a chap enjoy a peaceful Sunday without scallywags spoiling the atmosphere with their bloody noise?

The bar goes quiet as everybody turns to look at ALAN. Suddenly the group of men laugh in unison. One of them begins to chant and clap his hands.

MAN
He's a scallywag, he's a scallywag

The MAN'S FRIENDS join in and the chant continues.

GROUP OF MEN
(In unison)
He's a scallywag, he's a scallywag

ALAN begins to hyperventilate and grips his glass tighter still. Suddenly the glass smashes in his hand and ALAN runs past the jeering group and out of the bar.

CUT TO:

19. Ext. Street. Evening.
ALAN is running along the street and ducks into an alleyway crying.

ALAN
(Alternating between personalities)
Stop being such a wimp old bean-
Algernon, please, let me be-
Balderdash! Let's go and have some fun-
I want no part of this-

Very well old chap, get to buggery then!

ALAN is no longer crying, his gait alters and his eyes dilate. He stands up straighter, almost more confident, he looks over his shoulder and smiles a wicked smile.

DISSOLVE TO:

20. Ext. Garden. Evening.
LISA exits her front door and walks into her garden holding a mobile telephone to her ear. She seems jumpy and agitated and she walks as she talks.

LISA
(into the telephone)
Are you in yet? Come on Kingy, am goin' out me head here, can I come round now? Please mate? Yes. Yeah, I've got the money, I just want a tenner's worth. Alright, twenty minutes yeah? Promise? Alright, see ya in a bit.

LISA snaps her telephone shut and waits around by a fence in a snicket. Her eyes focus upon a tall garden gate, and it's wrought iron circular handle.

CUT TO:

21. Ext. Street. Evening.
ALAN is walking and staring forward, is breath is heavy but focussed.

CUT TO:

22. Ext. Snicket. Evening.
LISA turns to look behind her, uneasily, there is nothing there. Her attention is taken by the fluttering of a bat which skitters through the trees above her head.

CUT TO:

23. Ext. Street. Evening.
ALAN continues to walk, he turns into the same snicket that LISA is standing in. He sees her in the distance, her back to him.

CUT TO:

24. Ext. Snicket. Evening.
LISA is in a world of her own, watching the trees over her head, she does not notice ALAN striding up behind her, concealing a knife in his hand, pointed up underneath the sleeve of his wax jacket. From ALAN's P.O.V. LISA turns to face him and he

punches her in the face. She drops to the floor screaming.

ALAN holds his hand over her mouth, and she whimpers as he kisses her head.

ALAN
(As ALGERNON)
Don't be frightened you pretty young filly, this old stallion will make it quick

LISA looks at ALAN with fear in her eyes. Tears stream over the hand that is clamped over her mouth. She closes her eyes and screams out beneath the hand as ALAN draws his knife across her throat and exhales in satisfaction as her blood sprays over the fence.

CUT TO:

25. Ext. Snicket. Evening.
ALAN is peeling the last of LISA's clothes from her lifeless body. He smiles down at the corpse as he stands. A flash of sadness appears in his eyes and then the wicked grin appears. ALAN pulls at the flies of his trousers, takes his penis out and appears to be masturbating furiously, after about ten seconds his eyes roll

up into his head as he reaches
climax, he smiles.

ALAN
(as ALGERNON)
That was bloody brilliant my dear.
Sweet dreams.
ALAN turns on his heels, carrying the
clothes he has taken from LISA.

FADE TO BLACK

Daniel (ii)

Saturday 2nd October 2010

"So what were it like when he had thee in thi kecks? Did thy have thi bollocks aart?" Laughter rocked through the dance floor. Another stupid question from the pissed up population of Barnsley. The degradation had got slowly worse this last few months. There was a time when he was driven from interview to interview, Mr Charles was at his side at all times. Now the man had stopped answering his calls, stopped returning his calls, stopped making calls. Everything was done through his assistant. Daniel remembered when he'd had an assistant of his own. Not anymore. He would receive a call from the ICO office, and his heart would skip a beat thinking that they had a good job for him, but it never happened anymore. The best he was getting were these shitty question and answer sessions at midnight in towns that had more charity shops and discount pastry franchises than they had actual population. Drunken scumbags who were so far beneath him they shouldn't even be able to see the tick on the bottom of his Nikes, let alone be allowed direct access to him, to be able to further ingratiate themselves with the slags they had come out with by degrading him with questions that came from the very bottom of the gutter. In an eighties-themed bar in Chesterfield he had been forced to walk off after a heckler demanded that they "Get that fuckin' poof off stage and get the fuckin' tunes back on!". The money was drying up already, Mr Charles had convinced him it would last forever, so he'd bought jewellery, rented a flash pad in the city

centre, sorted out some of his old crew, really gone to town on making his life as comfortable as possible. The apartment had to go last month, the fees he was commanding were barely enough to keep him in weed and coke, let alone somewhere to do the stuff, so he had to downsize, move to a five hundred a month apartment that overlooked Devonshire Green, every time he looked out of the window he was reminded of the few weeks that put him here, he would look down and watch the skate park, where he first caught sight of the NHS glasses motherfucker. That piece of shit arsehole went and selfishly died shortly after he got banged up, which slightly increased interest in Daniel again, but it had been declining, and he was forced to do ever more desperate things to stay in the limelight. He'd done a mental checklist of shows he would try to hook himself up with, Celebrity Big Brother; I'm a Celebrity, Get Me Out Of Here; Dancing on Ice. None of them would touch him. Not even the makers of Celebrity Coach Trip would go anywhere near him, it was like he had suddenly been cursed. His luck had left him, much like Isaac Fucking Charles had, and it looked like it was no coincidence. He was being phased out.
He looked down at the asker of the question, and smiled that smile he did when he was asked something that was intended as less than serious, that smile that humoured the enquirer, but also allowed any eagle eyed witness to see that he was pitying them, but something in him broke, he couldn't do this anymore. He was a somebody, not one of these losers, or the fucking pseudo-celebrity pricks he met on the circuit. He'd left his old life behind long ago, but it smelled like it was edging closer back to him. The people he'd been

avoiding, getting larger on the horizon. He was aware that he was now just staring at the guy in the audience, the laughter had died down, they were staring back. He stuttered over his words.
"What was it like?"
"Yeah, did thy have a stiffy?"
"A what? You're askin' me if I had a fuckin' boner when I was about to be fuckin' killed man?"
He moved his gaze from the guy in the audience and cast his eyes over a blonde girl in the front, holding a bright blue alcopop.
"Man's asking a man if I got a fuckin' boner? I'm about to get my fuckin' throat sliced open like a fuckin' fish?"
She didn't respond, the whole crowd waited with baited breath, like they could anticipate that they were about to witness something special. A breakdown of catastrophic proportions.
"You fuckin' idiots in your fuckin' council houses, fuck all to live for. Happy to get pissed up seven nights a week, no fuckin' ambition, have the balls to ask me if I got a fuckin' boner when I'm about to die?! Have you any fuckin' idea what it feels like to be that close to not breathin'? Man's are idiots man. Simple in the fuckin' head yeah?"
He tapped the side of his head, his cherry brandy splashed up over the edge of his glass and onto his face, it felt cool under the heavy lights that powered down onto him on the stage, then warmed up and he couldn't feel it anymore. The bouncers edged closer to the stage. A giant bald one, his waistcoat raised between the buttons from where his gut was too big to be held in properly, his rolled up sleeves revealing arms covered in tattoos, held back one of his colleagues, malice

coating his big rubbery head like the sticky coating on a toffee apple. He was enjoying the show.
"Look at you, standing there drinkin' your cheap watered down beer and sugary vodka shit. You ever made thirty K in four hours? You ever been to a film premiere in Paris?"
The room was silent. Beneath the glare of the red, green, yellow lights blazing down onto his sweating head he could see a hundred faces looking at him. A voice called out from the back.
"What tha doin' here then dickhead? Skint?"
Daniel dropped the microphone and jumped from the stage, swinging his fists at whoever he could. His right fist caught the blonde girl in the jaw and she dropped to the floor screaming blue murder. Arms gripped themselves around him from behind, the familiar tattoos of the shithead bouncer squeezing tight around his torso, lifting him from his feet and pulling him out of the trajectory of the many bottles and glasses being pelted his way. The jeering became drowned out by the DJ excitedly and rapidly placing a dance record onto his decks in an attempt to divert the baying crowd.
From his viewpoint he could see the blonde girl being tended to by another bouncer, and the whole of the club disappeared behind the fire exit doors he was being dragged through. The bouncer threw him to the floor.
"What the fuck does tha think tha wa' upta? Fuckin' dickhead! They'll rip thee apart!" he growled loudly as he pulled Daniels face to meet his own.
"Fuck 'em man, fuck you, nobody motherfucker"
"Yeah? Fuck me? Wanna go take em on yer daft prick?"
"Just fuckin' leave me alone yeah?"

The bouncer picked him up roughly and dragged him to his changing room, pushed him through the door to the dark, damp, grey room. Posters of The Chuckle Brothers, failed X Factor rejects and people who came sixth on Big Brother. Adrenaline coursed its way through his body, with his fists clenched tightly he threw a punch at the smiling gurning face of Barry Chuckle looking out and mocking him, the plastered wall cracked beneath his moustached head. The entire montage of minor celebrities was filled with moustaches. Without looking for them he knew that if the Chuckles were up there then Keith Harris and Orville would be up there too, no longer appealing to the popular audience, making a living out of performing to an adult audience who remembered them from childhood, turning his puppet from an innocent hero to the children, now earning a crust by delivering innuendo laden sets. The thought calmed him down, sitting on an orange plastic chair he lowered his head and watched the floor, allowing him the time to get his breath back, and reflect on what had just happened. Who knew? Maybe the outburst would drag him back into the limelight, a half page feature in the middle of The Sun, maybe some of them took photos of him swinging his fists, as much as he felt bad for hitting the girl, he couldn't help but think she'd probably sell her story for a few grand. The lucky bitch. A knock at the door brought his mind back to the fore.
"Yeah?" No response.
"I said yeah?!" he raised his voice, perhaps the person on the other side was slightly deafened by the pumping bass from the club floor. He wasn't going to move for anybody.

"Come in!" He roared. Another knock. Muttering profanities he finally relented and stormed to the door, pulling it open, his face set to scowl.
"Are you fuckin' deaf-?" Confusion took the reins in the Daniel's facial expression Olympics as he was faced with somebody familiar. He knew he'd met this man, but couldn't place where. They looked at each other briefly. The man smiled, and plunged a needle into Daniel's neck, pushing down heavily on the end. He felt himself drowning in a rush of beautiful proportions, a heavenly fire danced through his veins, his head swimming in euphoria. His knees buckled as the man pushed him into the room and stepped in, closing the door behind him.
"What the fuuuuuck man? Who are you?" he heard himself say, but he felt detached from his own head.
"Don't you remember me?" the man said, then an echo repeated the question.
"What have you done to me? It feels, it feels nice"
"It doesn't matter pal, for sure, I'm your devil, night night sweet prince" he smiled as he pulled Daniel's arm toward him, and plunged another needle into the inside of his elbow joint, and the second rush of smack surging through his veins was the last thing he felt. Convulsing on the floor the last thing he saw was the shape of his devil stepping over him and silently leaving the room.

Ada (ii)

Saturday 24th April 2010

"Oh god! Oh Christ! Yeah! Yeah! You like that? Is it good? Who's the best fucking journalist alive? Tell me! Tell me I'm the best journalist alive!"
She felt his cock pound into her from behind, the slap of his loose, curiously low hanging balls against her thighs had been at a steady rhythm for a few minutes and it was already beginning to bore her. Some part of her thought that this was a good idea. She had promised herself a fuck before her flight back out of the country, and figured that she may as well mix business with pleasure, but the creep of a journalist, Mr David Harston, had done nothing but talk about how important he was, during sex of all times. She had done her research, he was a very self-important man, who had a great sense of his own successes, who felt that those successes were entirely down to his own merits. The kind of man who would also take the most tenuous of credit for other peoples triumphs too. She had heard him after the awards ceremony, he hadn't won a thing but when speaking to the actual winner, who told him of how the committee had said his work was some of the best they had ever seen, Mr David Harston had retorted with "What? How can you big yourself up so much? Why is there no Thanks for being my inspiration Dave? Thanks for your hints and tips on journalistic writing?" and he had only met the man that night. He was a man who felt that he had inspired everything and everybody around him. The only reason he was even here tonight was because he had been short sighted in

his speculation of who could possibly be capable of serial murder, and of course everybody was entitled to an opinion, but when that person was a journalist whose words would be absorbed on a daily basis, then they should be slightly more careful with the opinions they purveyed, this short sightedness led to Ada feeding him information, to give him a red herring laden future, and he lapped it up. He had hungrily gobbled up what she had told him anonymously, and every word was printed the day after she had fed it to him. He deserved everything he was going to get tonight.
"You are the greatest journalist who ever lived, big boy, you are my hero" she declared monotonously, the man didn't even notice how bored she was, quite the opposite in fact, it spurred him on.
"Yeah! That's it! Call me daddy!" The things men would shout out during sex were sometimes ridiculous. Why would a man request that he be called "Daddy" during sex? Was this an English thing? Surely there could be something quite worrying about somebody who would like to be in a carnal situation with an offspring? But she obliged, to get through the occasion.
"Oh yes. Fuck me daddy. Do it to your daughter. Fill your daughter with your huge cock"
He wasn't listening, of course he wasn't. The man was entirely self-absorbed, his rhythm building up steam, the hotel mattress springs crunching beneath his bony knees as he thrust his cock as deep as he could inside her, which, admittedly, was quite deep, his manhood was long, but extremely thin, almost like a peperami sausage. It made Ada feel like her pussy was like a whore's, overused and wide, and that was not conducive to her enjoyment of this pre-murder fuck. After the

debrief, when Hoxton had been a little more mellow than they had anticipated, considering the massive fuck up, and the double-figured body count that they had not anticipated, Dietmann had declared that she had taken it perhaps too personally, condemning a man to death for being too liberal with his discriminations, and that maybe she should learn a lesson from last year's operation, which had appeared to be doomed the second they let Christophe loose in the city of Sheffield. But she was a stubborn woman when she wanted to be, like a dog with a bone when she had an issue with somebody. This Mr David Harston would be made to pay for his words.
"You love it don't you? You dirty slut! Tell me you fucking love it!"
"Oh yes. Yes. I love it. Fuck me daddy"
She was never a woman who placed any amount of emotion around sex, it was a joy that anybody could take if they wished. She also never placed any importance on it. Those people who waited years to have sex once they were married were stupid, they were depriving themselves of one of life's few remaining free pleasures that were an actual pleasure. Filling in a crossword puzzle was NOT a pleasure. It was a time consumer. Walking up hills only to come back down again was NOT a pleasure. It was an interest. Sex was a real pleasure. Most of the time.
"Oh God! I'm coming! I'm gonna fill you with my spunk!"
Which was not necessarily true, she, of course, had made him wear protection. He was going to fill his condom with "spunk". She was nowhere near a climax, not that she expected one. The man was not aware that

other people existed in the world outside of his own mind. The world did indeed revolve around him, again, in his own mind. There was no chance that he would spend any time teasing her with his tongue. Had she been spending time with any man without her ulterior motive she would have requested that he run his tongue over every inch of her body, up her the curve of her back and over her stomach. She would ask him to gently lick her thighs, to tease her clit, make her beg him to fuck her, then give her oral pleasures until she was brought to a climax, and as she would be shivering with post coital dreaminess, only then would she want him to put his cock in her. She felt Mr David Harston shudder behind her as he shot his semen into the condom, pulling her back onto his long thin cock, roaring into the hotel room.
"You fucking loved that didn't you?! You fucking loved getting fucked by the best journalist on this fucking planet! You're welcome baby, you're fucking welcome"
He pulled his thing out of her as she rolled her eyes at his ridiculous bedroom bravado, the sound of the rubber snapping from him as he removed the condom, followed by the gentle splat of him throwing it, untied, onto the side cabinet by the bed. The springs crunched some more, wobbling the bed, he was climbing from the bed. Ada rolled onto her side and watched him strut to the bathroom as if he truly thought that she should be grateful for the experience he had just put her through, that he was a lover extraordinaire. He was not.
"You know, I really enjoyed that, I know that you did, you're sexy" he shouted from the bathroom, the sound of his piss frothing up in the toilet bowl an underlying

soundtrack to his delusion. Ada said nothing. She allowed him the feeling, it was the least she could do. "I reckon I could go again, want to fuck again?" Ada had stopped listening, she was preoccupied by reaching into her bag. The toilet flushed and there was no sound of hands being washed. Of course there wasn't. The bathroom door opened and he stood holding his cock. "Got to clean the pipes out or it could get clogged!" he laughed. Just before Ada shot him in the head.

Tom (ii)

Saturday 2nd October 2010

So that's that then. For sure, I'm a hit man. I made my bed and now I'm lying in it. I can't go back to my old life, the bobbies are still looking for me. The papers have still got a reward on offer for my arrest. They think I killed my boy Justin. Did I fuck. That rapist cunt Christophe did it and now they've got it into their heads that Justin was a drug dealing hard bastard who went out of his way to hurt people. Did he fuck. He was a top boy and he was one of my best mates, but I have to move on from it. It's been almost a year since it all happened, and the boy Hoxton has kept me out of trouble all this time. For sure, he could change his mind after a while and pop a cap in my ass, but for now I'm a useful tool in his toolbox. It takes a lot of guts to kill a man, you know that? I mean, it takes enough balls to just punch somebody in the face, but to end their lives, for sure it takes some bottle. The way I get round it is to see Christophe in their faces, see what he did to my girl, build up this stubborn wall where I would do anything to end them, no matter how much they beg for their lives, or how much they offer to pay me to switch sides. Switch sides? Have you seen who I work for? There's nowhere they can't get to you. I'm not a bad man, I have to stress that, don't be thinking that I'm a cunt. I'm not. The thing is, I'm stuck between the Devil and the deep blue sea, a rock and a hard place. I don't want to be a hit man, my girl doesn't approve of what I do, but we're bound in this together, they have us over a barrel. So I'm a hit man. Simple as that. You want to call me a cunt then feel free, but the chances are our paths will cross one day, and I'll probably have to do what I seem to do best. The black guy from the day the rapist cunt Christophe shot my boy in the face, Daniel, waving his big knife around, I could see it in his face that he recognised me. You know that look that people do, where they just know they know you. A bit like the faces of girls I fucked in my old life, that look where, if I said hello a few weeks later in a bar, they'd just study my face, wondering if they'd known me at university, or maybe used to work with me. Chances are that I probably did used to work with them, call centres man, full of three week stints, the ever changing line-up of customer service representatives, everybody's worked in one of those fuckers at some point. Well, everybody that didn't think to get an education and actually use it. I'm going off on one a bit there, but yeah, Daniel, he was the last one from the big fuck up that the rapist cunt Christophe, and by association, I, caused. Obviously I count as one of those remaining from the operation, but they gave us a chance and we took it. Sticking the needle in his neck, I was sticking it in that big French fucker's neck really, like, when I wanted to say something cool when I was about to smash him in the head with the shoe, now I really get to say cool things before I'm about to take some poor fool out of the game. "I'm your devil, night night sweet prince", fucking classic that one, I will defo use that one again. Jess hates that I have to do these things, but I think she's a bit excited about it all too. How many people do you know who get to go to bed with a hit man who says cool stuff? Not many I'll wager. She told me how she felt when the old boy told her what I was doing when

Cristiano, aka Mr Beefy, he hates me calling him that but he does take it with a pinch of salt really, good bloke, and I know he loves a good bit of chee-chee up his nose now and then. Yeah, she said her heart skipped a beat, and how all that combined with what we'd been through and how I stood up for her at all times, she knew she was alright with me. I've told her I love recently, told her when we eventually get out of all this, that I want to put a ring on her finger, maybe stick some preggers up her, make a baby like. If it looks anything like her it'll be fucking gorgeous I can tell you now. Yeah, we're both a part of it, she's been given a job as researcher, she told the old boy straight, she wasn't gonna kill anybody, he buzzes off her. The others, you know? The ones who have been with him years, they all watch their mouths around him, show him this level of respect that blows my mind, like he's got them brainwashed, I won't even say the stuff to him that she does. She tells me she knows his first name, but she won't tell me what it is. I won't get upset about that little secret, or jealous that they get on with each other. Have you seen him? I bet his wrinkly balls are older than time itself! It is strange though. Ada told me he's never been like that with anybody, maybe he's been waiting for somebody to stand up to him? Who knows? Well, he does, I guess, but I sure don't.

I'm back in the car alongside Cristiano and we're driving out of Barnsley and on to the M1. We'll be out of the country again in about twelve hours, back to wherever, back to nowhere, and most importantly, back to my girl, my gorgeous red headed angel who chats shit at one of the most powerful men you've never heard of, and gets away with it. I call her Gingerbonce and she calls me Shithead, and that's how I like it. She stitches me up all the time, plays pranks on me, and for sure she has the most gorgeous smile I've ever seen on the front of a human head. What's not to love? I'll protect her until the end of time, longer if I have to. Yeah, I'm not a cunt, I'm just a man who's in love and will do anything it takes to ensure his girl is safe, and if that means killing some bad people, then so be it. So, yeah, make sure you're good, or you might be next.

Part 4 - ...And He Appears

Wednesday 11th October 2010

1

My name is Philip Hoxton. In Barcelona my name was James Wilkinson. In Paris I was Matthew McArthur. In Budapest I was Paul Glover. You will never know my real name. You've probably made guesses as to my motives. Geared yourself up to find out that I was, predictably, the Devil, or some such. Tried to anticipate a twist in the tail and allow yourself a smug grin when you find out that whatever you thought I was came true. I'm not the Devil. I am worse than the Devil. I know you, I know that you pick your nose and eat what you pull from your nasal cavity, but not before giving it a good old look, rolling it between your fingers to dry it out a little, collecting the dirt between the grooves of your fingertips, and then popping it onto your tongue, your mouth shaped in that tell-tale way that says you're having a little chew with your front teeth, and then you'll swallow it. I know that when you smoke you don't care that the person next to you at the bus stop is inhaling everything you blow at them, but they're too polite to ask you to stop, so you continue, even though you are quite aware that you are doing it. I know that you are so scared to go to the doctor to have him prod around your back passage that you would rather die of cancer. I know that you will lift your leg slightly to let out that flatulent urge you feel in a public place, allowing the gas to float into the ether, curling up your lip in disgust at the person next to you as if you are just as outraged as they are that somebody could do such a thing. I'm not a psychic, but I know people. I know humanity. We are an awful species, I do bad things because you do bad things. Some people may see that as a poor ethos, that not everybody is bad, but those same people will fail to thank the person ahead of them if the door is held open for them. They may even go to the extent of sliding through the open gap of that same open door, and allow it to slam into the face of the person behind them. I do bad things because of you. You are the bus driver who will watch an elderly lady struggle to get to the stop in time, and drive off as she finally reaches your door. You are the person who laughed when he did it. You are the idiot who made jokes at the expense of the disabled celebrity who tragically died in a curious fashion and sent the same joke by text message to thirty of your friends. You are the thirty friends sending the same message to thirty of your friends. You make racist comments on your Facebook page and defend those same comments when anybody takes exception. You are the self-righteous socialist protester who makes everything your business, one day preaching human rights, the next you will throw petrol bombs at police officers. You are the man who will bleed the country dry with your requests of money to assist with make-believe ailments and hypocritically blame the next man who just happens to be from a different part of the world to you. You wish pain on those who happen to be more fortunate than yourself. People who made something of their lives. And those people stepped on anybody they could to get to where they were. You are the celebrity who refuses to answer calls from childhood friends that you no longer have any need for, you are the same childhood friends who are only contacting the aforementioned celebrity in order to bleed them dry. To ride their coat tails to wherever they think they can be taken. You are the sportsman who cannot keep your penis in your trousers, you also happen to be the slut who sold the kiss and tell stories of that same sportsman for a piece of notoriety, the combination of the pair who helped to destroy his marriage to a woman who cannot get to sleep without the aid of drugs, made by an entire organisation of scientists and suited businessmen who will sit upon a cure for everything and let people die because they work in league with the companies which create the things which kill. These people are you. I will reiterate one last time, I do bad things, because you do bad things. Life is one endless chain of Godlessness. Oh, but now you believe me to be a religious zealot who acts on behalf of the Maker. Far from it. There is no Maker. There is no Devil. There is simply life which is gradually being strangled by humanity. All I am is a very rich man who feeds on the greed of others, a leech on the wound, I make no secret of it, for me what is the point of being good when all around us is bad? I know who you are, and I know what you do, and one day my friend, our paths will cross.

***

When push comes to shove you're all guilty of something. I feel I've made my point already, so how about I tell you a little about the people you've made friends with? See if I can't get you on my side? Your friend Alan? Maybe you felt a little sorry for him? Maybe wanted to mother him? Well, be advised, if you wanted to be a mother to that man would it change your opinion any if I informed you that, before all of this, he killed his own mother? Yes, he did. As she lay in her bed, a twenty four year old Alan entered her room, and smothered her with a pillow, and this was before he went a little insane. The years of her messing his mind up with her bringing her work home finally cracked him. She lay for four days before anybody noticed the smell. We were quite happy with his involvement, the recordings of him alone would keep a lesser man awake at night. The fellow was a minefield of dysfunction, he masturbated until he advised himself that he was sore, he wore the same clothes day in and day out, this is without washing them, you must understand, he wore his wax jacket everywhere he went. He had given up on being accepted by fellow man so much that he became yet another disgrace to his species. This is the kind of person I look for. I look for inner turmoil, I look for what you don't want the world to know, yet you display it so very much that sometimes I do wonder whether you are even trying to hide it. I have seen your Facebook page. You tell us how sick you are of the people who make an issue of something, without even realising you are doing the same. How very self-aware you must be. Who else would you like to know about? Lisa? The heroin addict who mothered children by four different fathers. Children who were born out of addiction. She exchanged sexual intercourse for heroin, unprotected, and allowed herself to bring children into this world out of her own selfish needs. Do you see yet, why I do what I do? She stole so many times, from her mother, bled her dry. She was a drain on the resources of your country, in hospital so many times through her own misadventure. This was a woman who made lying an art form, she stole products to order so that she could feed her addiction. And don't bring to my table the argument that addiction is a disease, don't even think about it, the girl did not have to inject her first hit if she was not prepared to accept that she may enjoy it so much that she would become the creature that she eventually turned into. If you feel like arguing that she was a product of her upbringing then I shall retort that her upbringing was modest, yet relatively happy. The rich become heroin addicts too. Ask yourself how many artists have succumbed to opiates, and you will find the list goes back a long long time. Heroin is not a poverty drug. It is the drug of those who wish to remove themselves from reality, which guides me back to inner turmoil. Lisa Wallett gave up her life in order to 'chase the dragon' yet allowed herself to continue to procreate. Do you think this woman deserves to live? To breathe the same air as you? What about James? On the surface a respectable member of society, studying for a PGCE, aspirations of teaching your future generations. This was a man who demanded that his girlfriend sleep with strangers for his own gratification, who lingered in the corner of a bar and directed her toward the men he liked the look of, and because she thought she loved him she allowed this to happen for so long, until she eventually refused to be a part of his perversion, so he left her. A man who was so intensely self-absorbed, and so much taken by his own sexual desires that he would destroy the life of a woman who professed to love him. Yes, he destroyed her life, she became withdrawn, she declared she would never trust a man, that she would never love anything for as long as she lived, because she had put her heart in somebody's hands, and he crushed it. How do I know? The same way the newspapers know. I scour the internet for things you may have written, I intercept your telephone calls, I follow you. My people know every aspect of you. Nobody keeps things a secret anymore. Allow me to reword that. Nobodies, do not keep secrets anymore. And sometimes, nobodies become somebodies, and only then do you wish you had kept it all inside. You all wish to be somebody, you post your most intimate thoughts online in order to gain recognition from people you may have once known at school, or gave cunnilingus to on a beach at night in Magaluf one summer four years ago. You pour your heart out to a captive audience who could not care less. It does not take a great deal of digging to find out what you do. Daniel, for example, an aspiring musician who posted comments several times an hour pushing his output to people who could not care less. Who felt a grievance owing to the fact that he was not more popular than he was. He would declare that the world was being unfair to him, that he had a right to be famous when the simple facts of it were that he did not work for anything, he felt that if he created something then the world should pay attention, and he blamed everybody else but himself. I worked to be where I am. I have my reasons, and I have my justification. I even have a back story but you can go to Hell if you think you are going to hear it yet. But these are the people you encounter on a daily basis. Most of them protested when it was put to them that be involved in the game, but they all went along with it in the end, many of you would do the same, destroy others to save your own skin. I am a cleaner, my employees are the vacuums, and we remove all of the dirt from the world.

Eventually, of course, we will come unstuck, but for now, we will continue to plan your demise.

2

The operation was a unmitigated disaster. That much was true. Eighteen corpses this time round. A new record. Moscow provided twelve. Ideally there should only ever be seven. Of course he cried no tears over the deaths. They happened and that was that, but it was an ideal opportunity for Philip to dissect and deconstruct every aspect of the operation. He did it each time they completed one. Analysed every minute detail of what happened and where, to give him the chance to cut out the potential for mess-ups in future events. Christophe and his predilection towards seducing anything that moved, and then telling anybody that listened. He had long been a faulty cog in the machine, and had surprised all of those involved that he managed to get through Barcelona unscathed. Philip prided himself on allowing people a chance to prove their merit, and had almost been convinced that Christophe had proved said merit, he was an immaculate researcher in Barcelona, stayed in the shadows as much as was necessary, and provided back up when required. For Sheffield he had pleaded and begged to be permitted a more responsible role, and did his utmost to convince Philip that he had proved he had what it took, so Philip allocated him the role, gave him the opportunity to further enhance his worth. But when allowed out into the public, he approached it like the proverbial bull in a china shop. He refused to stay out of very public places, forcing upon the rest of them his ideas that they were the best places for him to blend in, reneging on the details that made previous operations the successes that they were. Everybody else involved trusted in Philip and his attention to detail, they respected the man that he was, and the power that he held. In comparison Christophe was a petulant brat. He was the reason that Sheffield had gone wrong. And the fact that it went wrong at all was what pained Hoxton the most. The financial gain from killing the gamblers was a fringe benefit, but on principal the perfectionist in Philip was a little hurt by the need to do it. Two years had been wasted. The reason he created these events was to test the morality of people, to learn more about them, and they never let him down. If he wanted to kill wicked people then he could simply instruct his team to kill indiscriminately, to walk into shopping centres with machine guns and pepper everything in sight, but that wouldn't be half as much entertaining, or half as educational. The people they had selected for the game were all ideal. They were an eclectic cross section of society. This was where Christophe had done well, his research skills had been fantastic, thousands of responses came back to them, and he had worked day and night to whittle them down to the last eight, liaised with Dietmann whenever he discovered a potential candidate to get them bugged and surveyed, and the eight he found were perfect.

***

The sea shimmered beneath the Mediterranean sun, disturbed by the coastal breeze. Tom and Jessica were playing daft games on the beach. Him chasing her around, pulling her to the sand when he caught her, kissing for a while, then rolling over to soak the sun up. Philip watched them for a while, a pang of regret touched him slightly, memories of a past life sneaking into his mind set. He cleared his throat and returned to the report. The matter of the gamblers. There were fifteen million Euros in the vault, fifteen million reasons to end the lives of eight greedy men. The deaths were regrettable to an extent but at the same time they were ultimately very necessary. The men had been carefully selected, much in the same way that the players had been selected. They were a mixture of corrupt politicians, gangland crime lords, and unscrupulous businessmen. The ones who did not jump at the opportunity to play along were gently poked into submission, via the time old manner of blackmail. The gangster from New York was photographed with the fifteen year old whore. The politician from Chicago was recorded fellating his personal assistant. They were always going to play the game, whether they wanted to or not. This was not an aspect which Philip felt the operation failed upon, these tactics had worked in all five of the previous events, and would work again in the future, of that there was no doubt. The gamblers, even the ones who initially refused, would find themselves pulled into the sport, the unusual nature of the game, and would begin to root for their players. In the past there had been foul play, when they were allowed communication with the outside world, they would make varied attempts at manipulating the outcome of the game, such as have an associate make contact with the players, guide them into the paths of others, the collisions taking another players out of the game, thus increasing their own chances of taking the eight million pounds prize fund. That lesson was learned in Moscow, and never happened again. The gamblers were holed up in a property, plied with drink, entertained, and given regular updates. They were warned that it could take weeks, and, given the correct amount of pressure applied, would realise that they were happy with the arrangement. Their deaths were the only way Philip could ensure that he was not out of pocket because of Christophe. Yannick and Lukas were consummate professionals, who barely knew the meaning of the word 'Question' when it came to requests from Philip and his organisation. They were paid handsomely, and they were happy to fulfil any needs. All being well their services may not be required in three years' time, the young new recruits showing a great deal of potential already. Ada was a remarkable judge of character.

Do you recall *Vladimir Golovkin*? Notorious serial killer who chopped off, and took a single arm of his victims, he collected them as mementos of what he had done. He was known as The Octopus, given that he murdered, and took the arm of eight people, he was sentenced to life imprisonment in 1997, and died in the same year, murdered by a fellow inmate? He was one of Russia's most famous killers. I'd hate to have to do this, but yes, Moscow, 1997, Lukas won that game. How about *Michel Lefévre*? Known as The Heart Breaker because he killed and cut out the hearts of seven people, in 2002 he was declared insane and sectioned indefinitely, he always claimed that he was innocent, but of course he was, you can trace the blame right back to Yannick. *Fabio Morales*, AKA The Bone Cruncher, smashed his victims arms and legs with a ball hammer until their bones were ground almost to dust, so that they were essentially a torso with flaccid limbs broken and bleeding, I'm sure you've heard of him, sentenced to life imprisonment in 2000, took his own life in his first week in prison after his failed appeal against the sentence, he died still declaring his own innocence. Was he innocent? Of course he was, Cristiano was a fantastic player in his game. Took to it very well, his size is very much a benefit in a game of strength, he killed all but one of his seven co-players, and he did it in record time, the average game will be completed within two weeks, Cristiano did it in eight days. *Werner Kuefer,* known in the German media as The Mad Man, he shot nine people in both of their eyes, in what was said to be important because Kuefer once walked in on his parents making love, and it scarred him for life, he wished he had never seen it, so he ensured that he made sure that nobody who ever see again, if indeed they survived. All of it utter rubbish, it was Dietmann. You see, there will always be a fall guy, a patsy, therein lies the beauty of these games. The premise remains the same, the template is there to do this every year if I wished, why do you think I keep counsel with Isaac Charles? The man is a genius, he can make you believe that black is white, he will twist your opinion of that blackness without you even realising that it is happening. Isaac Charles has been a closely held connection of mine for over thirty years, I believe the phrase would be that I scratch his back, and he scratches mine.

My employees are a very naughty collective. They are extremely good at what they do. They have been through hell and back, in order to grasp the opportunity to take you through hell and back, they are also extremely clever. Ada only actually killed one person in her game, and that was her finalist, she would follow her fellow players from a distance, watch them participate in the game, if they killed somebody she would continue to follow them, if they were killed then she would follow their predator, until there was one left, then she killed them. Very very clever.

Incidentally, *Kovácczné Piroska*, AKA The Spider Lady, found hanged in her bedroom throughout a nationwide manhunt in 2004, correct, that would be Ada.

***

Alan Foster, The Sheffield Ripper, how original. If I was still a native of this country I might cringe at the lack of imagination shown by the national media, and the predictable nature of their actions, but as the multinational businessman that I am, I find that they served their purpose to perfection. Of course they swallowed our lies, they took the baton and ran with it, turned the issue into a living breathing creature. They created panic amongst the public, everybody became a suspect, they forced the police to act rashly and make several arrests of yet more innocent men, it's hilarious to think that as I write this, they are the subject of a number of high class lawsuits. This is why I do what I do. You are the journalist who can change the moral climate of a country with your words and you do this indiscriminately. You are the editor who allows scurrilous rumours to circulate in your efforts to sell more editions. You are the witty wordsmith who sits upon a pile of headlines just waiting for a story to come out that you can tenuously attach it to. Of course, I sound like a very bitter man, I am a very bitter man, I will get to that in good time, you can skip on a few pages if you wish, ignore the middle, skip to the end, why not? You can always come back if you do not like what you read, this is the beauty of the written word. It is a very underrated form of communication. All of this television, radio, music, bloody games consoles for Christ's sake. A million different ways of entertaining you without you having to put the effort in of actually doing anything. The only things you read are the inked pages of your daily speculation treat, and even then you will probably only look at the bloody pictures. No wonder your children are illiterate, and obese, and carbon copies of your own stupid selves. Technology will forever be with us, it will forever evolve at a rate where it cannot keep up with itself, and you will be the first to rip it from the shelves and spend cash that you cannot afford on it. You will end up homeless and broke. Broken. All because you needed to take photographs that showed the smallest blemishes, because you wanted to hear your music at a decibel louder than you could with your old machine, you wanted to surf the internet faster than before, everything is always better than its predecessor, therefore you need it in your life. The only things I need, are the means to get from one place to another, a roof over my head, food in my stomach, and my employees. I enjoy reading a book, I like the silence, it calms me, but you will always want the noise, the ways and means of occupying your tiny minds between the times of you waking, and then sleeping. I suppose you could say that I hate humanity, and I surround myself with people who hate humanity enough to do what they do to it.

4

The skulls looked at him from the glass cabinet. The collection had risen to fifteen. Their previous owners ranged from old enemies, to mutinous former employees, and gamblers who had crossed him. Fourteen of them sat in chronological order along five shelves, and one sat alone at the top, atop a velvet cushion. Philip stood before the cabinet, his eyes slowly scanned the faces that looked back at him, their bones stripped of skin, sinew, muscle, and blood, boiled down to clean, smooth skeletal heads. His eyes came to rest upon the lone skull at the pinnacle of the cabinet, a sadness briefly passed over his features, his eyes blinked heavily, and he turned back to his desk. Thomas and Jessica had disappeared from the beach but they were still audible somewhere around the property, one of twelve properties that he had acquired throughout both of his lives, bought via a third party on his behalf, both when he was officially alive and kicking, and when he was officially dead, reportedly burned alive on his private yacht, alongside his daughter. Returning to his seat he looked at his papers, the reports almost completed. The files and reports from previous games locked away from potential prying eyes. Cristiano entered the room unnoticed, the old man always appeared to get like this after an event, only this time he had a lot more to consider. They both privately hoped that it really was solely down to Christophe, that a repeat would never happen again. Of course, lessons had to be learned, mistakes were the only way of truly knowing how to broach certain subjects again in the future, however much pain those mistakes caused. Cristiano cleared his throat to bring the old man's attention to his being in the room. Philip looked up and addressed him with his eyes, and gave his head a small shake, *not just now,* Cristiano took it as his cue and left him to it. They were very respectful of him, even if they didn't know his real name, they didn't know what his lives had consisted of, and they would only find out when he was dead, not that they knew that either. He was ultra-secretive, he spoke to most of them a minimum amount, give them orders and instructions, they would be within their rights to have sparked a mutiny, but they knew his ways, they knew what he was like, and he ensured that they would never be required to perform a menial task for minimum wage ever again. They lived the lives of fictional characters in a Hollywood film, they thought that what they did was cool, and this was down to Philip.

***

Four spotted balls remained on the red baize, seven striped and the eight-ball. Tom hid his grin behind his hands and watched as Jess made an effort to hit the white ball onto one of the striped balls but missed and rattled around the mouth of one of the pockets. Turning to see her boyfriend's daft smile she playfully threatened him, holding the cue up to his face.
"Don't laugh, you idiot!"
"I'm sorry baby, if you were better at pool I wouldn't" he chuckled, pulling the cue from her hands and bending over the table to take his shot. Closing one eye to take aim, he slowly drew the cue back, and-

"Pow!" Jess yelled as she slammed her hand onto the end of the cue, pushing it forward onto the white ball, sending it flying from the table and rattling loudly as it rolled along the tiled floor, coming to a halt by the doorway of the balcony, the rustling of palm trees in the breeze outside the window joining in with the sounds of her laughter.
"Foul ball!" she laughed, walking across the floor to retrieve the white ball, a gust of wind teasing her light dress up against her thighs, arousing a reaction from Tom.
"You're sexy baby, you are properly sexy" he sidled over to her, lifting her skirt slightly, holding his hands against her thighs, his fingers gently stroking her buttocks. Turning her round to face away from him he softly kissed her neck, whispering into her ear.
"What would you say if I said I wanted out baby?"
"What do you mean?" She whispered back, her eyes rolling in delight at the light kisses and gentle licking he was doing to her neck.
"Fifteen million in t'vault, we could get out of all of this, I know you hate me killing people, I hate that you hate anything I do, I want you to be happy"
"I am happy, but yeah, I do"
"We could take that money, we could get out of here"
"But, they'll find us"
"Not if we take the Hoxton out of the equation"

5

Hannah was my daughter, she was the light of my life, she was an angel, who, if you will allow me the use of a cliché, would never draw a bad word from anybody. She was so creative, a wonderful artist, she used to paint the most beautiful pictures, her favourites were of her musical instruments. She was elegant, she made me smile every single day, she did not even realise just how pretty she was, and she had a grace that allowed her to float gently through life, bringing a glow into the lives of all that she came into contact with. She was my only remaining link to, her. And you took her from me in 1992. Humanity. You were the man who poured petrol all over the deck of my boat. You were the hand that sparked the lighter. You are a pair of rogue journalists whose careers were destroyed after I dismantled your lives because you brought disrepute to my door. You allowed my newspaper to go to the dogs. You are revenge. You think that you can get away with attempting to burn me and my daughter alive as payback for ensuring you would never work again. You are a misplaced sense of justice. Your names are Marc Jewson and Simon Butterworth. I own your skulls. You were my crooked security guard who allowed all of this to happen underneath your nose in exchange for a little bit of money, even though I paid you well enough. You were the bastard who always wanted a little bit more, who felt that nothing was ever enough, you felt that you deserved everything whilst putting nothing in, that you could bite the hand that fed you and get away with it. Your name is Keith Mason, and your skull sits in my cabinet, along with the rest of the people who put me where I am today. Your face was a picture when you saw me, at my funeral. The shock in your eyes will live with me forever, the fear as my hands gripped tight around your treacherous neck. I survived, and Hannah didn't. And I made you all pay. I wish, with every thread of my being, that she had not been on that boat, by Christ I wish that. My heart aches for every single day that I continue to breathe and she does not, this contempt for every other soul that walks the Earth will never die. I will not stop until I crush each and every one of you. Nobody is ever perfect. Not one amongst you is worthy of ever breathing the same air that my Hannah once breathed. *She* was perfect. *She* was what made this planet a bearable place to be. No matter who I came into contact with, crooked politicians who would shake your hand with one hand, and stab you in the back with another, she would bring me back to a world where everything was good. She is gone, and so is that world, so to hell with all of you.

***

I survived it. Floating, face down in the ocean off the coast of Portugal, I almost died. I wish I'd died, and joined the thirteen people who perished. Hannah included. But I didn't. I found myself in a small Portuguese hospital having been dragged to shore by two fishermen, having the salt water pumped from my body. The authorities had no clue as whether I was alive or dead, the media made their speculations, my own newspapers printed tributes to myself and Hannah. They screamed foul play, and for once they were correct. What they could not anticipate was that the perpetrators were from their own flock. Those two bastards received their own tributes when they were discovered, naked, headless, and covered with lash marks all over their bodies, their fingers snapped, their penises coated in solidified lard, formerly boiling hot oil. Yes, you remember the story now don't you? I took my time with them. I wasn't alone. I had begun to form my new team already. For the right money anybody will do anything. I had already decided to stay dead, allow myself the freedom of death. I became a ghost. I became Elvis Presley, an extra-terrestrial. Stories of people who thought they had seen me were abound, but how could it have been me? I was dead for God's sake! Marc Jewson and Simon Butterworth did not leave this mortal coil before providing me with a great deal of information. They led me further and further up a chain of inequity, and I took more and more people away from their families, I gathered more connections in death than I could ever dream of acquiring in life. The people I dealt with were no longer morally bankrupt fools parading as figures of social importance, they were by then morally bankrupt snakes who wallowed in their own evil, but at least they *knew* they were bad people, and did not care who knew it also. The face of humanity sickened me, it still sickens me, how we as a race can pretend that we are good, and honest, and decent, and we blame God for what goes wrong in our lives. We blame everybody except ourselves. I blamed everybody else, so everybody would pay.

6

This life has been sort of good to me. For sure, I get to wake up next to the fittest bird I have ever met. That's not fair actually, I respect her way too much to call her a bird. That's something she's kept on at me about like. She says I need to respect women more. I actually am proper trying to do it an'all. So, I wake up next to the fittest girl I have ever met, let alone been allowed to kiss, or, you know? I spend my days on the beach with that same gorgeous girl, waiting for Hoxton to send me and Cristiano somewhere else in the world to do nasty things to nasty bastards. I've got four different passports, four different names, I live a pretty cool fuckin' life. I'm a dangerous cunt nowadays. Cristiano took me out to the hills to do some training like, nowt too Steven Seagal or anything like that, just a bit of self-defence, and how if you need to get out of a sticky situation, stab them in their kidneys, causes instant shock like, takes them right out of the game. He's helped me with guns and that too, but that's not how we roll, it's all about stealth, I mean, I know Mr Beefy's a big bastard, but he's light on his feet, and he's been giving me some tips, like how to walk with your legs bent, think about what shoes you've got on and stuff like that, so I properly am a dangerous bastard. I can drive now too, never thought I'd ever learn that, I mean, I tried a few years back but I was always rubbernecking at fit girls, and it nearly killed me and the instructor, nearly drove us straight into a massive lorry on the other side of the road! So I never thought I'd have the required amount of concentration to ever drive properly, but that was years ago, it seems I'm alright

now. Plus, why would I ever need to look at any fit girls now? No need at all.
The thing is, me and Jess are in a bit of a bind, I had this idea, like, she really doesn't like what I have to do to people. She's a lover not a fighter y'know? She'd much rather talk our way out of trouble that have me shoot our way out. So I was laid in bed thinking about things. We've got it good here, no need to worry about our future in one sense, Hoxton has snap sent in for us every week, and he's got this old French lass who knocks some proper tasty dinners up, and I mean some of the stuff she makes would blow your mind, but that's the French isn't it? They like to mess about with flavours, and I do like a good bit of flavour! The cellar's full of wines and strong stuff, I've got my own quarters and a fridge full of ale. Cristiano's got a mega coke dealer too, though, again, Jess frowns at me a bit over that, but she knew I was partial when she got with me, as long as I keep it out of her face she'll let me get on with it. Anyway, yeah, for sure we've access to some major luxury, but there's always been this niggling thought that burrows into my mind, keeps me up at night sometimes. That rapist cunt Chistophe. His fucking skull is still in the building, a constant reminder that if they run out of uses for us, then we'll join the fucker in that cabinet. No way to live that is it? In constant fear that you might do or say the wrong thing. I've had time alone with the old boy, and it always feels like a job interview, like he's always asking what would you do if? types of questions, like he's always testing me, and it gets on my tits a little bit. Yeah, Jess has this weird connection with him but it's more on his part, like

he really does see summat in her, not in a saucy way, no fuck that!
So I put it to her that we fuck off away from here. See, I have this dream some nights, where I'm snorting coke off my girl's belly, and we're laid on all this cash in a massive room where the walls are coated with gold, I can see our reflection in it, all yellow and white, and it all feels sleazy as fuck, but at the same time we're enjoying it, she's laughing 'cause she fucking loves it, and as I go up to kiss her, the doors burst open and Hoxton storms in, but it's not Hoxton's face I see, it's my boy Justin, but in my head I know it's Hoxton, and he's got two fuck off big guns, and just as he's about to blow my head off I wake up. It just feels like I'm scared that the bottom could fall out of the whole thing at any time, you know? I don't trust Hoxton really, as much as he dotes on Jess, I think he could order us both dead as soon as he's done with us, so my idea, is we beat him to the punch. Kill the cunt, take that fifteen mil that's sat in the vault, and just fuck off, disappear off the face of the Earth, and I reckon if he's not around, we'll free the rest of the guys from their chains. I'd never say owt to Cristiano, but I think he'd love it if the old boy weren't around anymore. Yannick and Lukas just float in and out of our lives as soon as there's a corpse to dispose of, so maybe they'd be happy of a rest. For sure, there's probably a landfill somewhere just full of the bodies they've cut up, and Ada, well, she's a chip off the old block as far as Hoxton goes, she could cause us some trouble, but she's out of the country just now, so I figure that now's as good a time as any. We get a head start and she'll be clueless. That's the plan anyway.

Jess has been a bit quiet since I told her about it, it put the stoppers on our game of pool anyway, yeah she looked right into my eyes, like, she's loves the idea of getting away from it all, just going somewhere and putting it all behind us, but she knows what it's gonna take to make it happen. She's looking up at me, her big gorgeous eyes blink, I know she wants to say summat, but is trying to figure out how to say it. I like to think I know what she's thinking a lot of the time, she's got these faces she does, like, if she's confused she looks to one side and chews her lip a little bit, I properly love that face, sometimes I confuse her just to see it! When she's annoyed but is trying not to show it she has this stony face, but the tell-tale sign is that her tongue explores her mouth, it drops open slightly, and you can see her tongue run over her teeth. When she does that face I just leave her to it, let her alone with her thoughts until she either says something, or lets it slide. Just now though, it's a new one on me.
"What about Cristiano? He's around somewhere, we can't go killing everybody Tom, there's been enough death around us for the last year, can't we just grab it and go?"
She knows we can't, she's just clutching at straws, if she wants out she knows what we've got to do.
"Baby, I've been up thinking about it every night, if there was any other way I'd be up for it, but there in't"
Her eyes are searching against my chest now, trying to think up some way magically, as if I haven't been trying for days, I leave her to it, she'll accept what's got to happen eventually, I did.
"When?"

"No time like the present" and I go to the pool table, duck underneath it, and pull one of the many shooters we've got strapped all over the place. That's Hoxton's thing that, makes sure there's a gun at least three feet from every fucking where. I look at her, she's properly shaking. For sure, I don't think I want her to see this. If anybody's gonna do it, I want her nowhere near.
"Go and wait outside" I tell her, but she's rushing up to me and throws her arms around me.
"I'm not sure about this Tom, can't we just carry on?"
"I wish baby, but I have these dreams, I just know this is all gonna go tits up one day, and I can't let it happen, I can't let owt bad happen to you, so I reckon we need to just go, get the fuck out of here like"
I push her gently away, and look her right in the eyes.
"Baby, please, go and wait outside, I'll not be long"
And I kiss her hard on the mouth, my heart is pounding, it's all I can hear now, this dull repetitive thud in my ears, my mind floats out of my head and I can feel myself walking down the corridor, doors pass at either side, I can sense Jess behind me, watching me walk away from her. This is for her, for us, for our future. The gun feels heavy in my hand and I'm gliding down the stairs, I'm on autopilot, this is how I get when I'm gonna kill some wanker that Hoxton's sent me for. His room's in front of me, the door's pulled ajar but not fully closed, and I come to a halt right there. I close my eyes, and take a deep breath, then knock on the door quietly, the knock he likes us to do so we don't make him jump while he's in there doing whatever. He doesn't answer, so I push the door slightly and it creaks open. The gun's tucked in my belt, I'm fucked if I'm gonna go in there waving it at him.

His room is empty, there's nobody here. Fucks sake. The plan is very nearly going to shit. I don't know what the fuck I was thinking, and now it seems like it could all get fucked very quickly. I slowly walk through the room, and as I approach his desk it's then that I realise exactly how fucked it is. The old fucker is there, laid out on the floor in a pool of blood. Five holes where the bullets exited his body. I flip him over and where his dead face should be it's a massive gaping hole, it's been smashed in. I feel my dinner burning up my throat and rushing out all over the place. It coats his corpse, and goes all down my front, but steaming hot vomit is the least of my worries. I hear a sound behind me and turn with a start, all I'm thinking is Please don't be Jess, please, do not be Jess. It's not Jess. It's fucking Cristiano, in one hand he's holding a big silver case, and if I had to have a guess at what was in that case I'd say it was probably about fifteen million euros, fifteen million euros that up until just this second had mine and my girl's names on each and every one, but now I'm having to reassess that situation because in his other hand he's holding his gun and he's got it aimed right at me.

7

I'm sure by now that you're bored of hearing about my gripes with you. I'm almost bored myself, but if I don't tell you then you will never know. You'll never be able to change your ways. Become a better person. A more helpful member of society. Perhaps my actions will create a better world. I doubt it. It was never my intention to create a better world anyhow, far from it. Nothing will ever bring her back. Of course, with most people the pain of the death of a loved one subsides for every year that passes, brought back to the fore for each anniversary, only to subside again once the banality of real life rears its ugly head and every-day problems that must be faced become the priority. For me, however, she was my last remaining loved one, she was my legacy, and she was taken by greed, and corruption. For that reason I shall not rest. I would hope that, in the event that you are reading this, whoever you are, you might begin to see why I do what I do, you might wish to continue my work. Look at that person you see every day on public transport, see the evil that lies beneath the surface. That person you see will hurt small animals, at some point in their lives they have wished harm on others, even if that wish was only fleeting. We all have it in us to perform the tasks that I perform. To order the deaths of a great many people. I do not care if you claim to love all living things, you will still have that briefest of urges to punch the person who is eating his food too loudly, you are only human, after all. I realise that I am writing as if I am the only person who has ever lost anybody, as if I do not understand that the people I take from this Earth are being remembered on

a daily, weekly, yearly basis by those that they left behind, but those people are the weak-willed bastards that will do nothing about their pain, they will go on, remembering with the half-hearted tribute of a rose on a grave on an annual basis. I urge you, whoever you are, to stand and fight the cruelty that occurs in every single inch of this bloody planet.
Perhaps the reason you are reading this, is because somebody did just that, finally stood up to me, I am only a man, after all. Part of me wishes that people *would* stand up to me, that they would not join my crusade against humanity, that they would finally put a bullet into my skull because I am a bad, wicked man. My blood courses with this over-riding urge for vengeance. I can never truly love anything ever again, because if I love something, then eventually it will leave me, whether it wants to or not, then my soul empties, and I am left the shell of a man that I sit here as today. Money can buy a lot of things but if you are strong enough, you can fight anything. My flesh is the same flesh as that of everybody else. I am not made of iron, or stone. A bullet can penetrate my bones just the same as it can yours. A knife can slice my skin just the same as it could an apple. Fists can break me. My outer is the weak part. My inner is immortal, it burns with hatred.
I do not believe I will ever see Hannah again. I am not naïve enough to believe that there is an afterlife full of dancing lost loved ones, I shall never accept that my little girl is up on a cloud watching my every evil move. She is burned, and she is disfigured, and she is the ground. The only happiness I shall gain from my own death, and know this please, is that my heart, and my

mind, will never feel the pain that it feels on each and every day. Do as you wish, you are your own person. Of course I feel foolish that I have given you so much information, that in today's Godforsaken technologically advanced society that we live in, you can quite easily use your internet to find out who I really am. So I shall tell you, and then I shall go back to my life, destroying the wicked. My name is Terence Wilcox. I was born in South Africa in 1947. I left for England with my wife Heidi in 1969, and worked my way up through the media industry. I owned my first printing press in 1975. Heidi died of a brain tumour in 1987, and I was the owner of a multi-million pounds media firm until my supposed death in 1992, where I perished along with my beautiful, angelic daughter Hannah in an "accident". Since then I have been so many different people, I have collected the skulls of every person that ever crossed me. I watch them to remind myself that I am the most powerful man you have never met. Death is a great liberator. I have watched you since you were born. I have followed your every dirty thought, I have seen the way you look at the person you do not like, that person you will tell that you love their shoes, only to turn to another friend and tell them how much you hate those shoes. I know how you think. I know what turns you on. I know what entertains you. And I know how greedy you are. We all want what we cannot have. I want Hannah back. It isn't happening. You want a fifty inch plasma television. That is not happening. There is no way you can hide from me. So don't even try.

8

We're thrashing it along the Boulevard Louis II out of Monte Carlo in a pristine brand new Lexus IS 350, with ten million euros in the boot, and I cannot fucking believe we pulled it off. Jess is looking at me and smiling like she wants to jump my bones right now and I'm feeling like nothing can touch me. This is immense. As the road turns into Avenue JF Kennedy I look to my left, beyond my girl's beautiful face to the marina, a hundred luxury yachts belonging to racing drivers, gangsters and film stars all moored up, bobbing up and down on the turquoise sea. We're not in the big league, some of those boats out there cost deep into seven figures, and our haul is small chips compared, but we don't need to be big league, ten million will do for us, we just need to disappear to somewhere quiet, out of the way, somewhere I can look after my girl by whatever means necessary. I'm playing out the events of the last hour in my mind, it could have gone tits up in so many ways.

I'm back at that room. Cristiano with his gun aimed right between my eyes, watching me, willing me to make a wrong move. The time that past between us felt like an age, I didn't have a clue what to say to him, I mean, what how many mixed messages could he give me? Did he think I was gonna take him out as revenge for Hoxton? Was he taking all witnesses out of the game? And what the fuck did he have planned for Jess once he'd killed me? These were the thoughts running, no, fucking sprinting through my mind. For sure me and Cristiano had got quite close, well, as close as two professional hit men possibly could get close, and I thought, in a situation like this, we would defo have each other's backs. So I was a little nervous about things, you can understand. After a time I slowly held my hands up, showed him I was gonna play ball, do whatever he wanted me to, I needed to get back outside to Jess, even if it meant leaving empty handed. No way I was gonna leave her here sat with her thumb up her arse with two dead bodies and no cash when Ada got back to find her job in something of a limbo.

"Look, Mr Beefy, Cristiano, I don't know what the fuck you did, or why, but I won't say owt, I promise, let me get back to Jess, please"

I'm trying to stay calm, not sound like I'm begging him, this was something he taught me, you let your voice go a bit pathetic and you're fucked. So I stayed cool, looked him in the eye, but didn't move a muscle. I had to let him know I was playing the game, but I wasn't shitting it.

"Don't be such a pussy little man, you are shitting in your little panties" he laughed, a properly evil look in his eyes, like I'd fucking shat in his boots and made him wear them to a party, like he fucking hated me. I only ever saw that look when he was looking down at a target, after he'd clobbered them with a heavy slap to the side of the face, and stood there, seeing red before he either beat them to death, or I stepped in and said something cool before I shot them between the eyes. He must have seen the confusion across my face, because his face suddenly lit up like a Christmas tree, his massive brown face grinning at me, a different vibe radiating from his massive brown eyeballs.

"I am playing a game with you, you focking idiot, I am not going to kill you" and even that didn't take the

confused look off the front of my head, I still didn't move a muscle, I just watched him as he approached me and patted me on the back, pulling the gun from my belt and tossing it onto Hoxton's desk.
"Seriously man, I heard you and yo' lady talkin' about this shit, you need to be careful what you say in this focking house man, you know there is surveillance everywhere, you focking locky it was me that heard that shit, I been waiting to kill that old motherfocker for years man, yo Tommy, put your fockin' hands down yeah?" and he pushed my flimsy skinny arms down with his massive shovel hands and pulled me close to him, my head crushed against his bulging chest and his booming laugh echoed into my skull, like I was at a disco, standing next to the speaker, and all they played on the decks was that big bastard laughing, so I pushed myself away from him and looked up at his face, a concern hitting me.
"What about Ada, and Dietmann? And Lukas and Yannick? What will they do?"
"I do not give one fock my friend, Ada is a cold bitch who can fock herself and Dietmann is her ass-licking poppy, the others, they do not have one brain cell to share with each other, they will be happy if you give to them a crayon and a book for colouring, they cannot find their focking dicks, they will not find you"
So he went into how Hoxton treated him like shit, he was the man who was sent to do the dirty work, whilst Ada, and Dietmann were floating around the old man, kissing his arse, telling him what he wanted to hear like they were smarter than Cristiano. Like he was the big dumb motherfucker who had to go out and do shit for them. He said that if Ada were around then she would

have been lying next to Hoxton herself, her skull broken and battered from his rage. Dietmann would have suffered worse, he wanted to pull his limbs from his body like I used to do with daddy long legs' in the summer, leave them flailing while they tried to figure out what to do without the integral part of their names. I always liked Cristiano, we were kind of similar, in a crazy kind of way, maybe it was just the love of coke, but a drug taker's bonhomie is pretty strong sometimes, sometimes it can be the only link you have to somebody, but it's still there. Like when you're at the supermarket and you pick up something a bit random, like, I don't know, a bag of charcoal in winter, and somebody else is getting the same thing, for a split second you're their best mate, then it's gone. He talked about when he was sitting in the surveillance room, watching Jess and me playing pool (he told me that I should have gone easy on her, by the way, a boyfriend's duty, he said), he was surprised to hear us discussing the plan, that he thought we might possibly go down the route of Ada, and the others, that we'd be brainwashed into doing all Hoxton's bidding, and end up dead like the rapist cunt Christophe before long, so he put his own plan into place. Hoxton was alone with three people who all wanted him dead, so Cristiano felt, after hearing Jess and me, that he should be the hand that destroyed a legacy, that I had killed enough people against mine, and my girl's wills. So he did. Walked in, pistol in hand, and shot him five times, didn't even give him chance to say anything. The old man was still breathing, so Mr Beefy went all Mr Beefy on him, and smashed a hole into his head. The crazy cunt!

He told me his plans, to go into the Pyrenees, the Spanish side, and set up in a cottage there, get a hot tub and sit drinking champagne in it whilst he looked out into the mountains, get a call girl in now and then, enjoy his own company like, but I totally agreed that for sure, a man's got needs. True fucking that! He never told anybody about his plan before, so he's feeling pretty safe with me, I certainly don't have any intention of telling any fucker! As far as the money went, Cristiano said he didn't need much, that he's already got millions stashed away, he just wanted to take five because it was fair. There were essentially three of us in this, so we should take five each. I did no complaining whatsoever, let me tell you that!
I left him to it, to do whatever he wanted to do to the house, or Hoxton, he just told me to take Jess, and one of the cars and get away. Ada would come back tomorrow, we might as well get a head start on her if she's got designs on tracking us down, but there's this big part of me says she won't. I think we all wanted the same thing, but nobody ever had the balls to do anything about it. I got out to Jess and grabbed her arse, kissed her beautiful pale face, the freckles always out now she was constantly in the sun. I love her freckles. I love her. She's an amazing girl and I wouldn't be where I am if it wasn't for her, she basically saved my life. I was chained to the desk in some piece of shit call centre, taking whatever everybody wanted to throw at me, like a mindless drone. Whatever bad things have happened since the day I quit that job, have happened, there's fuck all I can do about any of them. But what I can do for damn sure, is look after my girl.

And as we exit Monte Carlo for good, we still don't have a clue where we're going, I fancy getting onto a motorway and cruising through Europe, see what takes our fancy. Jess says she's never been to Italy, and we're not too far really, so we'll head north, cross the border and let her fulfil a dream. Why not? We've got the money, we've got each other, what else do we need?

Epilogue

2012

The room felt cold, a kind of cold feeling that you got when you climbed into a bath that felt fine when you swirled your cold hand around the water, but in actuality was slightly cooler than your body temperature. With that in mind, Liezel felt comforted to know that she had brought her knitted cardigan with her today, to wherever this was. She sat alone in this room, and hoped to God that somebody would join her soon. She had never felt such nervousness as she did today. She had no idea why she had even responded to the stupid advertisement. Okay, she conceded to herself, she knew exactly why she had responded, and why she had allowed herself to get this far, money. Her home in Pretoria was close to being taken from her, and this advertisement came to her at just the right time. All of her family in Cape Town could really do with a helping hand if she won the competition, whatever it might be. One million Rand. She could do a hell of a lot with that. Maybe she could even ride her success and steal a couple of interviews in the magazines. She had made a small fortune from selling counterfeit football tickets when the World Cup came to South Africa, but once the carnival had left town she struggled to keep up the things she thought she could afford when things were good.

The advertisement in Pretoria News read Attention Afrikaner. Win 1 Million Rand. And that was it, it was dubious, but it caught her eye. She followed all the steps, dialled the number that came with the notice, and waited. She had waited months, and had put it to the back of her mind, eventually conceding that maybe she was not going to be one of the lucky ones. Then out of the blue she received a call. It came from a lady with a European accent. All she said was "Liezel Esterhuizen, you have been chosen to compete for one million Rand, please wait in front of the statue of Oom Paul at twelve noon tomorrow, I will be there to meet you. Congratulations. You are the lucky one" and then she hung up.

Printed in Great Britain
by Amazon.co.uk, Ltd.,
Marston Gate.